CLETE

Also by James Lee Burke

CLETE

A DAVE ROBICHEAUX NOVEL

JAMES LEE
BURKE

Atlantic Monthly Press
New York

FIRST EDITION

Printed in the United States of America

First Grove Atlantic hardcover edition: June 2024

Library of Congress Cataloging-in-Publication data is available for this title.

ISBN 978-0-8021-6307-3
eISBN 978-0-8021-6308-0

Atlantic Monthly Press
an imprint of Grove Atlantic
154 West 14th Street
New York, NY 10011

Distributed by Publishers Group West

groveatlantic.com

24 25 26 27   10 9 8 7 6 5 4 3 2 1

To Nils and Amy Lofgren

Thanks for your years of support and the beauty of your music and the spirituality I believe you brought with you from the spheres.

Keep it in that old-time E-Street E major. We don't care what people say, rock and roll is here to stay.

Your friend forever,
James Lee Burke

CHAPTER ONE

This story about Louisiana happened in the late nineties, before Katrina and before the Towers, when my podjo Dave Robicheaux and I were splitting our time between New Orleans and New Iberia, down on the Gulf, in the heart of Dixie, where it's seventy-two degrees on Christmas Day.

Southern Louisiana is heaven, as long as you keep one eye closed and don't dwell on the corruption that's a way of life here. Louisiana is a state of mind, more like the Baths of Caracalla without the moral restraint. One of our politicians said we should put the Exxon flag on the capitol building. I don't know one person who thought that unreasonable. Our politicians are modeled more on the leaders of Guatemala than on Thomas Jefferson. Dave Robicheaux said a love affair with Louisiana is like falling in love with the Great Whore of Babylon. I said, yeah, but what a party.

Dave definitely did not like that remark, calling it crude and simplistic. Dave should have been a priest instead of a cop, and as a result he has made a mess of his life, and people like me have had to protect him from himself.

But I don't mind. I love Dave and I don't care who knows it. We were both in Shitsville and joined the NOPD at the same time and as rookies walked a beat together on Canal and in the French Quarter, bouncing our batons on the curb, the warm smell of Lake Pontchartrain in the wind, the clouds as pink as flamingos in a blue sky. By 10:00 p.m. we would end up at the Café Du Monde, across from Jackson Square, drinking café au lait and eating a sack of beignets, never talking about Shitsville.

We didn't have to. We had the same nightmares. When you come home from a war, you don't get a free pass. The same images hide in your head until you go to sleep. Here's the strip of film that gets loose behind your eyes: A column strung out on a night trail, the rain pattering on everybody's poncho and steel pot, the foliage dripping, green and dark and hot, heat lightning racing through the clouds without sound, then somebody on point snaps a trip wire and detonates a 105 dud. The explosion is like a sliver of glass in your eardrum. Somebody is yelling his guts out on the ground, and somebody else is yelling for a corpsman. Then you hear the droning of helicopters or the malarial buzzing of mosquitoes in your blood or the Gatling guns rattling or a door gunner strafing a rice paddy in a free-fire zone, all these things at once, all the sounds interchangeable, and when you awake you go immediately to the icebox, your hand shaking on the first bottle you can pull out.

But enough with Sir Charles and the NVA and memories of Shitsville. Dave's and my histories with NOPD turned out dramatically different. Dave never dishonored his badge, and I did. I took juice from the Mob and accidentally popped a federal witness and had to blow the Big Sleazy and join up with the leftists in El Sal. I also worked for the greaseballs in Las Vegas and Reno and up in Montana, where they tried to build a couple of Nevada-style casinos on Flathead Lake, which would have turned their state into a toilet.

Regarding the latter, an airplane packed with wiseguys crashed into the side of a mountain not far from the lake. Their remains had to be combed out of the trees with garden rakes. Then somebody spread a rumor there was sand in the fuel tanks. I thought it was a good opportunity to take a cruise up to Alaska and maybe later open a PI business back in the Big Sleazy.

So that's what I did. But as I write these words, I want you to understand something. The subculture of law enforcement and parole and probation and bail bondsmen and shyster lawyers and private investigators is a sewer, one where the pervs outnumber the normals. Actually, I don't know if the normals exist. I live with a slapjack, a .38 Special snub, and a badge holder on my kitchen counter. What that signifies is I blew my career as a real cop and became a lush and developed ulcers and a liver that probably looks like an eggplant. I also worked for people who turned my stomach. I also had a difficult relationship with the cops I once called friends at NOPD. I couldn't blame them, but I have to say it hurt.

This story starts at a car wash, can you believe that?

# # #

When I had the money, I always drove a Caddy convertible with fins and a rolled-leather interior. Of course, I didn't make a great deal of money, so I usually ended up with a junker I rebuilt. Then I got a real deal on a 1959 lavender-pink Eldorado with a starched top, one that had a few holes in it. I repaired the dings and repainted the body and redid the interior and bought a secondhand top that I turned into a starched-white beauty, and then I installed a stereo and loaded up my glove box with jazz and R&B and rock and roll tapes, and I left it at a car wash called Eddy's across the river in Algiers.

I'm talking about Eddy Durbin, who I grew up with in the old Irish Channel, when it was still a clean neighborhood where everybody got along, except for the turf beefs we had with the Italians, the kind of rumbles that went full blast in an alley or under a streetlight, with no adults paying any attention, with shanks and chains and chunks of steel pipe, a bonnet screwed on the end. That's how I got this scar through one eyebrow.

Eddy was a real Mick. Both of his parents were from Dublin and supporters of the IRA. Eddy had done back-to-back nickels in Angola but had stayed straight for seven years and had made a success of his car wash. I always liked Eddy and thought he got a bad deal by the system, but I have tried to stop judging about those things. It was Dave Robicheaux who got me out of El Sal, thirty pounds down with dysentery, jungle ulcers on my calves, zoned on weed and coke that could put you on the other side of Mars, the mosquitoes singing inside my head all night long.

I picked up my Caddy four days late because I had to chase down a dancer on Bourbon Street for a bondsman in Biloxi. I'll tell you more about that later. In the meantime, don't let anyone tell you that the life of a PI has anything to do with professionalism. Most PIs are just like me. They took juice or they drank it. For a cop, that one never leaves the blackboard.

# # #

I lived just two blocks from Jackson Square and St. Louis Cathedral and Pirate's Alley, which was full of tourists and drunks, so I always parked inside my courtyard, which had a piked gate I kept locked.

On a Sunday morning, two days after I picked up my Eldorado Caddy at Eddy's Car Wash, I heard a clanging sound that I thought was the Angelus ringing at the cathedral. No such luck. I heard voices inside the courtyard, like people arguing about something. I put on my bathrobe and fluffy slippers that had rabbit ears and plastic eyes sewed on them and went down the back stairs. For many years now after my wife dumped me, I've owned a pale-yellow two-story stucco house in which I live upstairs and run my PI office downstairs. It has a brick courtyard and a wishing well and flower beds full of banana plants and elephant ears and caladiums that make me think of pink hearts. My two balconies are hung with bougainvillea, as red as blood, and they bloom all winter. It has always been a special place for me.

My Eldorado Caddy was still parked by the wishing well and my barbells and weight set, but all four doors were open. A guy with ink all over him, to the degree that I couldn't tell his race, and two white guys were ripping the Caddy's insides out. Most of the rolled leather was lying on the bricks. The windmill palms and banana fronds were so thick around the stairs I didn't have a clear view of the courtyard, and I had to rub my eyes at what I was watching.

"What are you guys doin'?" I said.

The guy with the ink had a crowbar hanging from his right hand. He wore tennis shoes without socks and sweatshorts hitched tight around his buns and a leather vest with no shirt, a washboard for an abdomen; his skin looked like it had been painted with brown lacquer on top of his tats, like he was in a paint store when it got hit by a tornado.

"Who are you, Bluto?" he said.

"The guy who owns the Caddy you're destroying."

"Beat feet back to the shack, Jack," he said. "Don't be making any phone calls, either."

My .38 was in my bathrobe. There are lots of ways to confront lowlifes. But the last way is with a gun. Once it's in your hand, you will probably use it.

"How did you get in?" I said.

"Your lock was open."

"It was not," I said.

I looked at the two white guys. They were unshaved and dirty. One wore cargo pants buttoned below his navel. The other wore a T-shirt that read 6 MILLION ARE NOT ENOUGH. His hair was thick and greasy and uncut and hung in his eyes, but it didn't seem to bother him; his face looked like curdled milk, with pits in it. Like it wasn't skin.

"I'm going upstairs," I said. "Don't touch my automobile while I'm gone."

"Listen, asshole," said the man in the leather vest. "You left your wheels too long at the service. It got mixed up with another car. So we're straightening things out. We're giving you a break."

"Are you out of your mind?" I said.

"So far we haven't found our goods," the same guy said. "That means maybe you already took them. That's gonna be a big problem, rabbit guy."

"Rabbit guy?" I said. I looked at my slippers. The sun was just breaking over the roof; my eyes were starting to water. I felt a rubber band about to pop inside my head. "Where's Eddy?"

"In church," he said. "It's Sunday."

"You're going to pay for the damage you've done to my car," I said. "And you're going to pay for it now."

"Maybe later you can call State Farm," the guy in the vest said. "But right now I want to inspect the inside of your house."

"*You want to what?*" I said.

"There's three of us and one of you. I see that sag in your robe. Don't think about it. We can hurt you, Bluto. Or is it Blimpo?"

He flipped the crowbar and caught it.

I looked at the two other guys. I knew most of the lowlifes in Orleans and St. Bernard Parishes, but I had never seen these two. In the subculture I'm talking about, there's psychosis and neurosis; then there's evil. Most recidivists are lazy and stupid and can't function on their own. Most of them aren't half bad. Prison is a safe place. Like casinos. There are no clocks and no mirrors. These three guys were the kind the average convict doesn't want to cell with. The one with the 6 MILLION T-shirt bothered me the most.

"Where'd you get your threads?" I asked.

"I cain't remember," he replied. This man was not from New Orleans. New Orleans is Flatbush South because it was settled with Micks and Sicilians. This guy was a five-star peckerwood, like he had Q-tips shoved up his nostrils. "You're talking about my shirt, right?"

"Yeah," I said. "The six million are the Jews who died in Nazi extermination camps?"

He put a piece of gum in his mouth. "Yeah, I'd say that's a correct interpretation."

"Why would you want to say something like that?"

"I don't like them," he said, chewing while he smiled.

I nodded and looked at the bougainvillea hanging from my rear balcony, right next to a chain of yellow flowers called bugle vine. The sun felt hot on my forehead. A drop of sweat ran out of my hairline, even though the sun wasn't that warm. I could smell the spearmint that grew between the bricks in the shade, and the pools of water left over from last night's rain. That's the way the French Quarter used to smell in the early morning, with boxes of fruit on the sidewalk in front of the little grocery stores. Sometimes in the early morning I bought some beignets and ate them on a stone bench under the live oaks behind the cathedral, right there on Pirate's Alley. William Faulkner lived in what is now a bookstore there. Tennessee Williams lived not far away.

"You drifting off, pal?" said the guy with the T-shirt that was really starting to bother me.

"Y'all get down on your faces," I said.

"You got it backwards, Blimpo," the man in the vest said. "*You* get down. Not us. *You* get on your knees. Maybe with luck I won't piss in your mouth. Maybe if—"

That was as far as he got. Dave Robicheaux and I have a lot in common. My father was a milkman who came home with booze on his breath every afternoon and sometimes made me kneel all night on rice grains and hit me with his razor strop. Dave's father was an illiterate Cajun who wiped out Antlers Pool Room in Lafayette, and a half dozen other places, with a pool cue for fun, and died on the monkeyboard of an oil well in a blowout in the Gulf. He bailed on the Geronimo wire just before the flames swallowed the top of the rig and was never seen again.

I mowed lawns and dug leaves out of rain gutters in the Garden District, and usually got paid at the back door. I couldn't use the restroom inside their houses, either. Dave was a Cajun who couldn't speak English when he first got on the school bus. The same day, he washed his hands in the school toilet bowl because he had never seen an indoor bathroom. His mother worked in a laundry for twenty cents an hour and later let a pimp turn her out in a Breaux Bridge nightclub. Neither of us went to Shitsville for patriotic reasons. We went there to get even.

I broke the nose of the guy with the full-body tats. I caved in the stomach of the guy whose dirty cargo pants hung below his navel, and I ripped the T-shirt off the antisemite and stuffed it in his mouth and tried to kick him in the face but missed. I didn't touch my .38, but I used my sap, which I had also put in my robe. Then I got careless. I turned my back too long on the guy with the full-body tats. He caught me on the side of the head with the crowbar. I tripped across my set of weights and hit the bricks hard and didn't wake up until one of my cats curled up on my chest, his tail flipping in my face.

CHAPTER TWO

I called 911, but only because my automobile insurance required it of me. Even in the Garden District a car break-in got a three-hour response time. Plus, few NOPD cops liked me. But I told myself that was their problem. I told them I hoped their wives sprinkled kryptonite on their food.

I rented a car on a Saturday afternoon and drove across the bridge to Algiers and pulled into Eddy's Car Wash only two blocks from the river. Even though I was born in Orleans Parish, I've never gotten over the width of the Mississippi. It makes you dizzy, particularly in the spring. Farther down the river, back in the swamps where it starts to dump into the Gulf of Mexico, there are remnants of Confederate batteries and also the bones of British soldiers from the War of 1812. It's all right there, sticking out of the ground, or at least it used to be. Dave Robicheaux saw a column of graybacks walk through a brick wall and disappear in the mist. I believe him. Louisiana is a necropolis. If you don't believe me, walk through the cemeteries on Basin Street or Esplanade (make sure you're in company).

When I turned into the car wash, Eddy Durbin took one look at me, got into a car his employees were hand-drying, and drove away, right through a stop sign.

That wasn't like Eddy. I told you he did two nickels back-to-back. But I didn't tell you he did them straight up—no conjugal visits, no work release, no good time applied against his sentence. Ten solid years of prison, where you hear either the yelling of men or the clanging of steel twenty-four hours a day. The steady sounds are ultimately deafening, and not to be undervalued in terms of your sanity.

Eddy was a marginal criminal, the kind you find in New Orleans or Southie in Boston. Theft was a way of life with my friends in the Channel. Maybe it had something to do with the Irish and the coffin ships and the welcome they received when they landed in America. Eddy and his kid brother and some grifters out of New Jersey were laundering counterfeit and stolen money at the tracks and casinos all over Louisiana and Florida. Except one of the Jersey guys was a snitch, actually a plant, and he testified against the whole gang when they went down. Eddy lied and said his little brother, Andy, had nothing to do with the grift of over three hundred thousand dollars, and did the time for Andy.

In other words, Eddy was a stand-up guy. So why was he running away from me now? I hated to think about it.

# # #

He looked in the rearview mirror several times, then gave it up and pulled into a city park in a poor section of Algiers. Families were roasting wieners and kids throwing Frisbees and playing softball. I got out of my rental and went to the passenger side of Eddy's car and climbed inside without permission. Eddy had a round face and a small, pursed mouth, like a fish, and never smiled.

"You want to tell me why my Eldorado got ripped apart by three creeps who are evidently connected with your car wash?" I said.

"I'm sorry about that."

" 'Sorry' doesn't flush, Eddy."

"Another Eldorado was holding some stuff a guy was supposed to pick up. There was some confusion,"

"I've already heard that, Eddy. That's not a viable excuse. What was the 'stuff'?"

"I get the sense it was some heavy shit."

"What kind of heavy shit?"

"I don't know. Andy got in with some bad guys. I didn't know anything about it."

"Then why don't you find out?"

"Andy took off."

"I'm shocked," I said. "All he did in the past was roll over and give you an extra five-spot in Angola. Your little brother should have a telephone pole kicked up his ass. Where are these guys from?"

"I think they're Dixie Mafia."

"Dog shit. The guys who believe in the Dixie Mafia couldn't find Gettysburg if you tattooed a map on their stomachs. What are you hiding, Eddy?"

"Nothing."

"You're starting to make me mad, Eddy."

"You have personal feelings on the matter," he replied.

"Skag?"

"Could be," he said.

"But it's not?"

"Probably not."

"So what is it?"

"I'm just guessing. Andy is not even sure."

"I am about to hit you in the side of the head, Eddy. Then you can have thirteen stiches in your scalp, just like me."

"Fentanyl," he said.

I felt my hands ball on top of my thighs. I looked through the windshield. Some children were playing badminton now; others were eating hot dogs and ice cream; and some were turning somersaults in the grass. Their laughter was like a song.

"I know what you're feeling, Purcel. I just want to—"

"No, you don't know what I'm feeling. Not at all. So don't say you do."

"I apologize," he said.

"Don't tell me you apologize, either. My grandniece is dead because of that shit your brother is helping get on the street. Now, where is he?"

"I don't know. And if I did, I wouldn't give him up. So fuck you."

I stared into space and scratched my cheek idly with four fingers. Then I got out of Eddy's car and closed the door and leaned down on the window. "Think it over, Eddy," I said. "Don't end up on the wrong side of things. You never hurt anybody. The guys who visited me are mean. They hurt people for free."

His head was cricked to one side, like his neck was broken, his arms resting inside in the steering wheel, no expression in his face.

"Did you hear me?" I asked.

"Yeah, I did," he said. "Fuck you twice. And get your hands off my car. I just had it washed."

I walked away, then stopped. I couldn't take what he'd just said. I walked back to his passenger window and stooped down.

"Here's what it is, Eddy. I got another reason I want to see these guys in a cage. Maybe one you don't understand."

"Yeah? Then tell me about it."

"Maybe when I'm in a better mood. In the meantime, be thankful I don't walk you in the public restroom and pour the soap dispenser down your mouth."

"You had a badge and you blew it," he said. "Now you take it out on your own kind. Who's the real loser, Purcel? I feel sorry for you."

"Good try, Eddy. But I paid my dues. Don't ever talk to me like that again." And I pointed my finger in his face.

# # #

Before all this happened, Dave Robicheaux was fishing for green trout down by the Barataria Preserve. He had asked me to go with him, but I'd been working on the Caddy, and now I was in a mess. What kind of mess? The three creeps knew who I was and where I lived, and I knew nothing about them. So I called Dave on his cell phone and told him everything. Dave was a good cop because he was a good listener.

When I finished talking, he said, "You're at the house?"

"Yeah," I said.

"I'll be there in two hours. Don't go anywhere, and don't talk to anyone."

"Who would I talk to?" I asked.

He didn't try to answer that one.

# # #

One hour and thirteen minutes later he pulled his pickup truck and boat trailer into my courtyard.

"What kept you?" I said.

He looked at the bandage on the side of my head and the abrasions on my face. "Who are these bastards, Clete?"

"You got me, big mon."

We went upstairs and I gave him a Dr Pepper and cracked a beer for myself, which always made me feel guilty in front of Dave, because he had done real well with the program, except with a slip here and there over the years. His home group in New Orleans was just off the Quarter. It was the Work the Steps or Die Motherfucker meeting.

"Eddy got righteous about his brother?" he said.

"You can call it that. What's the word? 'Disingenuous'?"

"He has brain damage, doesn't he?" Dave asked.

"Yeah, he came out the wrong way. But what does that have to do with stealing, lying, and letting other people stack your time? He's pretty sharp at it."

Dave was standing at the sink, drinking his Dr Pepper, looking out the window. The shadows were sinking across the courtyard. Dave was a meditative and handsome guy, six foot one, his shoulders square, his skin tanned, a patch of white in his black hair. Other cops nicknamed him Streak. They didn't know he got his white patch from malnutrition as a child.

"You told Eddy you had a special reason for wanting to take these guys down?"

"Yeah. And I put it in his face. Fentanyl is the new killer on the streets. I kind of get a little unhinged when I talk about it."

Dave leaned on his arms and nodded. He was wearing a purple shirt with white fleur-de-lis emblems stamped on it and sharply pressed gray slacks and shined loafers, and I knew he was going out later, but not just because it was Saturday evening. He had lost multiple wives but mourned in a peculiar fashion. He stayed mostly celibate and walked by himself at sunset in the graveyards where they were buried. It was kind of spooky. A priest friend of his on the bayou in Jeanerette tried to help him, but Dave Robicheaux never had a door to his soul, even with his wives, all of whom he loved. I guess you could say he was the loneliest man I ever knew.

Hey, when it came to pain, Streak did his time in the Garden of Gethsemane. Fucking A. That said, he carried his own canteen, and respected people's privacy and didn't misuse his power or degrade the lowlifes, and that was why he said nothing about the creep wearing the 6 MILLION ARE NOT ENOUGH T-shirt and a photo I tore from a magazine and had been carrying in my wallet for at least two decades.

It showed a Jewish woman walking to the showers at Auschwitz with her three children following her. She was trying to keep the children together. They probably had no idea what was about to happen to them, but I think the mother knew. Her resolution and sorrow seemed to rise right out of the magazine. I have never gotten free of this photo. I don't think anyone can until we purge the earth of those who were responsible for the fate of this woman and her children. That's how I feel. I will never stop.

I am not going to say any more. Navy psychiatrists and therapists tried to treat me when I came back from Shitsville. They were good guys. But there is no pair of tongs you can use to lift certain images from your head. You're stuck, Mac, and neither the sugar shack nor four inches of Black Jack with a beer back will set you free. I know. I tried everything short of fragging myself.

"Clete?" Dave said.

"Yeah?"

"Nobody puts the slide on the Bobbsey Twins from Homicide," he said, and winked.

"I was just thinking the same, noble mon. But right now let's go have some fried oysters and maybe a catfish po'boy with mayonnaise and sliced tomatoes and sauce piquante on the side."

"I can't think of a better activity," he said.

I loved Dave Robicheaux. Like Waylon Jennings said, "I've always been crazy, but it's kept me from going insane."

CHAPTER THREE

L ook, I mentioned I had to chase down a dancer on Bourbon Street for a bondsman in Biloxi. I got that a little mixed up. The bondsman was named Winston Sellers, also known as Sperm-O Sellers, and sometimes the Octopus, because that's what the top half of his head looked like. He was from Jersey but tried to act like he was from down here. Sperm-O was drunk and tried to grab the dancer's ankle on the runway, but she kicked him in the mouth, breaking his bridge and causing him to swallow it. The bartender had to pull it out of his throat with his fingers.

The dancer bonded out but didn't show up for her court appearance, which got her in the can again. That is where I came in. Her name was Gracie Lamar, and she came from a shithole in Alabama that made you glad the South lost the Civil War. She caused so much trouble at the jail that a female guard maced her through the bars.

She was something to look at, though. The stripper bars on Bourbon always had the front doors open, unless it was raining, and you could see her up on the runway, smaller than the other women, silvery stars sliding all over her skin, her curly reddish-blond hair hanging in her face, with an expression like *In your dreams, buddy.*

So I tried to talk things over with my lowlife colleague in Biloxi, and he said he wanted Gracie Lamar busted on every charge possible and stuck in the worst rathole jail in Orleans Parish, one with stopped-up commodes and sex predators for hacks and the door welded so she could never get out. I offered to pay for Sperm-O's bridge and any medical costs, with an extra five hundred dollars to drop the charges. He said he had to think about it, and hung up.

An hour later he called back. "I had my accountant estimate my projected medical and dental costs and a proper indemnification for pain and suffering. It will come to forty-five hundred dollars. You can wire it to my bank. You got two hours."

Yeah, he played me, but what are you gonna do? Feed a young woman to some of the piranhas we have in our jails, both staff and general population? I wired the money to his bank, and didn't sleep two minutes that night. Sperm-O called me the next day, happy because he stiffed me, happy because he could make someone's day worse than his was every time he looked in the mirror.

"Your money came through," he said. "Congratulations, big fella. You got you a real prize."

"I read you loud and clear, Sperm-O," I said. "But let's stay clear of personalities and concentrate on principles, okay?"

"What the fuck are you talking about?" he said.

"That maybe you should go swimming in your pool. You still got one, right? Have your masseuse over. Be sure to put on some sunblock."

"I'm sensing a little resentment here."

"No, I like being fleeced. But if you come around, I'm gonna have a truckful of manure dumped in your pool. That means stay away from us. Even better, stay out of New Orleans."

"*Us?* Before it's over, she'll have you sticking your gun in your mouth," he said. "Enjoy."

# # #

I asked Dave Robicheaux to move in for a few days in case the three creeps decided to visit me again, and I put my Caddy in the repair shop and tried to find out how all this doodah got dropped on my head. Plus, Dave and I both love the jazz joints and the cafés in the Quarter and the strange people who live there.

The Quarter smells like medieval Europe probably did, always dank, and except for high noon, it's always in shadow. It smells like storm sewers and night damp and lichen on stone and kegs of wine stored in a cellar and smoked fish hanging in the open-air market. The same with the people. Their eyes are different, like they're walking past you but they don't see the modern world, like Quasimodo clomping along on the cobblestones.

Anyway, Dave and I hung out at the cafés on Decatur and in Jackson Square, where you get a grand view of the sidewalk artists and the jugglers and mimes and musicians and unicyclists and the myrtle in bloom, all at once. Also, I wanted to take a break here and explain why I took a financial hit for Gracie Lamar. I've got a lot of character defects, and I probably look bad for knowing somebody like Sperm-O, but here's the gen on that and it's the honest-to-God truth: I never took advantage of a woman who was in distress. Take it to the bank, Hank. I wouldn't put you on the glide, Clyde. F.T.S. on it, too, and you know what that means.

Plus, this woman had a great talent, and it wasn't on the runway. She could sing like Linda Ronstadt and had an accent like Loretta Lynn. How could you not help a woman like that?

In other words, I took the hit and wrote it off. Fuck me. I've done worse things in this world.

It was late in the evening, with the summer light trapped high in the sky and the wind wafting off Lake Pontchartrain, a Black guy up on a balcony in the Pontalba Apartments blowing a trumpet, the waiter serving us two big bowls of crawfish gumbo and French bread smothered in butter and garlic, when Gracie Lamar came around the corner looking like she had fallen out of the dryer at the laundromat, saying, "Why don't you answer your fucking telephone, Clete?"

Then, before I could wipe my mouth and speak, she looked at Dave and added, "Who are you, honey?"

"Dave Robicheaux," Dave said. "How do you do?"

# # #

"You don't have to stand up," she told him, then ordered a vodka collins and put an envelope in front of me. "There's thirty-six dollars in there. I can pay you that every week while I'm working, but that's about it. By the way, that asshole called me this morning."

"Which asshole?" I said.

"Sperm-O Sellers, who else? What a dickwad. His head looks like a penis. It's unbelievable."

"How about it on the language?" a guy in sunglasses at the next table said. His lady also wore sunglasses, even though the sunset was soft, with no glare.

"You don't like the First Amendment, go blow yourself," Gracie said.

"I need a napkin. I'll be right back," Dave said.

Gracie watched him as he went back through the French doors. "What's wrong with your friend?" she said.

"Nothing. What did Sperm-O say?" I asked.

"That I can make a lot of money if I can provide the where-abouts of something that was in your Cadillac. What's this about?"

"Forget it. If Sperm-O calls again, let me know," I said.

"That's not good enough. I don't want to get mixed up with any of the crud in this city. I thought Alabama was bad. The inmates in that jail I was in should be issued hazmat suits or full-body condoms. I told that to the guard, and he said I ought to see the kitchen."

The waiter set a vodka collins in front of her, then went away. Dave came back to the table and sat down. He had a paper napkin in his hand. "Excuse me for eating in front of you," he said.

"That's all right," she said. She watched him lift his iced tea to his mouth. "You don't drink?"

"No," he said. Then he smiled. Dave always had a good smile. "That's because I used to."

"You're a detective in Iberia Parish?"

"Right now I'm on suspension without pay," he said.

"Suspension for what?" she asked.

"Punching another detective in the face in the department men's room."

She made a pouch of air with one cheek, then the other cheek. "You do that regularly?"

"Just with this particular guy," Dave said. "Since he got out of the state asylum, he's been on a mandatory diet of steroids and gator tail and swamp cabbage. A lot of us coonasses are like that. Frayed around the edges."

She didn't smile, but her eyes were full of lights.

"You don't believe me?" Dave said.

She continued to look at him without speaking. When the waiter passed by, she raised her collins glass at him. "Another one of these. On my tab?"

"You don't want something to eat?" Dave said.

"What, I look thin?"

"No," Dave said. "You look fine. I didn't mean to tell you what to do."

"You didn't," she said, then looked at me. "I'm really happy for what you did, Clete. I'll do everything I can to pay back your money. But I have to get this cocksucker Sperm-O out of my life. If he comes around, I'll shoot him."

"That's it with the language," the man in shades said, rising from his chair. He was much taller than he'd looked sitting down, and he had big hands and big knuckles. He snapped his fingers at the waiter. "We need some help over here!"

"Sit down, Mac," I said to him. "We didn't mean any harm. It's a beautiful evening. We'd like to treat you to a dessert."

But the tall man kept snapping his fingers, his face turned away from me. Gracie rose from her chair and picked up her purse. It was made of denim and had an Indian design sewed on it. "Sit down, Bozo," she said to the man in shades. "I'm leaving." Then she turned to Dave and me. "I mean it about Sperm-O. I'm not gonna have these geeks in my life. I'll blow him out of his socks."

Then she squeezed Dave on the shoulder with her fingers and walked across the flagstones in the coolness of the evening, the sun's last red rays catching in her hair.

# # #

Dave and I walked to my house, which was only two blocks from Jackson Square. Both of us like to read. I had a collection of paperback Civil War books, and also books about the American West, such as A. B. Guthrie's *The Big Sky* and *The Way West* and John Neihardt's *Black Elk Speaks*. But I didn't have my mind on my books.

"She likes you," I said.

"She's a kid," Dave said, looking up the back steps, the banana and palm fronds dripping. "Kids like everybody."

"She likes you in particular."

"It was you she thanked about her problems with Sperm-O."

"Yeah, making me a party to a homicide if she cools him out."

"That's all talk, Clete."

Right.

Dave was always protecting my feelings. It's him who needed protection. I never could get that across to him. I unlocked the house and turned on the lights. Rain was clicking on the foliage in the flower beds, which sometimes gave me memories of Shitsville. Dave's rig was in the courtyard, but my vehicle was not. It was at the repair shop. That gave me a lonely feeling for some reason, as though my life wasn't under control, and time was slipping away. I put my hand on the doorknob. Then I felt it with my fingers, then I felt the plate.

"Everything okay?" Dave said.

"No, somebody tried to get in."

"You're sure?"

I stepped aside. "Take a look."

Dave felt the scratches on the brass. "Who are these guys?" he said.

"You got me. They're con-wise. By now they know I don't have their fentanyl."

"So maybe that's not what they're looking for."

I had no answer, nor did I know what to say. I was a private investigator. In the world of law enforcement, that's like saying I drove a garbage truck. Back then you could buy a badge in a pawn shop for twenty dollars. I didn't have computer access to the FBI or the NCIC, and NOPD hated my guts. Want my advice? When you see a PI office, run, or don't go inside unless you spray the chairs first. And leave your credit card at home. That culture really blows.

"You still don't want an alarm system?" Dave said.

"It's junk. The oversight guy is in Tennessee. All he does is notify the locals. I'd like to go back to the good old days."

"What were the good old days?" Dave asked.

I had to think a minute. "I'm not sure."

Dave took a book off my library shelf and turned on a lamp and started reading in the living room. I went to my desk and took a ballpoint pen and a fresh yellow legal pad from the drawer and set them on my ink blotter and sat down, determined to find out who tore up my Caddy and why Sperm-O Sellers was trying to insert his way into Gracie Lamar's life. I have to say Gracie kind of stuck in my mind.

# # #

After I finished writing on my yellow pad, it looked like this:

1. I tried to give Eddy Durbin a break by letting him detail my newly acquired Caddy.
2. Eddy let his little brother, Andy, use Eddy's customers to mule some high-grade shit that the Big Sleazy certainly does not need.
3. His brother, Andy, who is a snitch and gutter rat who rolled over on his big brother, gave my Caddy to some fuckheads by mistake.
4. The fuckheads, who claim to be members of the Dixie Mafia, loaded my Caddy's panels with fentanyl or China White or the Colombian coke that's coming down Highway 10 from Miami.

5. Then somebody boosted the whole load and laid the problem on me. Or maybe some other shit is going on.

6. They waltzed into my courtyard and commenced ripping out my rolled leather in my Caddy, like it was no big deal, like nobody was going to believe me or care, particularly not NOPD, the rotten motherfuckers that they are.

7. Which leads me to think what?

8. That the three throwbacks are familiar with my history at NOPD and the contempt in which I am held for tagging a federal witness, who was also a professional rat and not worth the air he was allowed to breathe.

9. The other probability is these guys are scared shitless. Which means they will be back. But not here. Someplace in a swamp. Maybe a shack in Bayou Lafourche. Maybe a place where there are tools you don't want to think about.

# # #

I pushed away from the desk, my mouth dry, and tried to clear my throat. I couldn't. I once saw a photograph that was taken in Mississippi of a Black man who died in the fashion I just suggested. Like the image of the Jewish woman with her three children, the photo of the Black man has stayed with me for many years. There are times when I wonder if there is a bad seed among us, one that will not perish.

"Did you work it out?" Dave said, looking over the top of his book.

"Work what out?"

"Whatever you're working on."

"Yeah," I said.

He nodded, then put a cough drop in his mouth and rolled it around behind his teeth. "Want one?" he said.

"Nope."

"I think the key is the guy with the T-shirt, Clete."

"The guy with the message that six million people in Hitler's ovens aren't enough? Why him?"

"You know."

"He'll work for free and enjoys it?" I said.

Dave closed his book. The book was *Twelve Years a Slave*. It was published by LSU Press. "Want to take a ride over to Mississippi tomorrow?"

CHAPTER FOUR

E arly the next morning we crossed the state line in Dave's pickup and headed north toward the Pearl River. That name might be familiar to you. As Dave says, the South has changed greatly, and the state that has changed the most is Mississippi. But the Pearl and Tallahatchie Rivers and the rural areas along their banks will be remembered for what is worst in human beings.

I don't like to talk about it. Neither does Dave. The people who did the killings and the bombings and the burnings were not ordinary people caught up in the times. Don't believe that. As Dave says, people are what they do. These were the scum of the earth. I think some aeras had a special affirmative action program for white trash.

Look, past is past. But the past has a way of hanging around. The guy Dave and I wanted to see was a character named Hap Armstrong. What picture do you see when you hear that name? The pilot of a B-25 bombing the Japs with Jimmy Doolittle in '42? A GI wading through a red surf on D-Day, his dead friends bobbing in the waves? A GI back home with a duffel bag on his shoulder,

looking up at his tenement building, the whole neighborhood waving, a happy man Norman Rockwell would like to paint?

Nope, our Hap would never be on the cover of the *Saturday
Evening Post*. Our Hap and his cousins owned a tin-roof welding
shed and a shade-tree car repair business that barely made them
a livelihood. Hap's customers were Blacks and poor whites and
old folks. The only distinction in his life was his thirty years as a
Klavern officeholder in the Ku Klux Klan. I first met him when I
returned from Shitsville. He hated Jews, people of color, what he
called "mud-people," Asians, Mexicans, Catholics, Yankees, and
most women. Then he and eight other men from his Klavern were
charged with bombing a church. Two children died. Another was
terribly burned.

Hap claimed to be innocent. Others said he was a ringleader.
Hap's wife swore he was at home, in bed, "making a baby." The jurors
grinned and tittered and accepted her word, because no Christian
woman would embarrass herself in such a way if she were not telling the truth.

We pulled into the shell drive that led into the oak grove where
he had his welding shed. I could see an acetylene torch burning
like a hot, red poker inside the darkness of the shed. Hap cut the
torch, thumbed his goggles up on his forehead, and came outside.
His sleeveless denim shirt was drenched under his armpits, his skin
wrapped like wet dough on his bones. Four or five years ago I heard
he had cancer. In my opinion he'd contracted it long before that.
Hap's cancer was hate. Like all of his kind, he nursed it day after
day, for no reason I could ever see. As I looked at him now, I could
only pity him.

"How you doin', bub?" I said.

"All right," he replied. I waited for him to go on. But he didn't. That was it. No expression, no interest in the question, no curiosity about anything.

"Remember Dave Robicheaux?" I said.

"Yeah," he said, nodding. "What do you want?"

"Some guys tore my Caddy apart," I said. "There's one guy I thought you might have heard about."

"I don't know anything about any of this," he said.

"We know that, Mr. Armstrong," Dave said. "But you've lived around here a long time and know pretty much what goes on."

"What are you talking about?"

"We're talking about a mean-looking dude with a headful of grease and skin the color of a shirt board with pits in it. He's got a thing about Jewish people. Like killing large numbers of them."

"I ain't got nothing to do with them people no more," he replied. He rubbed his nose on his sleeve, then, to cover his butt, he said, "On either side."

"I heard you got river-baptized," Dave said.

"What about it?" Hap said.

Uh-oh, I thought. Dave had just slipped things into overdrive. You do not get into a theological discussion in the South with people like Hap Armstrong unless you enjoy talking to people who have the reasoning powers of the Ayatollah Khomeini.

"In Vietnam I saw a real fuckhead call in Puff the Magic Dragon on a ville that may or may not have had some VC in it," Dave said. "I think the VC set us up and let the ville pay the price. Regardless, the ville got naped. I couldn't sleep through the night for a long time. Not in Shitsville, not in Louisiana. You know what I'm talking about, Mr. Armstrong?"

"You get the fuck out of here," Hap said.

"Do a solid for yourself, Mr. Armstrong," Dave said. "If you got baptized and you're on the square with the Man Upstairs, you can lay down your sword and shield and not fight the war anymore."

"You don't know what I went through, you son of a bitch." He wiped his nose again, heavier and wetter this time.

"You're right," Dave said. "I apologize. I can't carry your canteen. But at some juncture—"

"What do you mean, 'juncture'?"

"When you find yourself at a crossroads, why not just walk into a town meeting or a church or a bus station or a beer joint, and say what you did, then screw the rest of it?"

"Get off my property!" Hap said.

"You got it, podna," Dave said.

Thanks, Streak, I thought. *You really know how to do it.*

We started walking toward Dave's pickup, disheartened and tired. The wind was cool, the trees rustling over our heads, the Pearl River just across the horizon. Then I heard feet running and turned around, expecting Hap Armstrong to plow into us with a sickle or a mattock. But there was nothing in his hands. It was his face that made you flinch. It was twisted out of shape, one eye larger than the other, one eye holding a tear.

"There's a man named Baylor Hemmings," he said. "He's making a name among the New Rising."

"What's the New Rising?" I said.

"I ain't gonna say no more," he replied. "Stay away from us! Ain't y'all got no mercy?"

Then he ran into the woods, his steel-toed lace-ups coming down hard, the branches cutting his skin. I thought he would keep running, but he stopped and turned around and yelled at the sky, then yelled at us and dragged his fingernails down his face like he wanted to take the flesh off the bone. Then he beat his fists against a dead tree and began running again until he was invisible.

Tell me there's more pain in a soul anywhere. And I mean anywhere. If these were the "good old days," they sucked.

# # #

Dave drove us back on the highway.

"Did you ever hear of a guy named Baylor Hemmings?" I said.

"Nope."

"How about the New Rising?" I said.

"Nope."

"You're a blabbermouth today, aren't you?" I said.

"He sounds like the kind of guy who wants to burn down the city to make it a better place."

"Can you run him for me?" I said.

"There's no 'me' or 'you' in this," Dave said. "The pronoun is 'we.'"

"Thanks, big mon."

"I've got a bad feeling about this crap, Clete. From the jump, all this, including racism, has gotten bigger rather than solvable or containable. Like with Hap Armstrong shifting into suicidal mode."

"You think Hap might kill himself?"

The left wheel on the truck hit a deep hole in the asphalt, shaking the whole frame. "You don't screw around with depressed people," Dave said. "The depression is there for a reason. You've got to be gentle and let it run its course."

I told you Dave had a way of finding guilt. But in this instance I couldn't argue with him. We had unstrapped a pitiful illiterate to his own craziness, then left him running through the woods toward the Pearl River. The thought of it drilled a hole in my stomach. You know why an education, formal or self-acquired, is worth more than Fort Knox? Other people can't wind up your clock. Not unless you let them.

"You want to go back?" I said.

"No, I'll call him later."

But after ten minutes had passed, I knew it was still on his mind.

"Come on, Streak, get out of it," I said.

"I'm sorry," he replied. "I didn't make myself clear. Like I said, everything about this seems to get uglier. What's the only thing in this world that does that?"

"You don't have to convince me about evil," I said.

We hit another bump. He was staring right at me, his eyelids stitched to his brows. "But there's something going on that's self-creating, repairing itself as it goes along. We think we see the players, but these guys are Kleenex."

"You don't think it's narcotics?"

"Maybe, but I'm doubtful," he said.

I felt sick. You know why cops and newspaper people drink? They see things that don't go in the newspaper, things they can't tell their families about. I knew both cops and journalists who worked the BTK case in Wichita, Kansas. They still won't talk about it. "Pull into that convenience store, will you?"

"What for?"

"To use the bathroom," I said.

But he knew better. I wanted a couple of sweating six-packs and three or four tiny bottles of Jack. I couldn't get Hap Armstrong out of my head. I got out by the pumps. "I'll be just a few minutes. I'm gonna call Armstrong."

"Do it," he said. "But don't hump that guy's pack, Clete."

"I don't do things like that," I said. "We need to go to Biloxi."

"To talk to Sperm-O?" he said.

"No, Sperm-O needs to talk to us. That guy is dirty to the gills."

But before we left the convenience store, I called Hap Armstrong. No answer. Tell me this: How successful have you been when you've tried to save others from themselves?

# # #

We went first to Sperm-O's office. As with most bondsmen, his office was located close to police headquarters and the jail. This is the center of the subculture I was talking about. Dave always called it the Pool. Night and day you can count on the Pool. The Pool dwellers are untrainable and unteachable. Mounds of paperwork the size of Egyptian pyramids contain their life stories. The only people who know they're alive are cops, social workers, and parole officers; without these civil servants, no one would know they were on the planet. An army is assigned to maintaining them and listening to their woes.

But here's the other side of it. The Pool creates a shadow industry of shysters and bondsmen and police reporters who usually write in the passive voice, which means they received and believed a printed handout from the public information officer. The law is usually enforceable only when people obey it of their own volition. Professional criminals don't cooperate with the law; they lie, do not give their real names, don't file IRS forms, and are basically invisible. The poor jerk who tries to pay his taxes and conform to the law gets run over by a tank. At least that's how I see it.

Sperm-O Sellers was not in his office. I was shocked.

"When will he be in?" I asked his receptionist, who was filing her nails, chewing gum, and watching a soap opera on a TV set.

"He's off for the day," she said.

"Can you tell me where he is?" I said. "I'm an old friend."

"I don't know where he is," she said. "I'm a temp. What's your name again?"

We went to his house. As a PI, you get the whole story through visuals at a person's house. His home was white-stucco beautiful, with blue Spanish tiles and walls around gardens filled with flowers and palm trees, not far from the Gulf of Mexico and Beauvoir, the home of Jefferson Davis.

"Do you believe this bastard's house?" I said.

"No, I don't," Dave said.

"Is there something on your mind, Dave?"

"No," he said. "It's a nice day."

We went up a pea-gravel drive and parked by the carriage house. I could smell the salt in the air and feel the barometer dropping and see lightning flashing way out on the Gulf, purple clouds stacking up on the horizon. There was a warm smell in the air, like seaweed and shellfish trapped on the sand and the westward sun glowing on tarnished brass. Down here, these signs meant only one thing. People were already leaving the beach, gathering up their blankets and picnic baskets and their children.

I rang Sperm-O's bell. Then rang it again, and looked through one of the amber bubbled-glass panels in the door and saw a woman walking unsteadily to a back room.

Sperm-O opened the door with a big smile, in swimming trunks and a bathrobe. "You should have called," he said. "I was just about to have some food on the deck."

People down here don't use the word "deck." They say "verandah." It takes a pile of white inner tubes like Sperm-O to vandalize the dialect.

"Can we come in?" I said.

"That's Robicheaux behind you?"

"So what?" I said.

"I don't need any more grief in my life."

"Who ran off in your bedroom?" I asked.

"None of your business, Purcel."

"I'll wait in the truck," Dave said.

"No, you won't," I said. "Listen, Sperm-O, you were making certain overtures that are very disturbing. I'm talking about bothering my client Gracie Lamar."

He raised his hands in the air, like I was about to punch him. "Can you do me a favor? Don't call me that name in my house. Second, I got a friend I'm helping with some psychological problems. She's not used to vulgarity, so show some fuckin' respect. Better yet, how about coming back another time?"

"No dice, Sperm-O," I said. "Oops, I mean 'Mr. Sellers.'"

"We'll talk, then we'll be gone, podna," Dave said behind me.

Sperm-O's eyes rolled around in his head, then he said, "All right, follow me, boys. But I got your word on this, right? We talk, then you're gone?"

Boys?

"Yep, you'll never see us again," I said.

He turned and walked through the living room and slid the door on the verandah, his robe swinging open on his blubber. But Dave scratched his neck and just stood there. "What's wrong?" I said.

"I can't take that guy. I'll stay outside."

"Remember what you said about pronouns?" I said. "There's no 'you' and no 'me.' There's just the Bobbsey Twins from Homicide?"

He grinned on the edge of his mouth and nodded. That was the old Streak. You swallow your blood and grin your enemies to death.

But I got a caveat here. You know what always scared me about Dave? Every day, without warning or without reason, I thought he was capable of going to a place inside his head he would never return from. That was Dave Robicheaux, a guy with a smile and a kind word, protecting people who had no power, but one who had triggers nobody saw coming. But what really bothered me was the world he lived in. He saw three crosses on a hill and the mass murder of Carthage and legionnaires plowing the earth and Atlanta and Hiroshima burning. Dave blew the minds of the psychiatrists at the VA. People think *I'm* a drunk. Dave can get drunk and out of control without getting drunk.

# # #

Sperm-O waited until we were seated at glass-topped table under an umbrella, then went back to the kitchen and returned with a silver tray of pickled shrimp and tomato sauce dip and celery with cream cheese stuffed in it. He also brought a bottle of Cold Duck. He didn't ask if we wanted some other kind of drink. He had to know what Dave's history was, and mine, too. Can you imagine this shithead talking to you like that? I felt like telling him. Dave's deeds left him with blackouts and delirium tremens and the smell of burnt gunpower in the air, and the greaseballs climbing out the windows, I mean guys who were serious button men for the Mafia, all of it without two fingers of Jack in a shot glass.

"You got any Dr Pepper?" I said.

"Sorry," Sperm-O said.

"Well, shitcan the Cold Duck and bring us some iced tea," I said. "Or just a glass of water."

"I got some lemonade," Sperm-O said. "How's that?"

"I don't need anything," Dave said.

Sperm-O spread his hands wide, smiling. "What can I do for yous?"

"You got a hold of Gracie Lamar's private number and told her she could make a lot of money if she could provide you with information about the break-in of my Caddy."

"Gracie Lamar's got Swiss cheese for a brain," he said. "I was just trying to lend a helping hand."

"Yeah, a helping hand is right," I said. "That's how you got kicked in the mouth."

"What did I do to you guys?" he replied. "Why are you always on my case?"

"I've got a problem with you, Mr. Sellers," Dave said.

"Oh, yeah?"

Oh, shit, I thought.

"Yeah," Dave said. "We've got a number of morons mixed up in a car break. But the intensity of interest is far greater than dime bags in the projects. I have the strange sense there's a political edge to this. Have you heard of something called the New Rising?"

"You mean like getting a hard-on?" Sperm-O said.

"Answer the question," Dave said.

"No, I have never heard of any such thing as that."

"How about an anti-Semite by the name of Baylor Hemmings?"

"No, and I don't hang around anti-Semites, either."

Sperm-O kept his eyes on Dave's, without blinking, even though the sun's glare was in his face. Big mistake for Sperm-O. Liars try to stare you down, like Hollywood actors. The wind was popping the fringes of the umbrella; the air was humid and full of electricity and the smell of iodine. There was a tingling in the arches of my feet, and my hands were curling and uncurling under the table.

"Take the mashed potatoes out of your mouth, Sperm-O," I said.

"You're not gonna insult me in my own house," he said.

"Who's Hemmings, Mr. Sellers?" Dave said.

"Is he that famous author who wrote a book about catching a marlin off Cuba?"

"Nobody is this stupid," I said.

"Get out! Both of yous!"

"Who's the woman in the bedroom?" Dave said.

"Fuck you."

Then Dave did something I didn't believe he would do, and it bothered me. He handed me a shrimp, then pushed the platter into Sperm-O's lap, the shrimp and mayonnaise and tomato sauce sliding down his thighs.

"Two blocks from here over two hundred Confederate soldiers are buried under Jefferson Davis's lawn," Dave said. "Maybe you should give that some thought."

Then he walked back into the house and opened the door to the bedroom we had a seen woman enter earlier. I followed right behind him. The woman was sitting sideways on her legs on the carpet, one shoulder propped against the bed, a hypodermic needle in her lap, the tourniquet still tied on her arm.

She was Asian, and not young, but neither was she old. She was also beautiful, despite her age and the tracks on her arm. I pinched my hand on my mouth, because I did not know what to say, nor could I believe what I was seeing, nor could I deal with the dropping sensation in my stomach, like an elevator plunging down a shaft. I had suddenly traveled across the seas, into a neocolonial world I never wanted to see again. A place where the sun rose like thunder, and where death ruled and the innocent and the poor and the charitable were murdered from night to morning, and where thieves broke in and stole away the only woman I ever truly loved, and by "stole" I mean they blew her to pieces while her body was entangled with mine.

The Asian woman on the floor raised her face and tried to smile. "My name Chen," she said.

"Something's wrong, Streak," I said. "I'm losing my mind, and the whole fucking room is about to slide into the Gulf. I think maybe I'm dead. Don't look at me like that. I'll hit you."

I had never talked to Dave like that before.

CHAPTER FIVE

We got her into the truck, sitting between us. The wind was starting to blow, the few raindrops in it as hard as drops of lead, the sky darkening. "Haul butt," I said to Dave.

"To where?" he asked.

"Anyplace except here. There's a guy looking at us with binoculars down by the beach."

"I don't see him."

"Take my word for it. I saw him from the verandah."

Dave turned around slowly by the carriage house, looking at his mirrors.

"Dave, will you trust me?" I said.

"You want to take her to a detox or a hospital?"

"Negative on both," I said.

"Are you insane? We don't have any idea who she is. Or how much junk she has in her arm."

We were approaching the four-lane, which could lead us into Biloxi or Gulfport or to New Orleans. I shook my finger at him. "Sperm-O is into white slavery. I heard about it before, but I didn't believe it. She's probably an illegal. The locals will put her in a cage."

The clouds were black. I could hear myself breathing, a drum thudding in my ears. A bolt of lightning splintered the sky.

"Dave, if you take us into town—"

I shouldn't have doubted Streak. He turned left and headed us toward the Louisiana line. Then the heavens burst open and the rain twisted like spun glass on the highway and steel signs vibrated like soda straws.

"Your name is Chen?" I said to the woman.

She smiled but didn't respond.

"Where do you live?"

She continued to smile and look at the rain sliding under the tires.

"*Nee how ma,*" I said.

She turned her face to mine, then touched my cheek. "*How,*" she said.

Then she rested her head on her chest and went to sleep.

"What did you say?" Dave asked.

"I asked her how things were. That's all I know of Mandarin. She said she was okay."

Dave started to speak, but I cut him off. "Dave, I know this sounds crazy, but it really disturbs me," I said. "Yeah, the guy you dumped the shrimp on is a degenerate and a fat shit, but you don't put yourself on the same level with a guy like that."

He kept his eyes straight ahead as a semi passed us, blowing water all over our windshield. "I guess I need to go to a meeting."

"That's not a bad idea. You want to stop somewhere?"

"No," he said. "You have Sellers's number?"

"You're gonna call him?"

"That's what people usually use phone numbers for," he said, grinning now, the old noble mon back in E major.

"Yeah, I got his number in my phone," I said. "Here."

He pulled into a rest stop and got out in the rain, with no coat or hat, still grinning.

"Are you trying to catch pneumonia?" I said. "You're gonna get washed into South America."

But there was no changing Dave's mind about anything. He walked to the rest stop and talked a few minutes under the roof, then walked back to the truck, hopping inside, slamming the door, blowing out his breath.

"Did you get ahold of him?"

"Yeah," he said, starting the engine.

"What'd he say?"

Dave looked to see if the woman named Chen was still asleep. "He said, 'Eat shit and fuck you.'"

"Sounds like Sperm-O."

"What are we going to do with this lady, Clete?"

"I'll make some calls. In the meantime, she can stay with me. I'll have a third person there too."

"Who?"

"How do I know?" I said. "I'll take care of it. You look like a sponge."

He drove deeper into the storm, lightning popping on the bays, palm trees and live oaks shredding, the mystery lady couched between us, sleeping the sleep of the dead.

# # #

It rained all the way into New Orleans. We parked inside the court-yard and went through the French doors on the first floor to keep out of the rain. I changed the linen on my bed and put the lady to sleep in it, then made up a bed for myself downstairs and let Dave stay on the couch in the upstairs living room. I didn't know if Dave was going back to New Iberia that evening or not. I did not want him to go, but I didn't want to make his life any more difficult than it was. Plus, I had to feed my cats and clean their litter boxes. I love cats. Anyone who doesn't love cats, I think, should be killed.

Sorry, I don't know why I worried about Dave leaving. Dave Robicheaux was stubborn, but he never left a friend behind or failed to back his play. And I mean never. He would carry the Statue of Liberty on his shoulder if he thought she was in trouble.

I got on the phone and hired a Black cleaning lady, who was also a long-time friend, to help look after Chen, and I also hired Gracie Lamar, who was happy to have an opportunity to pay back the money she owed me for getting her free of Sperm-O. I also called a former navy corpsman, who in my opinion was as good as any medical doctor I ever knew, and asked him to check out the woman named Chen, no questions asked.

I know this sounds strange. But there are millions of people in this country who live off the grid and do nothing that is in sync with the rest of the nation. You can do it in fifteen minutes. You drop by the courthouse and apply for a copy of someone else's birth certificate. Then you get a library card and rent a post office box and order all kinds of trash mail. In fact, you don't even have to do that. After Vietnam, there were thousands of nameless vets holed up in the Washington rainforests. Thousands more joined the street populations in Los Angeles and Portland and New York City. An urban jungle is a jungle, and its rules are the same as those that apply in the heart of Africa. You survive.

But there was another story going on there. It was white slavery, and it still is. Most of the victims are from the Third

World. They work in sweatshops and they work in whorehouses. They suffocate in locked vans, in the holds of ships, and in steel containers on loading docks. For some of them, their environment is probably worse than the Middle Passage was in pre–Civil War times. Chen spoke Mandarin, so my guess was she came from North China or Taiwan. But I didn't care where she was from, and here's why.

I fell in love with a young Vietnamese woman who lived on a sampan in a marshy area on the edge of the South China Sea. She had no politics, and neither did her family. They were fisher people and lived simple lives. A trip into a city twenty klicks away was a grand event. The sampan they lived on was comfortable, the wood hand-carved and notched and calked and strung with mosquito netting. At sunrise and sunset, the sea and the flooded bamboo glowed with a bronze radiance that I never understood. It reminded me of pictures I had seen in an Old Testament Bible.

If I could have had my way, I would have never left. To this day, I am not sure what took place. Her family was gone. It was evening tide, the water high inside acres of flooded reeds, the sun like a smithy's forge, sliding off the side of the Earth. The monsoons were over, and there were storks and pink spoonbills pecking themselves in the bays. We were on a pallet, one with quilts folded on it, inside the mosquito netting, her thighs spread across mine, her breasts hanging above my chest, her eyes lidded, her lips parted.

Then I heard the first burst, maybe an AK-47, maybe not, maybe NVA, maybe VC. Then someone was firing from a boat. I knew this because tracer rounds were streaking across the water, like disconnected pieces of neon. I don't know whose rounds hit her, or where they came from. She shuddered all over, as though she were being electrocuted, her head back, as though in orgasm.

I can't talk about this any longer. I live with this every night of my life. I hate every son of a bitch in the world who cheers on a war he doesn't attend himself. If I had my way—

I won't say any more. I apologize.

CHAPTER SIX

It was cool and sunny the next morning, the courtyard pooled with rainwater. Dave went back to New Iberia, where I'd be going soon, because I had an office on Main Street and a room I rented at the Teche Motel on the bayou, right next to the live oaks. In the meantime, during the next few days, I got my Caddy back from the repair shop, bought clothes for Chen, took her for a ride on the St. Charles streetcar through the Garden District, and tried to find out where she was from. I also waited for the monkey to get loose.

Recovering alcoholics call it "restless, irritable, and discontent." Junkies have it a lot worse. Why? Because most of them started off as drunks, so they have a double problem. Hey, this is what you learn. Don't let that shit get you. I'll never forget what a pusher in the Desire project told me about his relationship with customers: "I don't got to dial them up. They're two days away. On their knees."

Chen got the shakes. She locked the bathroom door and cried. She puked in my office wastebasket. I sat on the couch at three in the morning and watched her writhe on the rug while heat lightning leaped in the sky. She slapped at my face and body when I forced her into the bathroom and locked the door and didn't unlock it until I heard her turn on the shower.

Then the monkey went away. My guess was it would be back, but right then she was on what recovering people call "the little pink cloud." It doesn't last long, but it's lovely while it does. You probably already know what Mark Twain said about his experience with smoking: "It's easy to quit. I've done it hundreds of times."

She seemed to bloom. Her hair was shiny and thick and soft-looking, her eyes clear. She woke before I did and made breakfast for us both. But she would not give me her last name or tell me where she came from. Maybe she was afraid of the law. Or maybe she had memories she never wanted to revisit.

I'll give a sample of our conversations:

Me: How did you come to the United States?

Chen: I not know.

Me: Who brought you to Biloxi?

Chen: I not sure.

Me: What's your family name, Chen?

Chen: A nice name. What "cocksucker" mean?

Me: Where did you hear *that*?

Chen: Outside on sidewalk.

Me: Don't use that word again. It's a bad word.

Chen: I no do. You no use?

Me: Uh—

Chen: You nice man, Mr. Clete. Mr. Dave too. But you
   nicer because you comb hair like little boy.

Me: Enough with the compliments, Chen.

Chen: Compliments are bad?

Me: This is giving me an aneurysm.

Chen: You always gentleman, Mr. Clete. Your cats sleep on
   your face and you no mind.

She picked up my hand and kissed it. "The world kill men like
you because you brave and you kind."

Then she ran into the bathroom and locked the door. Jesus
Christ, how do you handle that?

# # #

I had to get to New Iberia, which was a little over two hours on
the old highway, but I couldn't take Chen everywhere I went. No
situation is perfect. Plus, both the cleaning lady, whose name was
Miss Dorothy, and Gracie Lamar liked her and took her places
and helped her with her English. Plus again, they were a good sort
themselves. Life is funny that way, isn't it? On a dark day, you can
call good people to your home, and suddenly the world becomes a
fine place, well worth the fighting for, as Ernest Hemingway said.

Then I got the phone call from an NOPD vice cop named Earl
Banner, a shithead who never found a gutter he didn't love.

"Glad I caught you at home, Purcel," he said.

"I'm not at home," I said. "I'm in my office."

"From what I hear, you turned your place into a fuck pad. With
two or three broads around."

"What did you say?"

"Lose the attitude, Purcel. Nobody is interested in your private life. I got a couple of calls from Biloxi PD and the Mississippi State Police."

"So?" I said, taking a breath, trying not to exhale into the phone. Banner was a son of a bitch. He did nothing unless it benefited him or caused injury to others.

"So you're buds with Sperm-O Sellers?"

"No."

"How about your buddy Dave Robicheaux?"

"Why don't you call Dave and ask? Or do it in person and see what happens?"

"How about your dancer friend on Bourbon, Gracie Lamar, if that's actually her name?"

"I'm about to hang up," I said. "Is there anything else?"

"Yeah, at about six thirty yesterday morning, somebody dropped Sperm-O on his verandah from about two hundred yards out. One shot. A thirty-ought-six. The round toppled and keyholed his face. A black Ford pickup was seen in the vicinity about the time of the shot. Doesn't Robicheaux have a truck like that? Your prints and his are all over the house."

"Sounds like you're playing with yourself again, Banner. Your mother didn't talk to you about that?"

I eased the phone back onto the cradle. I knew the drill. Dave and I were on a shit list. I had no idea who dropped Sperm-O. He was a creep and probably a sexual nightmare and possibly involved in white slavery, but he seemed an unlikely and expensive candidate for the crosshair talents of a professional killer.

The vice cop, Earl Banner, knew all this, too. That's what shit lists are for. To besmirch innocent people. Banner was a sewer rat. He'd be back, like Chen's monkey.

I went upstairs. Chen and Gracie and Miss Dorothy were fixing lunch. Dorothy's mother nicknamed her for the Judy Garland character in *The Wizard of Oz* because she was always dancing around the house when she was a little girl.

"Join us," Gracie said. That girl had the most beautiful hair I had ever seen—it was like reddish-gold fire. Or bronze. Or anything. Some women are like that. Whatever they are is beautiful. I've got kind of an obsession with this. Anyway, the three women were all looking at me, waiting. Earl Banner was going to cause trouble. I knew it, and had a hard time speaking. This might seem like an exaggerated fear. It was not. Every soldier who has been in a war zone knows this terrible truth: The innocent suffer the greatest, from Nanking to Hiroshima, from Dresden to Wounded Knee, from the Polish ghetto to the deliberate starvation of the Irish. "Thank you," I said. "I have to run a few errands."

I went down the back stairs to my Caddy, trying to keep my smile in place, then drove out on the street into the noonday traffic, heading for Eddy's Car Wash. All this had started with Eddy's little brother, Andy. Maybe with dumb luck I could catch him there and then have a chat and, when that failed, tie him to the chain that moved the cars through the wash shed into the soap brushes, followed by a wax job.

# # #

I circled Eddy's twice. Neither he nor Andy was there. Nor were any customers. Some Black kids were popping chamois cloths at each other. I got out of the Caddy and walked over. "What's the haps?" I said.

They stared at me blankly.

"That means 'what's happening?'" I said.

"You want a wash?" one kid said. He was shirtless, and the elastic on his boxer shorts was pulled up higher than his trousers.

"I was looking for Andy."

"He ain't here," the kid replied.

"I gathered that. Do you know where he is? I owe him twenty bucks."

"He's eating lunch."

"Where?"

"In Holy Cross."

"Where in Holy Cross?"

"By the levee."

"We're making progress," I said. "Where by the levee?"

"In a li'l bitty park. You're axing about Andy, right?"

"Right," I said.

"Then why ain't you hearing what I say, man? I think you got a li'l thinking problem."

I drove there in eight minutes. Across from the levee that paralleled the Mississippi was a grove of live oaks littered with trash and a street where the houses were decayed and looked like machine-gun bunkers built in the early 1950s. This was a poor area in the Lower Ninth Ward. There was something haunting about this particular spot, but not for poetic reasons. There were open spaces, filled with weeds, few of them naturally attractive, many of them barren. The asphalt streets had no curbs, only rain ditches. The proximity to the Mississippi and the height of the levee made me wonder what a twenty-foot tidal surge could do to the neighborhood. There was a canal that went directly from the Gulf deep into the land, as though waiting for a storm.

I turned into the oak grove. There were two concrete tables and seats among the trees. Some old men were playing horseshoes and some kids slinging a Frisbee. Andy Durbin was sitting at one of the tables, a lunch bag pressed flat in front of him. He made me as soon as he saw the Caddy. I could see him breathing through his mouth as I approached him, but that's how he always breathed, his eyes like a pair of green Life Savers—unblinking, as hard as candy. He was in his late thirties, but you couldn't tell it. He made me think of a child sitting inside the body of an adult.

"I know who you are," he said.

"How are you doin', Andy? Mind if I sit down?"

"You want to talk to me about me and my brother, don't you?"

"Could be."

"We ain't done nothing wrong."

"I can dig that, but somebody laid some pain on me, and I could really use your help."

"You got any soda?"

His sentences sounded like they were put together with tweezers, his tone like blocks of wood hitting each other.

"I'm not trying to burn your kite, podjo," I said. "I know Eddy is a little mad at me, but you gotta remember, some bad dudes did a number on me. See the side of my head?"

"Somebody broke into the Coke machine," he said.

"What?"

"Down the street, at the little grocery. I couldn't get a Coke and a ice cream cone with my lunch. I didn't get a piece of frozen cake, either."

"That's a heartbreaking story, Andy. But I think you and these three dudes were transporting fentanyl in my car. Fentanyl killed my grandniece, Andy. That's hard to take."

I thought he would get angry and throw a tantrum. I had seen him do it before. Instead, his face became sweet, his green eyes brighter. "No fentanyl. Fentanyl is bad."

"Somebody made you their mule, Andy."

"No."

"Yes," I replied. "They used you."

"No," he repeated. "I want a vanilla cone. One with a chocolate dip. I don't want to talk about this anymore."

"Who's Baylor Hemmings, Andy?"

An angry moment clouded his face. From somewhere nearby, I could hear horseshoes clanking against a steel stake.

"Baylor Hemmings doesn't like Jews, does he?" I said.

"I want my Coke. I want ice cream and cake, too."

"What's going on over there?" one of the horseshoe throwers said.

"I'm a friend of Andy's family," I said.

"The hell you are," the horseshoe man said.

Andy's face went quiet, his eyes serene. His transformation reminded me of other occasions when he'd gone through dramatic changes, like when he was caught setting a fire inside a filling station, or the time he put poison in the neighbor's pet bowl.

I smiled at the man who had just called me a liar. "We've got no problem here," I said.

"Yeah?" he said.

"Cross my heart and hope to die," I said.

He gave me a dirty look and went back to his game. But my interview with Andy was a dead end regardless. Maybe I overloaded on Andy. Maybe I even mocked him. However, I was never convinced that Andy was a sweet kid, as many people called him. Dave Robicheaux doesn't believe the human family evolved from a single tree. I think Dave has it right. I think the real question is how many trees.

Rain clouds were gathering again on the horizon, like purple fruit rolling inside a golden bowl. I put up the top on my Caddy and drove away. In the rearview mirror I saw Andy light a cigarette and blow out a smooth white plume, his head bent back, grinning to himself.

# # #

Later that afternoon I gave contact numbers to the ladies at my house and took the old highway through Morgan City to New Iberia. South Louisiana doesn't have a past, a present, or a future. You won't find sequence here. The weather, the light, the wetlands, and the Gulf change constantly, like you're inside a dream. At Morgan City you go over a bridge that makes your stomach drop, like a camera swallowing you. All at once you see the Atchafalaya River flowing through miles of swampland and small cottages along the banks and shrimp boats docked in the middle of town and, far to the south, the magnificence of the Gulf of Mexico, where every night in the summer lightning leaps through the clouds without making a sound.

It's not a place; it's magic.

Dave won't admit this, but he sees more out there than I just described. At night, during the Civil War, the blockade runners would have a go at it, carrying mostly food but also Enfield rifles. Two or three times Dave saw their cannons firing from the gunwales, and the ships' masts and sails collapsing, the faces of the cannoneers suddenly illuminated when they jerked their lanyards.

Of course, Dave also saw Confederate soldiers in the mists on Spanish Lake, just outside of New Iberia. A drummer boy tripped in the shallows, and when Dave tried to grab him before he fell, his hand plunged through the boy's arm.

I believed Dave, and not because I had any evidence. I believed Dave because he never lied.

The sun was still up when I drove into New Iberia, the tide rising over the banks of Bayou Teche, the surface chained with rain rings, East Main Street deep in shadow, canopied with live oaks, the antebellum and Victorian houses just as they were in the nineteenth century. I wondered what it was like back then. Did the Christians have problems of conscience? How could they not? But that's not really my point. I had a feeling that something terrible was going to happen. And not just among us. Maybe a great darkness was coming from a place no one ever suspected.

When I had thoughts like these, I got drunk. I wasn't going to do that this time. Never, never, never, I said, hitting the steering wheel with the flat of my fist.

CHAPTER SEVEN

I had an office in the center of town, one block from Burke Street and the drawbridge over the Teche, and I had a permanent room at the Bayou Teche Motel down the street from the Shadows, a two-story, double-chimney plantation house with a second-floor verandah, built in 1834. William Faulkner and Henry Miller used to visit there. The owner back then was a drunk and once went out on the verandah in his robe and flipped a cigarette over the banister and went over with it, slamming into the flower bed and breaking his arm. Welcome to bayou country.

My room at the motel was the last one on the driveway and had chickens in the yard. From my window I could see the sun spangling on the oaks and the Teche running high and yellow and full of mud, a red pontoon plane anchored on the other side. I was in my skivvies, fixing a pot of Community Coffee, when I heard a vehicle park in front of my door, then a moment later multiple footsteps on the little wood stoop. My door didn't have a window, so I had to wrap a towel around myself, put on the night chain, and open the door four inches.

It was Earl Banner, the vice cop from NOPD. I told you he'd be back. Banner had the personality of a mousetrap, always trying to keep you off-balance and mess you up and embarrass you in front of other people. He had his badge hanging from his belt to ensure the neighbors would know I was in a beef of some kind with the government. A man wearing gray slacks and oxblood loafers and a light-blue long-sleeve shirt stood behind him, his hair neatly clipped, his face rosy, a dimple in his chin. He was tall and had a college ring on his left hand.

"What do you want, Banner?" I said.

"I'm doing a favor for our sister state and the United States government," he said. "This is FBI Special Agent Samuel Hawthorne, from Mississippi."

"How you doin'?" I said to the agent. "I'd invite you in, but I just got up."

"Sorry for the inconvenience, but I'd really appreciate it," Hawthorne said.

"How about later?" I said.

"Are you the fella who used to refer to us as 'Fart, Barf, and Itch'?" He grinned when he said it.

This was not good. My face was burning. I still had the night chain on and felt like a jerk being taken to task by the Fuller Brush man. "Yeah, I'm the guy," I said. "Y'all put me in the can a couple of times. But c'est la vie, right?"

"While we're on the subject, is it true you drove a bulldozer through a mobster's house on Lake Pontchartrain, then dumped all the rubble in his swimming pool and dug out his tennis courts for good measure?"

"No, it was an earth grader."

"Mr. Purcel, I would consider it an honor if you could talk to me for fifteen minutes."

I looked at the mallards wrinkling the water on the edge of the bayou. "You drink coffee?"

# # #

I unlocked the chain, and the two of them came inside. I closed the door behind them. Banner sniffed at the air. "It smells like a soiled jockstrap in here," he said.

"You can wait outside," I said.

"Don't be so sensitive," he said. "You made a crack about my mother over the phone."

"No, I didn't," I said.

"Fuck you didn't."

That was Earl Banner, with his thumb always on the jugular.

"You want a beignet?" I said to Hawthorne, the FBI agent.

"No, thanks. Know why anyone would want to kill Mr. Sellers?"

"Not in the way it was done," I replied.

"Too professional?"

"Yep."

"Does Detective Robicheaux have any ideas?"

"I wouldn't know."

"Even though you're best of friends?" He was smiling now.

"I like your college ring," I said. "Where'd you go?"

"Vanderbilt."

"I went to a juco," I said.

"How about we get back on the fucking subject?" Banner said.

He had a face made of bone, peroxided blond hair he said he needed for his role as a degenerate, a flat chest like a boxer, and a dangerous energy that sparkled in his eyes and took your inventory. "Why's this dancer Gracie Lamar mixed up with both you and Sperm-O? By the way, you know she's in the life, don't you?"

"You're full of shit," I said. "Tell you what, Banner, I've got a question for you. Why's a vice guy worried about a homicide in

Mississippi?" Then I let my gaze drift to the agent named Hawthorne. "And why is the FBI interested in a worthless hump like Sperm-O?"

"Trafficking in human beings is a federal crime," Hawthorne said. "But we don't think white slavery had anything to do with his murder. We think he bumbled into some information that some extremely bad people don't want others to possess."

"What kind of information?" I said.

"What is it you can't understand, Purcel?" Banner said. "We ask the questions. Got it?"

The gas flame was curling around the bottom of my coffeepot. I couldn't take much more of Banner, and I felt foolish standing in my kitchen in my skivvies and rabbit slippers. "Excuse me, I'm going in the other room and dress," I said to Hawthorne.

"We're on a schedule here, Purcel," Banner said. "Why don't you pull your head out of your hole and think about other people for a change?"

"It's okay, Earl," Hawthorne said. "You and I will wait for Mr. Purcel down by the water."

Banner stuck a cigarette in his mouth. "Yeah, I could use some fresh air. How do you stand it in here? You should hand out nose plugs, Purcel."

As soon as they were outside, I dressed and called Dave on my cell. "Streak, a Fed and Earl Banner are here. The Fed seems like an okay guy. Banner is a shit. He's gonna haul your pickup truck. I know it. Don't argue with me."

"Roger that," he said, and hung up.

I opened the front door and motioned Banner and Hawthorne inside. I had forgotten to turn off the burner. The coffee boiled over and sizzled in the flames. I turned off the stove.

"You cocksucker," Banner said.

"*What?*" I said.

"You called Robicheaux, didn't you? Your cell is right there on the table. It wasn't there when we went outside. You motherfucker!"

"Let's slow it down," Hawthorne said.

"No, let's get this straight," Banner said to Hawthorne. "You don't know these two assholes. There was a black truck seen at the exact spot where the shooter smoked Sperm-O. Robicheaux and Purcel have had shit on their noses for decades. I don't know how they're still around."

I picked up the coffeepot, a washcloth inside the handle, and looked at Hawthorne. I could see the alarm in his face. Banner didn't have a clue. "Ever hear of a guy named Baylor Hemmings?" I said to Hawthorne.

He raised his eyebrows. "Yes, I have," he said.

"You know about the break-in on my car?"

"Yes," he said.

"I think Baylor Hemmings was one of the burglars."

"How did you get his name?"

"From a former Klansman up by the Pearl River. Ever hear of a group called the New Rising?"

Hawthorne smiled. "You've been busy."

"What the fuck is going on here?" Banner said.

"This doesn't concern you, Banner," I said.

"I might have my problems, but I never took juice and I never ran guns to leftist spics," he said.

I could feel my fingers tightening inside the handle of the coffeepot, the washcloth squeezing into my palm.

Hawthorne rested his hand on Banner's shoulder. "Oh, don't be too hard on our friend, Earl. I hear Mr. Purcel had quite a history in the Marine Corps: two tours in Vietnam, three Purple Hearts, the Silver Star, and the Navy Cross. He's been quite helpful, so let's leave him alone right now and thank him for his time. Top of the morning to you, Mr. Purcel."

Then he guided Banner out the door and closed it behind him, never looking at me.

I knew he would be back, though. I also knew the Feds were not going to tip their hand on this one. But what was the issue? White slavery? A five-and-dime drug deal? Hate groups run by people who think brushing your teeth is unmanly? Hawthorne didn't ask me if I had an opinion regarding the object of the break-in. Which meant he already knew and he was not going to share it. I called Dave and told him what had just happened.

"You handled it okay, Clete," he said. "That's what counts, podna."

"This is creeping me out, Dave, but I don't know why."

"It's because others can't see what you take for granted. Secondly, you don't give yourself any credit."

"Credit for what?"

"For being you."

"Dave, I gotta ask you something. And it really hurts."

"Go ahead."

I cleared my throat. "You didn't lend your truck to somebody who went over to Mississippi and punched Sperm-O's ticket, did you?" My heart was pounding.

"You mean did I pop him?" Dave asked.

My feet were tapping up and down on the floor. "You've had blackouts without the flack juice, big mon. Not once, but at least a half dozen times that I know about."

"No, I've had no blackouts recently, Cletus."

"Blackouts are called blackouts because you don't remember them."

"I guess that's right. But trust me."

"You're not mad at me, are you?"

"Name one instance I ever got mad at you."

"Dave, this is what makes it worse. This feeling I got now, it's like my chest is on fire and I can't breathe and something real is about to happen, and it's so bad I wouldn't think it was wrong to cap a guy like Sperm-O."

"It's called psychoneurotic anxiety. It can tear your head off."

"Tell me about it."

"Let's get a spearmint snowball in the park," he said.

That was Dave. The man who created our short version of the Serenity Prayer, namely, "Fuck it, we're the Bobbsey Twins from Homicide."

# # #

He picked me up and we rumbled across the steel grid on the drawbridge at Burke Street and went into City Park, which in New Iberia is really a lovely urban forest. During summer the snowball man would set up his stand by the seesaws and the jungle gym and the softball diamond, and Dave and I would buy a spearmint snowball and watch the children play. It was a good world to be part of. The morning was cool, the breeze wrinkling the Teche, the oaks filled with robins, the squirrels jumping from limb to limb, and I had brought along my binoculars so I could enjoy all these things. Know what Robert E. Lee said right before his death? "I only wish to be a simple child of God."

"Don't let Banner get you down," Dave said.

"He's a psychopath, big mon," I said. "He's waiting for his moment."

"Let him."

"Wrong attitude, Streak. This guy should be salted and tacked on the barn door."

What people don't understand about Dave is that he has two Daves living in one skin. One Dave is a mummy. The other contains a train about to run off the tracks. One is meditative; the other lives in the year 778 and is riding at Roland's side up Roncesvalles Pass.

"This is how I read it, Clete," he said. "The Feds and the locals in Biloxi have the equation turned around. They're wondering who would hire a professional hitman to kill a pathetic man like Sperm-O, and they've concluded that he had some important information about drugs or something worse. The truth is he didn't know anything. But somebody saw you and me through binoculars at Sperm-O's house and decided he needed a tag on his toe. In other words, Sperm-O's connection with us cost him his life."

"Thanks, Dave," I said. "Great way to put it."

"Yeah, that doesn't sound too good, does it?"

"What is it we know that is so valuable other people are killing each other about it, although we ourselves don't know what we have? Where do you get these ideas, big mon?"

Then I realized he wasn't listening. "What are you looking at?" I said.

"That red pontoon plane."

"Yeah, it was moored across from my cottage last night."

"Who belongs to it?"

"I don't know. I never saw it before. Who cares?"

"It's against the law to fly airplanes on the bayou," he said.

"People fly them up and down the bayou all the time."

"Yeah, and it's dumb," Dave said, and stood up. "There's a woman in the passenger seat. She's got binoculars on us."

"I'm gonna get another snowball," I said.

Dave watched the plane lift up, then disappear behind the trees on the next bend. In the Atakapa language, *teche* means snake, because of the many curves in the bayou. I walked over to the snowball stand, wondering if Dave was starting to lose it. I'm not kidding about Dave losing it, either. It's a good thing I keep his dials turned down. Anyway, I saw a man down by the duck pond, which was a miniature swamp inhabited by nonmigratory birds. I rubbed my eyes and looked again, then wondered if I, not Dave, had the vision problem.

It was Hap Armstrong, the former KKK officer, who gave us our first lead in our search for the men who tore up my Caddy and knocked me unconscious. The last time we saw him he'd been running toward the Pearl River, yelling incoherently, leaving both Dave and me with a shitload of guilt. Now he was back. Lucky us.

I put my binoculars to my eyes. He was standing on an arched wooden bridge over the duck pond, dressed in clean strap overalls and a pressed white cotton shirt with tiny purple flowers on it, the sleeves buttoned at the wrists. His cheeks were shaved, his hair wet and combed. His mouth was moving, but no one was around him. His eyes were lidless, like two lead washers.

"Mayday," I said.

"What's going on?" Dave said.

"Hap Armstrong is at the duck pond. He looks like he left his bread too long in the oven."

"Is he carrying?"

"Not that I can see."

"We need to get him away from these kids, Clete."

"You got it, noble mon. Shit, what the hell is with this guy?"

"I think you just said it. He lives in hell."

Dave wasn't trying to be smart. He'd witnessed two electrocutions in Angola. He would never talk about it, and he would walk out of the room if others did.

We headed toward the duck pond. Neither of us was armed, nor was either of us wearing a coat in which we could hide a weapon. As we got closer to the pond, we increased the distance between ourselves, looking at everything in the environment except Hap Armstrong. Dave smiled and so did I, as though we were talking about the weather.

"Don't y'all come no closer," Armstrong said.

"What's that?" I said, cupping my ear.

"I been to the river," he said. "I done washed off all my sins."

"We're happy to hear that, Mr. Armstrong," Dave said. "It's nice to see you. What brings you to New Iberia?"

"If you'll shut your goddamn mouth a minute, I'll tell you."

"Dave's on the square, Hap," I said. "We were worried about you. We left you a message or two to that effect."

"You don't git it. My sins are gone, but that don't hep the children we killed."

"Why don't you sit down with us and have a snowball?" I said.

"Jesus wept in the garden. He sweated blood. I cain't sweat blood, but I can tell y'all what's coming."

"You're not carrying a weapon, are you?" I said, trying to grin.

"Weapons don't do no good when the devil's in charge."

"Let's sit down in the shade, Mr. Armstrong," Dave said. "Remember the words of Stonewall Jackson when he died? 'Let us cross over the river and rest under the shade of the trees.' That has a nice sound to it, doesn't it?"

"I don't know nothing about no damn trees. I got to stop them people."

"Which people?" I said.

"They ain't just after the Jews."

"Who's 'they'?" Dave said.

Armstrong looked both ways. "Them that's gonna steal the light from the world, them that's gonna bring us to a new reckoning."

Dave and I looked at each other. "We'd like to be your friend, Hap," I said. "How'd you find us?"

"Went to your private detective office."

"How'd you get here?" Dave asked.

"Colored woman drove me."

Right there, in one short statement, was the great irony of the American South. The individuals the poor whites trust with their children, whose churches they share, whose dialect they speak, who work side by side with them in the same fields and for the same meager wages are the same people they fear and denounce as a group.

"Want to have some lunch, Mr. Armstrong?" Dave said.

"Y'all think I'm a crazy man, but I've seen things nobody else has seen, I don't care what kind of wars y'all been in. I've seen the devil. Know how I know it's the devil? Ain't no human beings capable of the cruelty I seen."

"Why are you here, sir?" Dave asked.

"Y'all seen that pontoon plane?"

"Yeah, it was parked across the bayou from me this morning," I said.

"Then you seen them."

"Seen who?" Dave said.

"Don't take a step toward me. I'll cut you, boy."

"Boy?" Dave said.

"What's wrong, Hap?" I said.

"Them on the jungle gym. They ain't children. You just think they are."

He began walking backward down the little bridge. Somehow, in this man's tortured mind, the children on the playground had turned into demons. How do you deal with someone like this? How do you deal with the culture he comes from?

"You need to sit down, Mr. Armstrong," Dave said. "We'll find the lady who brought you here and make sure you get home okay. Are you hearing me on this?"

Armstrong started walking fast, then broke into a run.

"Oh, boy," I said.

Dave took out his cell phone and called 911. We had done all we could. I hoped he'd find the woman who had brought him to the park. The system is not kind, and jails are not good places for the mentally ill. But padded rooms aren't, either. We got in Dave's truck and drove out the park exit, then turned toward the drawbridge. I thought we would see Hap Armstrong riding in the woman's car or running along the strip of pedestrian walkway on the bridge. But that was wishful thinking.

A dump truck coming fast from the opposite direction drove head-on into Armstrong, the bumper slapping him horizontally onto the grid, the driver never letting up, Armstrong's body catching in the undercarriage, doubling up, his limbs grinding and thudding with a dull sound, the bones in his body breaking like sticks, splitting the skin. Then the truck swung away on a side street and sped toward the west side of town and the highway.

The grid on the drawbridge was dripping with blood and sinew. Some Black people who were cane-pole fishing among the pilings were staring up at the gridwork, stupefied at what they had witnessed, a mother putting a hand over her child's eyes.

CHAPTER EIGHT

I t was hard to watch the medics scrape up Armstrong and put him in a body bag, even though I'd seen what a Gatling gun could do to a village made of straw. So I didn't. I let Dave deal with his own people, namely, the Iberia Parish Sheriff's Department, and walked down below the bridge onto the yard behind the Shadows, a plantation that had been home to over two hundred slaves. Just the thought of that number was a mindfuck. How could anyone have the arrogance to own the lives of that many people? Or maybe a better question is, how do people like Dave and me admire men like Robert Lee and at the same time hate the cocksuckers who ran the system?

You've got me.

I sat down on a stone bench behind the plantation house and once again took the photo of the Jewish mother and her children from my wallet. For me, that image symbolized everything that was wrong on the earth, and I swore that one day I would find a way to make the world a better place. Did you ever read John Grisham? He wrote a story about a Klansman about to be executed in Parchman Pen, and the warden asks him if he has any final words. I don't have the quote exactly, but it was something like this: "Yes, sir, I do. There's many a man I have hated, but the one I hated the most was myself."

That's how those asswipes made it work. If they had their way, we'd all be in the cotton field, white and Black, working for Mr. Charlie up at the big house while he sat drinking his mint julep on the verandah.

I was just about to get up and rejoin Dave, when I heard a single-engine plane and looked up to see the pontoon plane coming from the south, low over the bayou, the wings tilting, then the pontoons skimming the water, the pilot cutting the feed, drifting into the canebrake, the propeller suddenly locking in place. A woman stepped into the shallows and walked through the cattails onto the lawn. She was wearing tight gray jodhpurs and a white blouse and a cute cap with a chinstrap on it. She took off her cap and shook out her hair and combed it with her fingers. Her face was heart-shaped, her eyes dark brown and childlike and round, her hair light red, a nimbus around it, her chin tilted up, her shoulders slight, as though she were begging to be kissed.

I got up from my seat and removed my hat. I wear a porkpie. Very few people do. A porkpie hat looks like something an ugly dog might wear.

"Hello, Mr. Purcel," she said. "I'm Clara Bow. Your neighbor across the bayou."

"Like the actress?"

"You must be a student of film." She turned around and looked at the bridge. "What happened up there?"

"A fatal accident, I'm afraid."

"Oh, I'm sorry. Did you know the person?"

"Not real well."

"Aren't you a detective?"

"A private detective, yes, ma'am."

"I'm looking for one."

"I'm pretty stacked up right now."

"Hmm," she said, and looked at the drawbridge again. "What's your retainer?"

"I don't ask for one."

"How about two thousand dollars?"

"I take a case or I don't," I said. "What's the trouble?"

"My former husband, who deserves a bullet in the mouth."

"Yeah, I've heard about that kind. You want to drop by my office? I'm right by the old Evangeline Theater."

"If you don't mind my asking, Mr. Purcel, what's that photo you have in your hand?"

"A mother and her three children on their way to the showers at Auschwitz."

Her face drained.

"I'd like to catch the Waffen SS who killed these innocent people," I said. "But they're probably all dead. So I don't know what I'm gonna do. I really don't."

"I don't quite know what to say, Mr. Purcel. I hope I didn't intrude upon you."

"You didn't," I said, and put my business card in her hand. "Come by anytime. In the meanwhile, don't shoot your husband."

"Pray you don't ever meet that son of a bitch," she said.

If she had cut her hair, she would have looked very much like her namesake, the silent film star known as "the It Girl." Her language didn't go with her face, though. However, I didn't want to deal with the complexities of someone who resembled a silent film star, so I let them go.

# # #

I put on my porkpie hat and tipped the brim at her and walked through the gardens, under which probably lay the bones of colored people who would never have rest or justice, just like the family at Auschwitz. I got to the front of the property, deep in the shadow of the live oaks, and opened the piked gate and stepped out on the sidewalk, which was broken by the gigantic roots of the oaks, then continued on to the center of town, past my office, and into Clementine's, where I loaded up—I mean the full-tilt boogie, what Dave calls the drinking man's horizontal bop, a frosted mug of draft beer, with four fingers of Jack back, a painless swack of the ultimate flack, like puffs of black smoke seen through the plexiglass nose cone of a B-29.

Yeah, that's right, for people like me it's death. It is for all drunks. We commit suicide one day at a time. Ask Dave. He tried to kill an MP in Bring Cash Alley in Saigon. A whore saved the MP's life. Those are the kinds of things he and I have done to ourselves.

That night I stumbled into Streak's front yard on East Main. That's where he lived by himself in his shotgun house on the bayou, surrounded by trees that were two hundred years old. The lights were out, so I went into the backyard and lay down with my arms outstretched and stared through the trees at the moon. Only minutes earlier the moon had been the color of ivory, but it changed before my eyes and became marbled with bruises, then it turned a bright orange and then bloodred, as though there was no haven from man's self-delusion and cruelty. I thought about Armstrong and the dump truck and the innocent people he had killed and the pitiful man he had become, serving the cause of men who taught him that light was darkness, and darkness was light.

Then I felt Streak kneel down beside me. "What's the haps?" he said.

"No haps," I said. "I couldn't sleep."

"No kidding?"

"Yeah, I didn't want to wake you up."

"I have some pecan pie on the kitchen table, and some coffee I can reheat," he said.

I sat up and tried to brush the leaves and dirt and pecan husks off my arms. "I sure did it, didn't I?"

"Screw it," he said, and helped me to my feet and put my arm across his shoulders.

And that's the way we walked to his back door, out of step with the world, uncertain of our next breath, a great white fog rolling up the Teche, about to wrap itself around both of us.

CHAPTER NINE

I showered and changed clothes and went to the office the next morning, not feeling the best. Dave said the dump truck driver got away, and Armstrong's death was now considered a hit-and-run homicide. No witnesses, including Dave and me, were able to get the truck's tag number because it was filmed with mud.

What I could not get out of my head was the moment of collision. The truck never slowed; in fact, the driver may have accelerated. Most hit-and-runs are motivated by fear. But this man had no criminal liability, even if he was under the influence. Armstrong was running in the middle of the bridge, obviously deranged. Why would the driver take on the burden of a fatal accident he didn't cause?

I had another question, too. Was it possible that Armstrong recognized the driver and was deliberately running at him? That did not seem reasonable, but nothing in this case was.

Just as I was about to go to lunch, the lady with the name Clara Bow came through my door, the little bell tingling overhead. She wore a white dress and red heels and black shades and a floppy straw hat like an antebellum woman would wear. "You have time for me, Mr. Purcel?" she said.

"Always," I said, and put a chair in front of my desk.

"Well, you're very nice," she said.

"How can I help you, Miss Clara?"

"My husband, from whom I am separated, is trying to blackmail me. Of course, he calls it suing."

"For what?"

"Take a guess."

"Things on tape?" I said.

"Of course. But in these times no one is particularly shocked about that. My husband has forged evidence implicating me in an enormous tax fraud. Perhaps fifty million dollars' worth."

Then the name hit me. She and her husband had created a Ponzi scheme. The people at the top of the pyramid got rich; the ones at the bottom lost whatever they invested.

"Y'all sold soap franchises or something like that?" I said.

"I didn't sell anything. I went to the eleventh grade. He put my face and name on the soap boxes."

"If you don't mind me asking, how long were y'all together?"

"Fifteen years."

"Long time," I said.

"You mean, why didn't I catch on? I was trusting and dumb."

"Why would you come to a guy like me, Miss Clara?"

"Your reputation."

"Reputation for what?" I said.

"Throwing some pornographers off a roof. Handcuffing a congressman to a fireplug in New Orleans."

"I'm not the right guy for you."

"Do you mind telling me why?" she asked.

"Most of the people I deal with are common criminals. I live most of my life in a septic tank. Look at my office. The floor is littered by ten a.m."

She got up from the chair and unbuttoned her blouse and leaned on my desk. "That's where he put out his cigar. Do I qualify, Mr. Purcel?"

I had no response. There are some things you don't get used to. If you do, one day you'll look in the mirror and be frightened. That's why cops, welfare workers, and journalists drink too much, and why they don't hang around with people outside their own circles.

Maybe I rubbed my forehead with the heel of my hand. Or sucked my teeth. Or cleared my throat. Looking at a cigar burn on a woman's breast isn't easy for guys like me. I'm from another generation. When we were young, jukeboxes all over the country played "Ragged but Right." We loved it. That may sound like a digression, but it's not.

One thing I was sure of, though. I opened my desk drawer and put a clipboard and ballpoint pen in front of her. "If you think my terms are all right, sign at the bottom."

"Thank you, sir," she whispered.

Oh boy, I thought. *Why did I just do this?*

Search me, you clod, I answered myself.

# # #

After she was gone, I called my house in the Quarter to see if Chen and Gracie Lamar and Miss Dorothy and the cats were all right. Are you that way? You know, when you have a family or a group of pets or close friends who come into your life and become part of your tissue? It just happens, like osmosis. They're part of you and you're part of them. It's the best feeling in the world. I don't know how people can live in solitude. I really don't.

Gracie said everything was fine.

"I should be back there next week," I said.

"If not, we'll come get you," she replied.

Then I called up Dave again and asked if he wanted to meet me for a late breakfast at Victor's Cafeteria.

"Sure," he said. "Some Cheerios and tea and skim milk and maybe a piece of dry toast?"

"That's not funny."

Just as I was about to lock the door and head across the street, the phone rang. It was Gracie. "I didn't look out the back window," she said. "Someone dug up all the beds. There's dirt and elephant ears and flowers and banana plants all over the courtyard. You want me to call the cops?"

I had to think. "No," I said.

"Why not?"

"You know a vice detective named Earl Banner?"

"Yeah, he's not only a geek, he takes freebies," she said.

"If you dial 911, he'll be out there."

"Why would a vice cop come here?" she asked.

He had told me Gracie Lamar was in the life. But I wasn't going to let Banner's lies hurt an innocent person. "He's a bastard, Gracie."

I gave her the name of a lawn and garden service, then asked to talk to Chen.

"Chen's already cleaning up the patio. Do you have a gun in the house?"

"Yeah, there's one in the top of the closet and one taped under my desk in the office. You worried about these guys coming back?"

"I'm not. But you should watch your butt, Clete."

"*Me* watch *my* butt?"

"Yeah, you don't take care of yourself."

"You know how that makes me feel?" I said.

"Hey, the only argument you ever win is the one you don't have. Know who said that?"

"No, who?"

"Charlie Manson."

# # #

I finally got across the street and went into Victor's. Dave had not arrived, so I thought I'd get started early. I was still hungover and wanted to unscrew my head and float it down the bayou. You know what I have never figured out about booze? Without exception, every experience I ever had with it was bad. It was the same for Streak, and the same for every lush I ever knew. How fucked up is that?

Anyway, I got a tray and went through the serving line and sat down and was tying a napkin like a bib around my neck just as Dave walked in. What does he get? A Diet Coke, a small bowl of dirty rice, and a piece of fish the size of a sardine. He sat down and scanned my food.

"*What?*" I said.

"Got enough cholesterol? Why don't you order up some ninety-weight tractor oil? Or a whale burger?"

"I was dehydrated this morning."

"So you're eating biscuits sopping with butter and milk gravy, mashed potatoes, a porkchop, deep-fried shrimp, and a wedge of chocolate pie with whipped cream. And you wonder why you have high blood pressure. How about a dozen fried oysters on the side?"

"Dave, you should join some antifood movement. Or figure a way to rain on the Mardi Gras Parade. Or outlaw Christmas."

"Did something happen this morning?" he said.

Oh, boy, Dave had this way of reading my mind. I don't know how. It was really embarrassing. "I just talked to Gracie Lamar," I said. "Somebody dug up the flower beds in the courtyard."

"The same guys?"

"Probably."

Then he saw my eyes slip off his.

"What else happened this morning?" he said.

"Who said anything else happened?"

"Come on, Cletus. Don't hide things from your best friend."

The people at the next table were starting to look at us.

"The woman from the red pontoon plane, she came into the office this morning," I said.

"What did she want?"

"Protection. Her husband is a mean motor scooter. Her name is Clara Bow."

Dave pinched his temples. "You didn't let her hire you, did you?"

"Yeah," I said.

"Oh, Clete—"

"I don't turn down desperate people, Dave. If I can't handle the action, I nullify the agreement and give them back their money. What's wrong with that?"

"She and her husband are bad news, Clete."

"He burned her breast with a cigar."

The people at the next table got up and moved.

"What the fuck, Dave? I mean, why do you fuck up everything when everything is going along fine? For no fucking reason."

"That woman and her husband are sociopaths. They'll be your ruin."

"The problem is you hate rich people, Dave."

He got up from his chair and dropped a ten-dollar bill on the table. "See you later," he said.

"Come on, Dave, sit down."

But he went straight out the door. New Iberia is a polite town, and the people around my table looked the other way as I tried to finish my food, my face red and hot as a light bulb, my blood pressure through the ceiling, the midday Angelus clanging in my head.

I felt miserable.

# # #

I crossed the street and tried to do some paperwork on the terrace behind my office. I had a wood spool for a table, a beach umbrella for shade, and a grand view of the drawbridge and the old Carmelite convent and the live oaks on the lawn across the bayou. The breeze was warm; a drop of perspiration was sliding down my forehead, my heart was thudding, my breath was short. Dave and I never had words. We had taken on every kind of situation, every kind of foe, and painted the walls and grinned and walked through the cannon smoke. I carried Dave down a fire escape with two bullets in my back. Dave let himself be tortured rather than give me up to some sadistic bags of shit trying to re-create the German-American Bund. Together we never gave an inch.

I knew the problem, though. One wife was murdered; one wife died of lupus; and his adopted daughter, Alafair, was at Reed College in Portland on a scholarship. Dave was lonely and wouldn't admit it. He had pulled Alafair out of a downed plane piloted by a Maryknoll priest south of Southwest Pass. Everybody else in the plane was dead, and she was drowning in a bubble of air, in the dark, thirty feet down, and only five years old. Dave went over the gunwale with a tank that had three minutes of air in it, got into the cabin, and took them both to the surface, their lungs on fire.

Hey, dig this. You know what he gave me for my birthday about five years back? A bumper sticker he'd had custom made. It read, CAUTION: HEAVILY ARMED BADASS LEFTIST MOTHERFUCKER ON BOARD.

I haven't tried it out yet.

I gave up on the paperwork. Maybe Dave was right and I had made a mistake getting involved with Ponzi people. Know why? They are as low as they come. They not only steal the money from their victims, they steal their victims' faith in their fellow man. And worse, the victims resent themselves for the rest of their lives. How much damage can one person do to another?

I closed the office, put down the top of my lavender-pink Eldorado Cadillac, and, like Chuck Berry said, motorated down the bayou to Jeanerette, Louisiana, in St. Mary Parish country, where, in a snap of your fingers, you can be back in the fourteenth century.

# # #

There are several antebellum homes in Jeanerette. Like the ones in New Iberia and New Orleans, they look like wedding cakes, the icing immaculate yet soft, the carriage lights flickering at evening tide. Sometimes Dave said he almost wished the South had won the war. But he was only kidding. He knew what those people in those houses were like. They stole the short time a child or woman or man was granted on this earth and thought nothing of it. Still, you wonder, when the sugarcane is bending in the wind, and you can smell the salt from the Gulf, and the sky is like a great bruise, can all of this be bad, is the lightning in the clouds a message, can we correct what our ancestors did and keep the magic of the moment, the deep, oceanic coolness that seems to electrify your skin?

I pulled into the driveway of a two-story house, built in the 1850s, one with the biggest pillars I've seen in Louisiana. I didn't know if Clara Bow or her husband had custody of the home. I didn't care. That's the way I've always done things. Just go do them and see what happens. Actually, I think that's the better way to go. Most of the things we plan don't turn out too well, so what the heck. How about World War I? The royal families who started it thought it would be over in a few weeks. Four years and twenty million deaths later they were still thinking on it.

# # #

I knocked on the door. The man who opened it looked like a golfer in his fifties, with the cap and two-tone shoes and pegged pants and muttonchop whiskers that could have been pasted on his cheeks, and a bright smile that seemed to have been in place before he opened the door.

"Hello, may I help you?"

"Are you Lauren Bow?" I asked.

"Yes."

"How do you do?" I said, taking off my hat. "My name is Clete Purcel. I'm a private investigator in Iberia Parish and New Orleans. I've been retained by Ms. Clara Bow. Is she here?"

"She is not." His smile never left his face.

"Could I come in?"

"For what purpose, sir?"

I had to think about it. I could hear dogs barking in back. "Endangerment?"

"My heavens, about what?"

"Physical injury caused by a hot cigar."

His accent was Anglo-English, a bit like the Aussies or the Scots. He studied me, his eyes never blinking, his expression like a car grille. The wind was blowing from the sugarcane field, but not a hair on his head fluttered. Then I knew what I was dealing with. Every cop, every psychiatrist, every parole and probation officer knows that moment in a perp's eyes. He had locked the lens in the camera; inside, his brain was whirring warp-speed through the galaxy.

"I don't know anything about hot cigars," he said. "I certainly don't smoke them. Anyway, come in and have a drink."

"Thank you," I said. "I'll just take a glass of water."

"All righty, let's go out to the kitchen. Grand day, isn't it? The kind that puts a fierceness in a man's stride."

The kitchen was spotless, every surface glittering in the sunlight.

"How many dogs do you have?" I asked.

"They come and go. Rottweilers, pit bulls, and Dobermans."

"They're rough guys, huh?"

"I don't think so," he said, pulling open the refrigerator.

"I've got cats," I said.

"Good for you, fella." He pulled out a pitcher of lemonade. "Now, what's this about an injury with a burning cigarette or something?"

"Miss Clara showed me the scar on her . . . skin."

"You mean on her breast, don't you?"

"I'm talking about a wound on a person's flesh and how it got there."

"Well, you're a gentleman," he said, pouring a glassful from the pitcher. "Mr. Purcel, my estranged wife is a thespian, God bless her soul, who could upstage the sinking of the *Titanic*. Believe nothing she says. Her previous full name was Natalie Klaus. As soon as the minister gave her the name 'Bow,' she became 'Clara Bow.' You're not the only person taken in by her. I think she hauled the ashes of two or three IRS accountants. She had a lot of practice, too. Fifteen bloody years of it."

He poured three inches of vodka in a glass and dropped two ice cubes in it with his fingers, then swirled it and knocked it back like a pro. Then he did it again. "Fuck!" he said. "That's a little better. You're a stout fella, aren't you? Clank a little iron, do you?"

If he was an actor, he was really good. If he was not, I needed to tear up Clara Bow's check as soon as I could.

"How do you feel about your troubles with the IRS?" I said.

"That's like asking someone how he likes his job at Buchenwald."

I put down my lemonade.

"Something wrong?" he said.

"Light references to extermination camps bother me."

"Sorry, I know what you mean. What else can I do for you, Mr. Purcel?"

I scratched my eyebrow. "Can you give me a tour? I've never been through a house like this."

He stared up the stairs. They were made of recovered cypress, probably two hundred years old. In the sunlight they had a soft golden-brownish glow. He bit on a thumbnail. "You were in the service?"

"In the Crotch. That's the Marine Corps."

"Good for you, pally. I have an appointment," he said. "I'll take you around another time. Let's go through the carriage house. I'll show you my dogs."

When we went through the garage, or carriage house, his dogs began crashing against the wire of their cages, the weight of them shaking chains and locks, their breath so hot you could almost feel it.

CHAPTER TEN

A s I was driving away, I saw a man trying to start the outboard motor on an aluminum boat that was tied to the dock. He was wearing only swimming trunks and tennis shoes and a cap. His body was deeply tanned and looked woven from whipcord. Each time he jerked the lanyard, his torso and thighs rippled with muscle. He was covered with tattoos.

I stepped on the brake just as the motor caught and the man and the boat split the bayou's surface, sending a frothy, wide wake into the cattails and bamboo and floating elephant ears.

I turned out onto the back road to New Iberia, one that follows the Teche through the LSU experimental farm. The pastures were emerald green, the occasional willow tree by the bayou's bank freckled with birds. In the distance I could see a black pickup truck headed toward me. No one else was on the road. The truck began slowing. I felt a gladness in my heart that these days I seldom have the opportunity to experience. It was Dave.

He pulled to the shoulder, his window down. There was not one other person on the road or on the farm. "What's the haps?" he said.

"I was checking out Lauren Bow," I replied. "He's a beaut."

"Yeah, I've heard he's the kind of guy St. Mary Parish understands. A guy like Joseph Stalin."

I cut my engine. So did Dave. "He's a hard guy to read," I said. "He asked me if I had been in the service. Out of nowhere."

"That's a little weird."

"More important, I saw a guy leave in a bass boat who brought back bad memories," I said. "The guy who hit me in the head with a crowbar."

Dave looked straight ahead, then back at me. "You're sure?"

"How many guys look like a walking bottle of ink?"

Dave widened his eyes. "The wife wasn't there?"

"Not that I saw. But I had the sense there was someone upstairs he didn't want me to see."

"We need to get inside," Dave said.

"You're kidding?"

"No, I'm serious. You're too kind, Clete. That man and his wife are going to hurt you."

"You're suspended indefinitely without pay, and you want to creep the house of a billionaire?" I said.

"If need be, we'll start a fire."

"Have you lost your mind?" I said.

"I had you going."

"No, you didn't. I know you, big mon. You're far more reckless than I am, so quit it."

"This one is different, Clete. The perps seem like regular shitheads, but they're puppets. Two people, Sperm-O and Hap Armstrong, are already dead, and over what? Answer: We don't know."

"You think this guy Bow is behind all this?"

"Scammers are scammers. They've been around since the pyra-mids. This one has really got a stink on it."

"You're scaring me, Streak."

# # #

I went back to the office. My temp, who I employed four hours a day, three days a week, was there. Her name was Sally Boudreau. She weighed over two hundred pounds and worked out at Baron's Health Club every day at 7:00 a.m. She had a round, pink face and dyed-white hair and shoulders and upper arms that sometimes tore her shirt when she bent over. She also smelled like garden flowers and ate cupcakes and candy bars all day. She told me Gracie Lamar had left two messages.

"Where are the messages?" I said.

"I was busy doin' two t'ings at the same time, Mr. Clete. I'm sorry."

"It's okay. Just tell me what Miss Gracie had to say."

"She said that Miss Chen was climbing the wall. And somet'ing about a monkey."

"Thank you, Miss Sally."

"She's got a monkey in your house?"

"I'll call and find out," I said.

I went out on my small deck and sat under my beach umbrella and called Gracie.

"Hello?" she said.

"How bad is it?" I said.

"Cold sweats, vomiting, curling up in a ball."

I gave her a number. Then told her the name of the number. "That's the Work the Steps or Die Motherfucker group," I said.

"Is there something wrong with this phone?" she said.

After I hung up, I changed into my swimming trunks, put on my beach sandals and shades, smeared myself with sunblock, chugged an ice-cold Dr Pepper that I kept for Dave, spread a quilt on my deck, lay down and stuck a pillow under my head, put in my earbuds, closed my eyes, and listened to Tommy Dorsey and Albert Ammons and Benny Goodman and the Platters and Doris Day.

I changed my mind about the good old days. They were great. Or think about it this way: Would you rather listen to Lionel Hampton or a guy bouncing up and down while grabbing his crotch?

Gee, I don't know.

# # #

The evening sun was a molten-red ball in the west when I woke up. Sally Boudreau, my temp, had locked up the front and gone home. Actually she had been my temp off and on for two years and was not really a temp but a poor soul who had lost her son to drugs and lived by herself and did the best she could and belonged to the choir at her church—in large part, I think, for the companionship, even though she gave it her all.

She called me when I got home. "You all right, Mr. Clete?" she said.

"Sure, why wouldn't I be, Miss Sally?"

"I seen some man out there on the bayou. Man wit' tattoos all over his face and neck and arms. I kept my eye on him while you was sleeping. But I t'ought I should ax you if you knowed who that was."

"Did he have a dark tan?"

"I don't know. I couldn't see t'rew the tattoos."

"Thank you, Miss Sally. Do you know where this fella went?"

"No, suh. I'll see you in the morning. I hope you didn't get fried. You looked red all over. Good night."

The line went dead. You know when you're in Southwest Louisiana.

# # #

The presence of a heavily tattooed man behind my office on the same day I saw a heavily tattooed man behind Lauren Bow's house was too much for coincidence. Worse, I thought somebody was making a move. Even worse than that, neither Dave nor I was doing anything about it. Let me put it a little more strongly. People were wiping their feet on me. So was the system. My Caddy had been vandalized; I had been knocked unconscious; the same people had returned to the scene of their initial crime and torn up my gardens and terrorized the women staying at my house.

In the meantime, Eddy Durbin and his little brother, Andy, were getting a free pass, even though it was obvious that Eddy's Car Wash was an outlet for narcotics at the least.

Lastly, the FBI agent who had some real power had disappeared, after I gave him information and he gave me none. I was very disappointed at that.

Look, everything I'm saying here is subjective. I'm the stink on shit. I accept that. But Andy Durbin was selling dope, and his brother knew about it. I'd always thought Eddy was stand-up for doing double nickels to keep his little brother out of Angola. I no longer felt that way. I was stacking their time, even though I wasn't in the can, which is something you never do.

I left messages with three federal agencies and asked to speak to Samuel Hawthorne. Guess how that worked out.

I don't like talking about my two tours in the Crotch, because I came back home and friends of mine did not. But they wouldn't mind me passing along these things you learn in the Corps and never forget, whether you're on the firing line, in prison, or in any other kind of institutional or civilian situation. You don't silhouette on a hill; you don't wear civilian jewelry; you don't make enemies with people in records or people who handle your food; you don't make enemies with people who know where you are when you don't know where *they* are; and lastly, you don't let your enemies know when you're hurt; instead you swallow your blood and spit in their faces.

I believed the clock was ticking on Dave and me. A button man of some kind took out Sperm-O in daylight from over two hundred yards away, in a tourist area and among homes that cost millions. That meant he didn't have time to set up a tripod or a stand. That meant he probably stepped out of his vehicle, wrapped his sling around his left arm, squinted one eye and used the other to aim through the crosshairs of a telescope, and pulled the trigger, then got back in his vehicle and drove away without drawing any attention.

There were other things about this guy's professionalism, too. A thirty-ought-six makes a sharp pop, so obviously the shooter was not using a silencer. The round keyholed through Sperm-O's face, which meant the bullet was toppling. That meant the round had tipped on an object, maybe a wash line or a picket fence, before it hit its target. This guy knew everything about guns, and beat all the odds when he squeezed the trigger without a dramatic loss of velocity, blowing the back of Sperm-O's head all over the verandah.

I apologize for all this morbid material. I don't mean to shock anybody's sensibilities. What I'm trying to say is if you get caught in the world of crime, you might find out you're on your own. I'm talking about victims of rape and robbery and sadistic beatings, people who find themselves defenseless and confused and unable to work and support their families. People who know nothing about the incompetence of the system, one that puts a perpetrator back on the street without warning the witnesses or victims who can send him away for decades. You get pretty fucked-up in the head when that happens.

# # #

Dave talked about creeping Lauren Bow's house. I told him that was crazy, but we had done it before. There are worse things in law enforcement—planting evidence, lying under oath on the witness stand, dropping a throw-down on a corpse, even putting it in his hand and firing it to ensure exoneration of a guilty cop.

My problem was not with Dave, though. Through no fault of my own, which was a rare condition in my life, I was a target because I took my Eldorado Cadillac to Eddy's Car Wash, and now any number of innocent people could be hurt or killed. How could this happen? It was like putting a penny in a gumball machine and discovering you just bit into cyanide. Do you have dreams in which you're trying to run in wet concrete? That's what it was like. People like Chen and Gracie Lamar and Miss Dorothy and now my temp Sally Boudreau were in peril, just because they were my friends.

Let me tell you a big truth. The world of crime is not a mystery. There are two kinds of people inside the gray-bar hotel chain. Deadbeats and people who beat other people until they're dead. The people I'm talking about are people like Whitey Bulger. How did he do so much damage for so long? He did it with the knowledge of the FBI and most of Boston.

Fuck. That. Shit.

That night I went to a secondhand gun store in Lafayette run by a gunsmith who had burned off half his face in an oil-well accident. His skin had shriveled, so his glass eye bulged from the socket and made him look like he was trying to tell others of some terrible danger. He worked late hours and had few friends, and often smelled of alcohol. No one else was in the store. "What's happening, my man?" he said.

"No haps, Mike," I said. "Can you put together an '03 with a sling and a telescopic sight. Or a Mauser."

"I got some AR-15s and an early modified M-16."

"I'll pass."

"They're popular now."

"I'd like to shove them up the ass of the people who are popularizing them."

"When do you need it?"

"Now."

"How about tomorrow?"

"That'll do."

"You into some shit, Clete?"

"Why would you think that?" I said.

I started out the door.

"Hey," he said.

"What?"

"Slow it down, gunny." He tried to smile.

"Copy that."

I got in my Caddy and drove back to New Iberia, then caught the old road to Jeanerette and parked my vehicle on the edge of a sugarcane field about one hundred yards from Lauren Bow's home. The wind was blowing, the sugarcane waving, and the moon was streaked with clouds that looked like black rags. At 5:14 a.m., the door on the carriage house rolled up, rattling like a junkyard, and a big Buick came out with three or four men in it and a woman behind the wheel. They drove to the far side of the house and sped down the driveway through a tunnel of oaks onto the asphalt road, one of them flinging a beer bottle into the bayou.

I started the engine, then shifted down and pressed the accelerator to the floor. The Caddy bounced onto the road, then the frame dipped and the right rear wheel came down on the tire, slicing a strip that whipped under the fender. I pulled to the side and cut the engine. A hawk flew overhead, its feathers gilded by an orange sun, then circled and splattered a load of bird shit on my windshield.

CHAPTER ELEVEN

D ave knocked on my cottage door at 1:04 p.m. the next day. "Come on in," I said. "I got to hit the shower. There's a diet Doc in the icebox."

"No hurry," he said, staring out the side window at Bayou Teche.

I knew that look. Dave never showed his feelings. I told him that after he croaked I was going to tell the mortician to shake him to make sure he was dead. Then he said the same thing about me. Can you believe that? No sense of humor.

I came out of the bathroom dressed. "Hey, let's go to the doughnut place. I got some stuff to tell you."

"Better sit down,"

"What is it?" I said.

"Eddy Durbin's dead," he said. "He was killed in his car wash."

"Eddy?" I said. "Eddy's dead?"

You know how it is when you hear a kid you grew up with suddenly dies. It makes your heart drop. It's not supposed to happen. Kids are eternal. Even if the guy is like Eddy, maybe a bum sometimes, maybe even selling you out, like Eddy did. I didn't want to think that way about Eddy, though. Eddy took a shank off an Italian kid who was going to put me under in a rumble in the cemetery on Basin. All of these things were going on in my head.

"When did this happen?" I said.

"Two days ago."

"In the car wash?" I said.

"It had something to do with the chain and the brushes and the wax squirters."

"That doesn't sound right," I said. "Eddy was smart."

Dave sat down on the bed. I was still standing. "I talked to the coroner. Eddy went out hard," he said.

"How hard?"

"He was torn apart."

"Jesus," I said. "Why didn't Eddy tell us what was going on? Where was his brother all this time?"

"Andy's impaired, Clete. Eddy may have been your friend, but he stiffed you just the same. Eddy made his choice. Don't eat yourself up because of his mistakes."

"You don't water it down, do you, mon?"

"The worse lie we tell is the one we tell ourselves."

I sat down and blew out my breath. "Jesus, what a mess, huh?" I said.

"Hey, you know what Stephen King said about the kids you used to know? 'I never had any friends later on like the ones I had when I was twelve.' Eddy should have read Stephen King."

I wiped my eyes and got up. "Let's get something to eat while I tell you a couple of things."

"Like what?" he said.

I sat back down again. "My temp says the tattooed man was behind my office yesterday. I also staked out Lauren Bow's home last night. A woman driving a Buick with three or four men left at sunrise."

"Going to early Mass?"

# # #

My desk phone at my office rang just after 1:00 p.m. "Purcel Investigations," I said.

"I'm glad you picked up," the voice said.

"Banner?"

"Yeah, Banner, you fuckin' idiot."

"I'm glad to know you're in a good mood today. Is there anything I can help you with? Maybe tickets to the Books Along the Tech Literary Festival?"

"We had a surveillance in place and you queered it."

"What are you talking about?"

"You parked your shit-mobile and your fat ass in the cane field across from Lauren Bow's house so you could look through his windows. Our guys had to pull out. You piss me off so bad I want to beat the shit out of you."

"You don't have any jurisdiction around here, Banner."

"Number one, you're wrong. Number two, you don't have any jurisdiction anywhere, Purcel."

"What do you know about the death of Eddy Durbin?" I asked.

"A guy who helped spread crank throughout the projects? We're all broke up."

"Eddy wasn't selling dope."

"How do you know that?" he said.

I didn't have an answer. But I didn't think that mattered. "I don't believe any of this is about dope, Banner. It's something else.

I don't think you have any idea about what it is. That said, neither do I."

I could hear him breathing against the phone. "Eddy Durbin's guts were spilled out on the floor of the gantry. You want to do our job, come over here and fill out an application. By the way, that broad of yours?"

"What broad?"

"The one you got a hard-on for, the one that's in the life, Gracie Lamar. Keep hanging around with her and see what happens, asshole."

Then he hung up.

# # #

I went down to Clementine's and had a piece of pie and a cup of coffee at an outdoor table in back, with a view of the drawbridge and the old convent. Banner was scum, but that did not explain his obsession with Gracie Lamar and his conviction that she was in the life. She clearly was not. Hookers did not work as independents in New Orleans, nor do they anywhere. I decided to get Banner out of my mind. He was not dirty because he was a cop. He was dirty because he was a sociopath. He could be a door-to-door Bible salesman and would remain a sociopath.

But here's where I ran into trouble. For just a moment there was a flicker of compassion about the way Eddy Durbin went out. I hated the image Banner had left me with. It made me think of the medieval practice of drawing and quartering and evisceration in front of a crowd in the town square, and the possibility that the problem was not the era but the seed of depravity that was still alive, as was in evidence in the photo of Auschwitz I carried in my wallet.

When I got back to the office, Miss Sally said I had a message from "Mr. Mike, the gunsmit'." Like most hardcore Cajuns, Miss Sally had trouble with the *th* sound.

"What did he say?" I asked.

"He's delivering your gun."

"Did he say when?"

"Around four o'clock."

"Is something bothering you, Miss Sally?"

"Yes, suh. He said it was a hunting rifle. Wit' a telescope."

"That's right."

"Mr. Clete, you're not hunting, are you?"

"I don't hunt, Miss Sally."

"I knew dat. Knew it all along."

"You're a special person, Miss Sally."

"Suh?"

"You look after people like me."

She blushed, then went back to her desk. My friend Mike arrived at four thirty and came inside with a canvas gun case and laid it on my desk. "Want to have a look?" he said.

I didn't. Not in front of Miss Sally. She obviously sensed my feelings. "I'm going home now, Mr. Clete," she said.

"Good night, Miss Sally," I said.

Mike waited for her to leave. "Want me to open it up?"

"Yep."

He unzipped the case and lifted the K-98 eight-millimeter bolt-action Mauser with the mounted telescope and the leather sling gingerly in his hands and placed it across my ink blotter. "Can I ask you something, Clete?"

"Sure."

"What the hell are you doing?" The eye that bulged from the burned side of his face looked as hard as marble, the skin around it pink and diseased.

"I think we're living in dangerous times," I said.

"You just realized that? Look at the stamp above the chamber. Nineteen forty-two, with the swastika. Some Waffen SS son of a bitch could have lined up civilians with this, because that's what those cocksuckers did."

On the way back to my cottage at the Teche Motel I stopped to get a bottle of Jack and a six-pack back.

# # #

I got the call from Dave in the middle of the night. And Dave got it from the Iberia Parish sheriff's departmental dispatcher. Miss Sally had been attacked in her house, and had been taken to Iberia General, traumatized and unable to speak. A fireman had wrapped her in a sheet because all of her clothes had been ripped from her body.

CHAPTER TWELVE

Dave stood with me outside the door of Miss Sally's hospital room. He had arrived first. I had just come out. He looked at my face, then clinched my arm. "Take it easy," he said.

"My ass," I said.

"Get it out of your head. She's safe now. We'll get whoever did this."

"What did she tell you?" I asked.

"I couldn't make it out. Did she say anything to you?"

"'Tattoos,' that's all," I replied.

"In the plural?" Dave said.

"Yeah."

He squeezed my bicep again. "You need to dial it down, Cletus."

"You know what kind of life she's gonna have after this?" I said.

"Yeah, I do," he said. "That's why we're going to nail him. Were you drinking last night?"

"A couple of hits to go to sleep."

"Cut it out, Clete."

"Okay, you're right. I'm gonna take some vitamins and drink some orange juice, and I'll be okay," I said. "Yeah, that's all I need."

When I blew out my breath, Dave's face flinched.

"That bad, huh?" I said.

"Don't worry about it. Look, I'm going to talk to Helen about my badge."

Helen Soileau was the sheriff. She was not only bisexual, she probably had three or four personalities inside her, all of them supercharged and potentially dangerous if you punched the wrong button.

Dave shook my arm. "What are you thinking about?" he said.

"The tattooed guy who hit me with a crowbar did this."

"Yeah, I think that's a given," he said.

"Why did he go after Miss Sally, Dave?"

"She's bait," he replied. "He wants you to lose it and mess up so he can pop you from afar or—"

"Finish it," I said.

"Get you in private somewhere, a basement or an empty warehouse. His friends will be there."

Dave knew how to say it. But he was right. The guy with the ink was setting me up.

"I was drinking last night because I bought a Mauser rifle from Mike Fontenot in Lafayette," I said. "It's got a swastika on it."

There was a beat before Dave understood what I was saying. "It made you think of the Jewish woman and her children?" he said.

"Yeah," I said. "How can people do the things they do?"

"Come on down to Helen's office with me."

"Half the cops in the department would like to kill me."

"We'll just have to straighten them out," he said.

# # #

The Iberia Parish Sheriff's Department was housed in a large, white-columned, two-story brick building behind the city library on a long curved driveway shaded by oaks between East Main and the bayou. There's a fountain and a reflecting pond in front of the building, and not far away is a grotto dedicated to the mother of Jesus.

Dave deliberately made me drive the two of us from the hospital to the sheriff's department in the Caddy to make sure everyone in the city knew he was with me. Dave Robicheaux didn't have secrets. I always thought of Streak as the ultimate gentleman stomp-ass flatfoot, someone Wyatt Earp and Doc Holliday would admire.

I had to sit in the waiting room downstairs while Dave talked to Helen upstairs. There were orange peels on the floor and a Black woman trying to control her three children, a single bandage on her cheek. The smallest child was crawling under the chairs. An old man was sleeping with his chin on his chest. Two white teenage smart-asses I had seen taunt a retarded girl who worked at McDonald's on Main were whispering and grinning and sharing some kind of private joke. They looked like a pair of crows pecking on each other.

I had been there for twenty-seven minutes. I went to the food machines in the corridor and bought four candy bars for the Black woman and her children. Wally, the dispatcher, motioned to me from behind the reception window. "The sheriff wanna see you," he said.

"Sure about that, Wally?" I said.

"She loves you. It's the highlight of her day."

"Why don't you use some discretion, Wally?"

"What's dat?"

"I have a speech teacher I'd like to introduce you to," I said.

Actually Wally was more intelligent than he pretended to be, and knew better than to joke about me and Helen Soileau. Helen and I had been an item for a while. It didn't work out, but I still had feelings for her and great respect. I couldn't avoid it. She handcuffed me in Tee Neg's Pool Room in St. Martinville after some outlaw bikers got out of control and I had to talk things over with them. They were piled in a corner when she arrived, and she busted me by dropping the cuffs in my hands and saying, "You know the drill, handsome. Hook yourself up."

I got six weeks in the parish can. If not for Dave, I'd still be there.

Wally gestured for me to come closer to the reception window, looking both ways, lowering his voice. "Helen's trying to do the right t'ing for Dave," he said. "We're all sorry for what happened to Miss Sally. We'll get the fucker who done dis."

Actually I bought five candy bars. I never left the sheriff's department without giving Wally a candy bar. He ate them all day. I took a Baby Ruth from my shirt pocket and put it on the windowsill. "What are those two white kids doing here?" I asked.

"They shot somebody's cat wit' a BB gun."

"Tell Helen I'm on my way, okay?"

I stopped before I left the room and sat down in a folding chair behind the two white kids and leaned into their conversation. "I've seen y'all bait that little girl at the McDonald's. What do y'all have to say for yourselves?"

Their faces froze. Then the older boy's eyes sharpened, probably looking for an exit. The younger boy swallowed.

"Answer me."

"We ain't done nuttin'," the older one said. He tried to smile.

"You calling me a liar?" I said.

"No, suh."

"I'm gonna line it out to you guys, one time and one time only," I said. I put a five-dollar bill in the shirt pocket of the older boy. "When you leave here, you go to the McDonald's and order something. It doesn't matter what. But you be kind to that girl, no matter how long you have to sit there. Do you understand that?"

"Yes, suh," the older boy said.

"If I hear that y'all harmed another animal or if you disrespect the little girl, I will take y'all to McDonald's and shove your heads into the toilet bowl and wipe the floor with you."

"Yes, suh. As soon as we leave here," the older boy said. The younger boy nodded with him.

I went up the stairs to the second floor. I'd like to say I felt good about myself, but I didn't. Can you imagine the homes those kids came from? I hated to think about it.

I walked down the corridor and tapped on Helen Soileau's door.

"Come in, Clete," she said.

# # #

Helen had graying blond hair and was medium height and had an athletic body and eyes that were not hostile but unblinking and analytical and sometimes unreadable and made people look away. Her name was French (Soileau is pronounced "swallow"), but I always believed she descended from Vikings. I asked her about that once. Her answer was "Shut up, Purcel."

She wore slacks and short-sleeve shirts that were tight on her upper arms, and started out her career as an NOPD meter maid in the days when women, particularly masculine-looking women, were treated badly, in her case by a vice cop she took down in public and made a laughingstock. I'll tell you about that later.

"Sorry about Sally," she said.

I nodded. Dave was sitting in front of her desk. She was standing. Dave's badge holder was open on her desk.

"How have you been, Helen?" I said.

She shrugged. I never knew anyone who shrugged so well. It was the body language equivalent of "Who cares?" or "Get a life" or "Beat it, Bozo"—take your pick. But she surprised me. "From what I'm hearing, we have some mainline bad actors on our hands, and a lot more questions than answers."

"That says it," I replied.

"You saw this walking ink bottle get in a boat behind Lauren Bow's house?" she said.

"No doubt about it," I said. "He's the guy who hit me with a crowbar."

"And Miss Sally saw a guy who looked like him behind your office?"

"He looks like Spider-Man without as many colors," I said.

"How did a New Orleans vice cop like Earl Banner get mixed up in this?"

"I don't know," I said. "Maybe the Feds dealt him in. Banner's a good resource. He's on a first-name basis with every cockroach in Orleans Parish."

She looked out the back window, which gave onto Bayou Teche and City Park and the softball diamond and kids playing. A power-boat was splitting the water, tugging a skier, as though all were right in the world.

"It started with your Cadillac, huh?" she said.

"No, Helen, it started when a few assholes thought something of theirs was in my Caddy. There's a difference."

She bit her bottom lip, her eyes empty. It wasn't a smart thing for me to say, at least with Helen. I thought I had stepped in it.

"You make a point," she said. "We've got something in our lap that's much bigger than us. Lauren Bow situated himself in

Louisiana because we're an easy fuck. Outsiders have been doing it since Huey Long gave the state to Frank Costello."

Helen wasn't kidding, either. There were slot and horse machines everywhere, with boxes to stand on so they could put their lunch money in.

"Dave said Bow asked you if you'd been in the service," she said. "Out of nowhere."

"That's right."

"You think Bow has something to do with weaponry or militia groups?" she said.

"Could be," I said. "But billionaire guys like him don't deal with pinhead dope mules headquartered in a car wash."

She put her hands on her hips and looked at both Dave and me. "Yeah, I think you're right. This whole deal sucks. Okay, Clete, can you keep this friend of yours out of trouble?"

"Yeah, I think so," I said.

She picked up Dave's badge holder and handed it to him. "I'm going to Iberia General. Y'all think Miss Sally is gonna make it?"

"The guy who did this is not human," I said.

Helen's eyes locked on mine. For a second there was a great sorrow in them. Then she became the regular Helen again. "Watch your ass, Clete. We're gonna be on our own. That means we don't make dumb mistakes because we've got a private agenda. Do you hear me loud and clear?"

"Yes, ma'am," I replied, my hands opening and closing at my sides. "Helen?"

"What?"

"When you go to the hospital, prepare yourself," I said.

# # #

I returned to Iberia General later that day. Miss Sally was heavily medicated and swathed in bandages and attached to tubes and drip bags. I sat in the room for a long time as several of the personnel went in and out, not speaking, doing whatever they do, closing the door quietly. I hardly noticed them. I knew there was a reason for their silence and the nameless and remote way they did their work, but I wasn't sure what it was. Then I remembered a battalion aid station at night and the rain clicking on top of the tent, a single lamp hanging from a pole, and the anonymity of the corpsmen doing triage from cot to cot, their faces empty, knowing all the while they would live and some of their charges would die.

I wanted to drink, but I didn't. Instead, I returned to my office and sat at the spool table on my little deck and watched the sun descend like an ember inside a purple bank of rain clouds on the horizon. The wind was warm and made me sleepy and unguarded and vulnerable, but I did not care. If someone was looking at me through binoculars, he would not see any firearms on my person or on the deck. I even stood up and stretched my arms, expanding my chest, daring anyone to shoot at me. Then I walked down the slope to the bayou and watched some old Black men sitting on upside-down buckets, cane fishing at sunset in the bridge's shadows.

But I knew if my enemy was out there, in a vehicle or behind a tree or a window, he would not shoot. He was after information, the key to something big, something that bought power and money or the ability to terrify people. All the skells are after the same thing. And the worst are usually those we suspect the least or trust the most. And if my enemy was working for someone higher up in his organization, someone who was as cruel and depraved as he was, he could not allow mistakes.

I guess that was a pretty crazy way for me to behave. But not really. Mortality is mortality. It comes to you when it's ready. We don't set the clock. At least that was the way I felt.

I walked into the water, into the cattails and bamboo, the incoming tidal current sliding over my shoes and my ankles, then my calves. The red and green lights on the drawbridge switched on, and a water moccasin swam in its slithering S-shaped way inches from my legs. I could not have cared less.

I addressed myself to the bayou, the cars thudding on the steel grid, the old convent across the water, the trees, the gloaming of the day, the flooded canebrakes, a little boy flying a kite high in the sky. "I'm here!" I shouted. "Anytime you want me, I'm here!"

I received no response. The old Black men pulled up their lines and corks and baited hooks and swung them farther out in the bayou, studying the corks as they floated with the current and straightened the lines, as though that would keep them safe from a lunatic shouting at the wind.

# # #

I couldn't eat supper, so I lay on the couch in front of my television set and watched my DVD of the 1948 film *Joan of Arc*, starring Ingrid Bergman. When I finished it, I watched Ingrid Bergman in Ernest Hemingway's *For Whom the Bell Tolls*. I think both stories are about bravery that is beyond the limits of bravery; know what I mean? There are times when human beings run out of courage. There is only so much courage people are allowed. It's not an inexhaustible resource, and neither is hope. When you've bought it, you've bought it. But something happens when everyone else bags butt for the fort and leaves you behind. I'm not good at this, but other people are. They find a place that is beyond the Earth, beyond gravity, beyond the edges of both the universe and eternity. It's like breaking from dark water into light.

A soldier, although brave, has weapons and other forms of protection and can usually go out in hot blood. The two women in the films, Joan and María, had nothing to protect them and faced every form of evil that could debase them first and kill them later.

Hey, I'll tell you something. I met John McCain. He told me his favorite novel was *For Whom the Bell Tolls*.

I thought about Miss Sally and what she went through, and I wondered if her psychic fear was like the mother's fear when she and her three children were about to enter the showers at Auschwitz. I took the magazine picture from my wallet and hid it in a safe place and promised myself that I would not die until somehow I found justice for the Jewish family and now for Miss Sally.

I slept until two in the morning, then went outside and heard a gator slap its tail in the bayou, then a squealing sound, like a nutria caught in a gator's jaws. Across the bayou the red pontoon plane I had seen Clara Bow in was bobbing in the incoming tide. But I didn't care about Clara Bow, nor did I care about her airplane. Heat lightning was all over the sky, the way it gets in late summer over the Gulf, or in the hurricane season, when the barometer suddenly drops and the sky starts to rip apart, like a tin roof being peeled in half, and you know that a bad moon is on the rise.

A giant streak of lightning jumped across the heavens, lighting the bayou and the trees as bright as day, and I saw a man by the pontoon plane looking straight at me, shirtless, his skin dry and cool and strung with tattooed flowers, like an Oriental painting.

Then he ran for a pickup truck. The lightning died, the sky went dark, and I heard the truck door slam and the engine start.

I went into the cottage, grabbed the Mauser bolt-action and a cloth bandolier full of clips, and got into the Caddy and headed south toward Jeanerette, the only place the tattooed man could go unless he wanted to go back into the center of New Iberia.

CHAPTER THIRTEEN

I took one side of the bayou, and the tattooed man took the other, except he did not know I had followed him. His headlights were ahead of me, the only ones powering through the darkness on the two-lane that went through the LSU experimental farm. In less than fourteen minutes we were both in St. Mary Parish, not far from Lauren Bow's antebellum home and his acres of sugarcane, but on different sides of the bayou. I thought he would turn into Bow's home. I was wrong. He made me and took off for St. Martin Parish and swamp country.

The biggest swamp and marshland area in the United States is in Southwest Louisiana—bigger than the Everglades in Florida and the Okefenokee in Georgia. But this guy did not know his way around. He went up the top of the levee at Henderson and deeper and deeper into the swamp. I got behind him and kept my brights on and used a handheld spotlight that plugged into the cigarette lighter to fill the inside of the truck cab with an eye-watering brilliance.

It didn't take him long to make another mistake. He hit a pothole, lost control of the steering wheel, and hooked one wheel off the single dirt road on top of the levee and slid into the water. He jumped out, a bolt-action rifle in his right hand, one that looked like an '03 Springfield, and splashed into the cattails and began working his way across a canal to an island covered with cypress and willow trees. I stopped the Eldorado and cut the engine and went out the driver's door straight down the levee so as not to silhouette, then went into the water, sinking up to my waist, a huge cloud of mud mushrooming around me.

Up ahead I saw him emerging from the water and walking up the slope into the trees on the island. My eyes had adjusted and I could see him well. His rifle had a sling. He should have wrapped it around his left arm, gone to one knee, and gotten me dead-center in the chest.

But he didn't. And I think I know why. He was a coward and frightened to death. Every rapist and misogynist I've ever known, and there are far more of them than you think, was yellow from his toes to his hairline. Yeah, they probably suffered as children, but wouldn't that give them more incentive to protect the innocent than to torture them. In other words, F.T.S. again, which you know by now means Fuck.That.Shit.

I could hear him splashing through a chain of stagnant pools inside the trees. I eased down behind a cypress trunk, the butt of my rifle resting on a strip of dry sand. A wind began to kick up from the south, a bad omen for the tattooed man. When the wind blows, the trees do the same, revealing whatever is hidden inside them.

Maybe he had caught on. I couldn't see an outline or hear a sound other than the wind and drops of water scattering on the ground, and a distant train whistle, probably the Sunset Limited, headed for either New Orleans or Los Angeles.

I decided to take a chance. Not a big one. Just one that would leave me with a clean conscience down the track, like being on that train out there in the dark, riding through the Grand Canyon country, eating a big breakfast in the dining car while watching the sunrise streak across the desert and climb up the buttes that resemble tombstones. Everybody's got a code. But you've got to stick with it. Would you give up your principles because of a sadist who hates himself so much he disfigures his own body?

"I've already dimed you, bud!" I called out, then moved quickly to another position. "Why go out in a body bag?"

I moved again, into deep shadow. The bit about the 911 call was a lie. Back then there was no service in that area. I lobbed a piece of rotten wood at the shell of a half-submerged tupelo tree, the kind that flanges out at the waterline and sounds like a conga drum when you knock on it.

"I've got a frag, bud," I said. "Five seconds after I release the spoon your grits will be hanging in a tree."

My eyes were stinging and full of sweat, my armpits drenched with stink, my nose itching, my ears buzzing with mosquitoes, my heart thumping. I was back with Sir Charles again. Except I was lying about the grenade.

"I'm really getting pissed off with you, bub," I said. "Forget about fragging you. I'm gonna cut you up, you piece of shit."

I meant it, but it was a dumb way to think. I was losing it. I had seen what he'd done to Miss Sally, and I no longer cared about my own safety. That's a bad way to be. Sir Charles taught us that. In daylight the NVA could go underground and take a B-52 pounding that lit up an entire jungle, and by dark they'd have sappers cutting our wire.

"Last chance, asshole," I said.

No answer.

I stood up and started walking, in what's called a high-ready position. My mouth had turned to cotton, my heart as hard and heavy as a cantaloupe. Then my enemy rose from behind a tangle of willows and air vines, without a shirt, the moonlight like a net of silver coins, his arms straight up, a Springfield bolt-action propped across both hands.

"You win, Jack," he said.

I could see every detail of him. I felt like I was looking at a nightmare that had suddenly become real. His face was skeletal, his eyes cavernous, his torso both ribbed and plated with muscle. With his arms held stiffly in the air, he tipped his rifle out of his palms and let it fall to the ground.

"Lace your fingers and put your hands behind your head," I said.

"No problem, Blimpo. You're not gonna start knocking me around, are you?"

"Turn in a circle. If you lower your hands, I'll shoot you through the spine. That means life as a quadriplegic."

"You're a nasty son of a bitch, aren't you?" he replied.

"One . . . ," I began.

"You got it, boss man," he said, rotating in a circle, a smile on his mouth. "I got to take a dump."

"Good. I hear the toilets in the St. Martin Parish jail are first-rate."

"Hey, man, it'll just take a second. I'm trying to cooperate, here."

"Keep your right hand on the back of your neck. With your left hand, undo your belt and unbutton your pants and let them drop. Do not reach down for anything unless you want to get shot."

I heard a car engine up on the levee and saw headlight beams bouncing off the channel and the trees. The tattooed man was grinning. "A little jumpy?" he said.

"Say a prayer it's not one of your friends," I replied.

"Give it a break, Jack. You beat me fair and square. I don't deny that. As far as that Cajun broad, yeah, I took her out a couple of times, but when I went to her house at her invitation, somebody had already beat the shit out of her. My DNA ain't in the places you'd like."

"If you open your mouth about Miss Sally again, I'm gonna cave in all your teeth."

"Then do it, motherfucker. Because you ain't got shit, except some car damage over some weed that was left in it. It'll take Orleans Parish three fuckin' years to get that on the docket. In the meantime you're building a case against yourself."

"Whose car is up there on the levee?" I said.

"How the fuck should I know? I'm not from here."

"Kick your pants off."

"I'm gonna fall."

"Then fall," I said.

"Come on, man, what the hell. Lighten up, huh? I got mosquitoes on me from outer space."

He was telling the truth, but the mosquitoes didn't seem to bother him, like his skin was a lampshade.

"What's your name?" I asked.

He tilted his face up, his eyes locked on mine. "I ain't got one. At least not one you'd recognize."

"Where's the man who has an anti-Semite wardrobe?"

"Don't know what you're talking about. Here, I'm stepping out of my pants. You satisfied?"

He reached over to pick them up.

"Put your hands on your head!" I said.

I should have clubbed him with the buttstock, but it was too late. I had made a serious mistake. He ripped an expandable baton from the tape on the back of his calf and whipped it at a forty-five-degree angle across my face. The blow was blinding. Before I could raise my rifle, he had both hands clenched on it and was twisting it from my grasp. He bit my hand and kicked me in the genitals and spat in my face, then slammed the butt between my eyes. His strength was superhuman, like his muscles were made of spring steel. I got one arm around his neck and was going to break it, but I couldn't get a hold on it. The smell of his body and of the oil in his hair was like the odor of a grease trap. I tried to get my thumb in his eye, to no avail. His head slipped from the crook of my arm. Then suddenly he was free, my rifle in his hand. I was disarmed and about to die.

He was filled with delight, his expression fiendish, his index finger slipping through the trigger guard. "Get down on your knees, Bluto. Maybe I'll cut you some slack."

"Eat shit," I said.

How long is a second when a loaded gun is pointed at you? Answer: an eternity. Your skin feels like it's being peeled off your face; you fight to control your bowels and your urine; the degree of psychic pain is not measurable.

"Bye-bye, you fat fuck," he said.

The car on the levee had stopped. I heard a door creak open, then a spotlight attached to the door lit up the island. The tattooed man's face jumped in the light, his eyes watering, and I slapped the rifle barrel away from my chest just as he pulled the trigger. A searing agony like a red-hot poker seemed to lance simultaneously through every organ in my body. The only other time I'd experienced such pain and fear was when a navy corpsman dragged me down a hillside on a poncho liner in the middle of a monsoon, tracers from a solitary helicopter streaking the night sky, smoke rising from the shrapnel in my vest.

Then the person on the levee fired a round. The tattooed man fell down on top of me and left his brains on my shirt. The stars, the spotlight, the silvery shine on the willows and cypresses, and I slid down a long, dark drainage tunnel below the ground, one that smelled of rainwater and decayed vegetation and stone that could have come from a medieval dungeon or a prison tower. I knew I had gone to a different place, one not of this world, one that did not belong to the living or the dead, but I had no idea what it was.

Then I heard the shooter wading across the channel. It was a woman. I don't care if anyone believes me or not; I saw what I saw and felt what I felt and heard what I heard. She propped her rifle on a willow trunk and got on her knees and held my head in her lap and stroked my hair and my face with her fingernails and kissed my eyes and shushed me when I tried to speak. There was a luminosity inside my head and a coolness on my skin that I had never experienced, not even when the corpsman saved my life in Shitsville.

But I couldn't see her face, nor could I hear what she was saying. Maybe it was French. I just don't know.

"I know you, but I don't know from where," I said. "Please tell me who you are."

She placed a finger gingerly on my lips.

"Am I going to die?" I asked.

She laid her hand across my eyes and touched the entry wound in my side, then moved her hand across my stomach and chest. The pain went away, just like creek water flowing through a mountain stream. Then she kissed my forehead. For just a moment I saw her profile against the moon.

"You're Joan," I said.

I saw her head shaking.

"Don't deny it. Please. I've always wanted to be with you."

She picked up my hand with both of hers, then kissed it and rose to her feet. Then she said, *You're a good man, Clete Purcel. I would have loved riding side by side with you. God be with you.*

Then she was gone. She didn't walk or swim away; she was simply gone. I didn't want her to ever leave. I tried to speak, but passed out.

CHAPTER FOURTEEN

I woke up in Iberia General, with Dave Robicheaux sitting right next to me. It took me a while to know where I was and what had happened to me. There was a bandage on my side and on my head. The room was full of sunlight, the contrast with the island one I could hardly imagine.

"Where is she?" I said.

"Who?" Dave said.

"The woman who saved my life."

"You were talking about her in your sleep, Cletus. But the 911 came in anonymously from a phone on the four-lane."

"I ate a bullet," I said.

"No, you didn't. You got grazed in the side and knocked in the head with an expanded baton."

"Yeah, the tattooed man did it. He's dead, right?"

"Definitely."

"Brains all over the place?"

"You bet."

"I didn't do it. The woman capped him from across the channel. A bullet went through my guts and liver and stomach. It felt like somebody took out my insides with an E-tool."

Dave picked up a cup of crushed ice with a straw in it and tried to put it in my mouth. "You need to rest up, Clete."

"Don't blow me off, Dave. You see Confederate soldiers on Spanish Lake. I saw that woman drop that bucket of shit. I was dying and hating myself for doing it. She told me I was a good man. She came from someplace else."

"Where?" he said.

"She wouldn't say. But I know who she is."

"Who?"

"I'm not gonna say. What's the gen on the tattooed guy?"

"There's not any. We did an emergency request with the NCIC."

"Don't tell me that, Dave. A guy like that is not a blank."

"This one is. At least so far."

I remembered the guy said something about his DNA on Miss Sally, something ugly. But I'll tell you something, whether you believe me or not. If you're a cop, if you live in the world of these cocksuckers, you don't let them get in your head. It's not worth it. They win, you lose.

"How's Miss Sally?" I said.

"Better," Dave said.

"No kidding?"

"Yeah," he said. His eyes wandered around the room.

"What are you not telling me?" I said.

"A woman came to see her. Except we had a uniform on the door in case a perp tried to get to her."

"Yeah?"

"The uniform said the woman got into the room but never went through the door. He swore that up and down."

"What'd the woman look like?" I asked.

"He said he looked straight at her but couldn't remember. That's how he put it."

"Where'd she go?"

"He said she went out in the hall, then she was gone. In seconds."

"Sound a little strange?" I said.

Dave leaned forward in his chair. "Nobody is going to believe your story about the woman on the island, Clete. So don't tell it to them. Somebody popped the tattooed man from the bank. The only thing that's important is what the woman told you about yourself. You're a good man. Got it?"

"Do you believe me about the bullet inside me?"

He bit the corner of his lip. "Put it this way, Clete. The madness is not with us. It's out there, podna," he said. "How long do you plan on staying in the hospital?"

"I don't," I said.

I got out of the bed and almost hit the deck.

# # #

Nevertheless, I checked myself out and dropped by Miss Sally's room and found her sound asleep. I ordered some flowers downstairs and bought a straw hat at Walmart to shadow my face because it looked pretty beat up. I also called my house in the Quarter to make sure everything was all right. Chen answered and said Gracie and Miss Dorothy were out shopping and all the cats were in the courtyard and digging holes in the flower beds.

Then I went back to Henderson Swamp, where I'd messed up proper and gotten myself disarmed, which didn't make me feel very good. The day was windy and beautiful, the trees thrashing on the island, the leaves blowing high in the sky and floating down on the channel. I walked around on the levee, searching for a spent cartridge or footprints that led from the top of the levee to the spot on the bank where the woman had entered the channel. There were other prints, those of the ambulance and the medics, and my own, and the tattooed man's, but no prints where I knew I saw the woman.

I was having some other problems with my thought processes as well. The guy who I had decided to call Ink Man was smaller than I was, but he'd twisted my weapon out of my hands. I'm six foot and weigh 248 pounds. I don't know how he did it. Maybe my thinking was based on pride. No, that was not true. Either Ink Man was wired on crystal or some kind of chemical adrenaline or I needed to go to the fat farm, although I don't have that much fat.

I went back to my cottage at the motel and fell fast asleep face down on my bed, my clothes on. I dreamed about horses and men in armor that clinked when the horses trotted, their helmets as silvery as mercury in the sunlight. When I woke up, I didn't know where I was. I thought I heard horns blowing in the distance.

I popped open a beer just as Dave knocked on the door. Great timing.

I'll tell you this about Dave, though. He worried about my drinking, but he never fussed at me. He might ask me to take *him* to a meeting, trying to get me into the building, but that was as far as it went. No matter what I did, he never made me feel bad about myself. That's why I always believed in Dave Robicheaux. He was the knight errant and I was the grunt. I told him that once. He said that if he ever heard me denigrate myself again, he would throw me off the drawbridge at Burke Street.

He stood in the doorway at the cottage, the evening sun dull red on the live oaks. "What's the haps, Clete?" he said.

"No haps," I said.

"The sheriff wants us in her office."

"It's after hours," I said.

"Tell Helen that."

# # #

She was walking up and down by her back window, patting her knuckles in one palm after the other.

"What's up, Helen?" I said.

"Not much. The FBI called. So did Earl Banner. So did Lauren Bow's attorney. Our coroner is about to quit. I get the sense my office may be responsible for original sin. Before I go deeper into this, tell me Banner is totally nuts."

"What'd he say?" Dave asked.

"That Clete has a demon living in his house. A dancer named Gracie Lamar."

"Banner is obsessed with sex, Helen," Dave said. "That's why he's a vice cop."

"Duh," she said. "That doesn't make him a theologian."

"Who cares about Banner?" I said. "He's an asshole. Hang up on him."

Helen's mouth was crimped tight, a heat wave rising into her face. For a long time I had felt she needed counseling.

"Why did you take it on yourself to chase the tattooed man into St. Martin Parish?" she said. "You could have called it in. We could have coordinated and had him in a cage. We would have information now. Instead, we've got an unknown dead man in a body bag the coroner says has the worst stink he's ever smelled."

"I'm sorry," I said. "I thought I made the right choice. Ink Man was obviously there to kill me. That made me a little subjective in my thinking processes, I guess."

She rubbed her forehead and shrugged, this time cutting me some slack, which was often her way. "It's been a long day," she said. "You have any idea who the female shooter is?"

"I'll have to give it some thought," I said.

She shook her head like I had thrown a glass of water at it. "Some thought? That's it?"

"Probably," I replied. "Some people say it's an improvement."

Dave grinned. So did I. Helen did not.

"Ho ho, funny men," she said. "An FBI agent named Samuel Hawthorne wants our dead guy sealed up with everything that we can stick on him. What's with that?"

"Maybe they need a glow-in-the-dark doorstop," I said.

She slung her ballpoint pen at me.

# # #

I called her at her home later that night. Helen and I share a private country. We're both different. I grew up with Irish and Italian and Jewish street kids. New Orleans has a violent history, all the way back to its founding in the eighteenth century. In 1811 the biggest slave uprising in American history took place outside New Orleans and was put down by mass murder and decapitation. The man who led the uprising, the son of a white man, had his hands chopped off in a barn, then his thighs were shot one at a time, then his tormentors piled straw on him and burned him alive. There's not a lot of talk about that in our tourist brochures.

Anyway, Helen became an NOPD meter maid, then got promoted to a beat cop in the Quarter and over on Canal, the same area Dave and I patrolled. A vice cop named Baxter used to hound her every chance he had, particularly about her sexuality. One time he put a dirty jockstrap in her locker; another time he glued a picture of her face onto the photograph of a Detroit linebacker and tacked it on the corkboard. So when a sniper ensconced himself in the Howard Johnson's and killed nine people, including five officers, and wounded many others, Baxter took over and did a good job. But being the piece of shit he was, he decided to have some fun with Helen. He said something like, "All you guys and all you ladies are kicking ass spot-on." Then he paused and said, "Sorry, Helen, I don't know where that leaves you."

Baxter took freebies, oral ones, particularly from a prostitute named Scarlet Brown.

"Oh, I'm doing okay," Helen said. "I busted Scarlet yesterday. Did you know Scarlet's a male? Who would have guessed?"

Baxter never lived it down. He was also shot through the back of the head in a family restaurant off Canal; he fell face down in his linguine.

"I want to apologize," I said, looking out my window at the stars dropping from the sky.

"Forget it," she said.

Helen was tough, but she had soft places, too. What I always liked most about her was her nonjudgmental attitude, even with the worst of the skells. In fact, she liked them better than the socialites in the Garden District. Her favorite movie was *A Streetcar Named Desire*. Her next favorite was *The Rose Tattoo*; the others were *The Fugitive Kind* and *Suddenly, Last Summer*. She believed that monsters awaited all people who were gentle and kind. Sometimes Helen could make me afraid. If she was serious, she didn't take prisoners.

"This is what happened at Henderson Swamp, Helen," I said. "The Ink Man was about to kill me. A woman fired from across the channel and blew away most of his brains. How many people can fire with that kind of accuracy in moonlight? Then she waded across the channel and knelt by me and put my head in her lap. She said several things to me, but they had no bearing on the shooting."

There was a long pause. "What did she say?" Helen asked.

"That she would have loved riding side by side with me. I don't wish to say anything else."

I thought maybe she might mock me, but she didn't. "People see and hear all kinds of things when they're traumatized, Clete. You don't need to put it in a report. Okay, big guy?"

"Dave said the same thing. But both of you are wrong. I saw and heard everything I told you."

"I believe you. That's why I keep you around."

"What do you mean?"

"You never lie, or at least not about things that are important. Neither does Streak. You guys really fuck things up. See you tomorrow."

# # #

Someone knocked on the door early the next morning. I was already dressed, but hardly anyone I knew knocked on the door at 7:14 a.m. I looked through the window before I unbolted the door and took off the night chain. I was a little bit leery, but not for the usual reasons. It was Clara Bow, and she had cut her hair and dyed it so it was a dark walnut color and curled under her cheeks, accentuating the heart shape of her face. In other words, some of my cogs and wheels were waking up in the wrong fashion, dig what I'm saying?

"I'm very sorry to disturb you at this hour, Mr. Purcel, but I must talk to you," she said. "I'm scared to death."

"Well, please come in and sit down, and we'll see what we can do about that," I said.

Here we go, I thought. *Bombs away. Why do I do this? What a pinhead I am.*

CHAPTER FIFTEEN

"I heard what happened to your secretary and am deeply sorry," she said.

"Miss Sally is a little better now, so we're making progress," I replied, and moved another chair to my breakfast table. "What can I help you with?"

"I also know about your injuries. I'm sure they're associated with my former husband, and I regret having pulled you into his web, because that's what it is. He's a tarantula."

"That's pretty strong, Miss Clara. Did you say 'former husband'?"

"Yes, my divorce was finalized two days ago."

"You want some coffee and beignets?"

"Yes, I do. That's so kind of you."

You ever hear bells ringing at a railroad crossing? That's the sound I was hearing, loud and clear. *Clang, clang, clang!* "Do you have some information for me, Miss Clara?"

"The man who tried to kill you was heavily tattooed?" she said.

"How did you know?" I asked.

"The ambulance driver who took you to the hospital lives a short distance down the bayou from me."

"You knew the tattooed guy?"

"I think my former husband had a man killed, a CPA who caught on to Lauren's financial schemes. I think the assassin Lauren hired was the same man who tried to murder you."

"What's his name?"

"I don't know."

Here we go, I thought. She was informed, then uninformed. It's an old runaround, particularly with the clients of private investigators. Why? Because PI work usually revolves around spousal misbehavior, and usually both parties can't get enough of it.

She had already sat down at the table and was now moving the silverware around. She actually looked like Clara Bow, more child than adult, with a thought she couldn't handle hidden behind her eyes. Hey, this is the truth. PI clients are like people who commit themselves to electroshock therapy. They're at the end of the line. You have to feel sorry for them.

I thought maybe we should go to Victor's Cafeteria, but the coffee was already made and the beignets were in the oven. At least that's the reason I gave myself.

"I call the dead guy Ink Man," I said. "Right now Ink Man is in a body bag. An FBI agent named Hawthorne thinks we should be extra careful with it."

"I don't know anything about that," she said.

"Ever hear of an anti-Semite named Baylor Hemmings? He wears T-shirts that say six million Jews were not enough."

"No, I never heard the name."

When people say that with such certainty? Yep, you got it. Duck. But I don't listen to myself sometimes.

"What are your ex-husband's feelings about Jews?" I asked.

"Lauren doesn't have feelings."

"Pardon?" I said.

"He doesn't have feelings about anything except money. All kinds. Gold, silver, diamonds. He worships it, literally. He has a master's degree in chemistry. He used it to make soap, and as if that wasn't enough, he used it to con people out of all their savings."

The real question I needed to ask was obvious: Why did she marry this guy, and when she found out he was an asshole, why didn't she dump him?

I think she read my mind.

"You're wondering why I spent fifteen years with him, aren't you?" she said.

"Yes, that kind of concerns me, Miss Clara."

"I was a waitress at a truck stop in Amarillo. He knocked me up, made me have an abortion, and told me he would pour acid in my face if I left him. In the meantime he screwed every attractive woman he could get his hands on."

I put a napkin across my lap and accidentally touched her foot with mine. She lifted her eyes, then searched mine. "You don't use profanity, do you?" she said.

"Excuse me?" I said, trying to keep my thoughts straight. "No, I don't use it in front of women. Listen—"

"You're an exceptional man, Mr. Purcel."

"No, I'm not, Miss Clara. I'm a disgraced cop who accidentally killed a federal witness. I also worked for the Mob in Vegas and Reno and Montana. What I'm saying is I got lots of problems."

"I don't care about any of those things," she said, her eyes on mine.

"I'd better be going to town. I have clients coming in all day."

She didn't move and looked straight ahead. I rose from my chair, my fingertips touching the top of the table, my face burning, the Sunset Limited going through town on Railroad Avenue, a knot in my throat I couldn't cough up. I wanted to run.

"Please," she said. "Don't go right now."

"What's wrong, Miss Clara?"

"Everything. He's going to kill me. People will not even know I'm dead. He told me that. I would just disappear, maybe in a vat of acid. I want to kill him, Mr. Purcel."

She got up and stepped on my shoes and pressed her forehead on my chest, her hands placed loosely on my hips. "Oh, Mr. Purcel, just stay with me a minute. Just a minute. Please don't just walk away from me."

I was not very good at these kinds of things, and I'm still not. But if she had wished to channel her fear and dependency into a rising male problem, she had succeeded. I found myself placing my hands on her shoulders. "Miss Clara, you have many good years ahead of you. You don't need to get mixed up with over-the-hill jarheads who left their brains at the slop chute."

"The what?"

"A saloon."

Her response was to slide her hands over my ribs and sink her nails in my back.

Then someone beat on the door so hard it rattled the silverware. I stepped back from Miss Clara and almost fell down, and actually lost my breath. "Excuse me, Miss Clara," I said. "It must be an emergency."

Why do these things always happen to me? I thought. They never happen to Dave. It wasn't fair. I jerked open the door.

No one was there. I walked down the stoop. The grass was spangled with sunlight, the chickens pecking around my feet. Then I saw her in the shade by the edge of the Teche, wearing clothes that looked like a medieval peasant's, her feet wrapped with thongs and soft leather. I could barely make out her features in the leaves and moss, but her hair was beautiful. She was shaking her index finger at me.

"I'm sorry," I said. "My gyroscope got out of control."

I said you were a good man. That's not a compliment. It's what you are. Don't disappoint me, sir.

"No ma'am, I won't. You saved my life. You held me in your lap. That never happened to me."

Why do you pause? Go ahead and finish your statement.

"Are you who I think you are?"

Yes, of course, she said. *I came a long way for you.*

"I'm not drunk or asleep or maybe dead?"

No, you're my Jean d'Aulon. He stood up for me at my trial.

"I don't know who that is."

Goodbye, my friend, she said, and evaporated.

I went back inside the cottage and sat down, shaking all over, my teeth chattering, worse than malaria.

"What's wrong with you? Who was that?" Miss Clara said.

"You ever see Ingrid Bergman's films?"

"Yes."

"She made some great ones, didn't she?"

"Mr. Purcel, you're acting very strange. I apologize for my behavior. Please don't think bad of me." She got a wet towel and put it on my face.

"Let's go downtown and have some fried eggs, Miss Clara. It's on me."

"*Joan of Arc* is my favorite Ingrid Bergman film," she said. "How is that connected to your obvious condition?"

I decided to change the subject, and that's how I got through the rest of the morning.

# # #

After 1:00 p.m. I met Dave at his shotgun house not far down from the Shadows on East Main, right on the bayou. He had two magnolias, and live oak and pecan trees all over the property, as well as azaleas and hydrangeas and roses and hibiscus and purple phlox and red and gold four-o'clocks in the shade, all of it in full bloom. He sat down next to me on the back steps and put an ice-cold Dr Pepper in my hands. "Okay, start over again," he said.

I went through the whole thing about Joan a second time. I felt like a fool. When I was finished, he stared at the shadows in his backyard and the sunlight blazing on the bayou. "You've seen the same woman twice now," he said. He wasn't asking me a question. He was telling me what happened.

"Yeah," I said, my heart tripping.

"Don't dismiss what you've seen, Clete. And don't let others do it, either. Look at it this way. There are two ways to think of existence. One, there's nothing here but atoms. Two, there's a spiritual world as well. Did a couple of amoebas do the horizontal bop and create all that's on the land and in the ocean? For me, that's a bit challenging."

Tell me Dave Robicheaux couldn't say it.

"You want another Dr Pepper?" he said.

I shook my head. "I want to see Miss Sally at the hospital."

Dave looked down the slope at the bayou. "That brings us to another subject. I think I'm next on the hit parade. I think it's going to get a whole lot worse, too."

There was a hutch against a tree trunk in the yard, where rabbits and coons came and went of their own accord. He had cats named Buggs and Snuggs, and a possum named Lady Godiva.

"Did you hear me?" he said.

"Yeah, they didn't nail me. So they're going to keep chewing up people until they get what they want. With pliers and blowtorches and those kinds of things. What am I supposed to do about it?"

"I don't know," he said. "Worse, we're getting the lockout from the Feds and NOPD, the latter in the form of Earl Banner. I don't think that guy is just a simpleton. He knows something we don't."

"Like what?"

"Have you talked with Gracie Lamar about him?" he asked.

"More or less."

"What did she say?"

"She said he's a geek."

"I think it goes deeper than that," he said.

"Banner's on a pad?"

"Yeah, it's something like that," Dave said. "He's always looking for the big score. It doesn't matter in what form."

"What do you want to do about it?"

"Make all these guys pay a higher price."

Dave didn't talk like that often. When normal people are volatile, they make a lot of noise. Dave doesn't make a sound. He could be a hat rack. Then suddenly someone is on a barroom floor, tangled in the brass rail, mewing and begging for his life while I try to keep Dave from committing homicide. He always calls it a blackout. I don't think there's a name for it.

Ask Dave if he ever killed an NVA or a VC. He'll tell you no, he killed a pimp named Mack who made his mother a whore. And he did it more than once.

"Where do you want to start?" I asked.

"Ink Man's body bag."

"You're kidding, aren't you?"

"Doing anything else?" he said.

# # #

Guess what? Two hours later we were in Helen Soileau's office.

"Ink Man's body is gone?" she said.

"That about says it," Dave replied.

"Out of the locker? You're sure?" she said.

"Yeah," Dave said.

"Jesus Christ, I can't believe this," she said. "Who else knows about this?"

"The Feds were just notified," Dave said. "They're a little upset."

"Fuck them," she said. "They should have already picked it up."

"I've got a suggestion," I said.

"What?" she said.

"Get the FBI and Earl Banner in here at the same time," I replied. "Then get the coroner in here with his observations about the body. They have to make a response of some kind."

"What are you talking about, Clete?" she said.

"The coroner says either the refrigeration wasn't working or the body went into the fastest decomposition he's ever seen."

"Which is it?" she said.

"He has no idea," Dave said.

"This pisses me off," she said.

"Let me talk to this guy Hawthorne," I said. "He seems like a good guy. But I have a feeling he's on his own. Maybe he and us are on the same side. What's to lose?"

"Okay, we'll give it a try," she said. "I didn't mean to start knocking y'all around."

"We're used to it," Dave said.

The phone on her desk rang. She looked at the caller ID and frowned, then picked up the receiver. "Sheriff Soileau," she said.

We could hear the other party speaking, but not well enough to understand the words.

"Thanks," she said. "Maybe we'll see you, maybe not."

She replaced the receiver in the cradle. "That was the fire chief in St. Martin Parish. Somebody dropped a body from a plane in Bayou Bijou. An air bubble in the bag floated it to the top. Our parish code is stamped on it. Want to take a ride?"

CHAPTER SIXTEEN

The three of us took the Loreauville Road into St. Martin Parish, the home of Evangeline and the Acadians, who were expelled from Canada in 1755. The parish is deep green and full of lakes and bayous and swamps and palmettos and flooded tupelos and live oaks and Spanish moss. It was the right place for the Cajuns to be, because they surely did not have a good history. Exploitation, forced servitude, and illiteracy dominated their lives, which made them brethren with the slaves and Atakapa Indians, and few of them ever ascended to the plantation culture. But oddly they were happy, and it's been that way unto this day.

Cajuns love their families. They laugh all the time and have little interest in politics, and seldom leave South Louisiana. I know many people here who have never traveled farther than two parishes from their birthplace. They are proud to be called coonasses, and eat food with a cholesterol count that could clog an elephant's arteries. Even as a little boy in New Orleans, I spent a lot of time with them.

Bayou Bijou is a beautiful place. At evening tide the water rises among the trees in the sunset, and the birds climb inside the limbs, and small waves with a yellow-white froth on them slide through the trunks. Blankets of lichen rock with the current, and you can hear a hush all the way to the Gulf of Mexico.

I hated to see a place so grand contaminated by whatever was coming into our lives. It was not just one instance, either. For a long time, since our days in Shitsville, I've felt that something was aimed at us, something we created, something that was mean and ugly to the bone and was going to undo the paradise that early people lived in, when people took the fruit from the trees with their hands and shared it with the animals.

Helen had called ahead and asked the firemen not to remove the body from the water until we arrived. We drove along a levee, then drove down a slope to a dock and landing where Ciro LeBlanc, the assistant fire chief, and a helper in the boat were waiting for us. Ciro looked like a fire hydrant with a drooping mustache. Ciro was what I called a hardcore coonass.

(Let me clear something up about that name. The Cajun boys who went to France in World War I were given the name by the French as an insult. It has to do with the female anatomy. Thanks, France.)

"What's the haps, Ciro?" I said.

"Ain't no haps," he replied. "Except that bag bobbin' in the water. How you, Miss Helen? You know what's goin' on wit' dis?"

"We're not sure, Ciro," she said. "Who called this in?"

"Some kids fishing."

"Where are they?" she asked.

"Dey gone home."

"What kind of plane dropped the bag?" she asked.

"Dey said it was way up in the sky," Ciro said. "Dey couldn't make it out."

I had a feeling we were not going to get a lot of detail from Ciro and the witnesses.

"How you doin', Dave?" he said.

"Just fine, Ciro," Dave said. "You okay?"

"Yes, suh," Ciro said. Then he folded his arms on his chest and stared at the water and the dock and the powerboat that was waiting for us. "I seen t'rew the rip. There's somet'ing going on, huh? Somet'ing y'all cain't talk about?"

He waited for an answer. But we offered none.

# # #

We went due south across a bay, the wind stiff in our faces, the propeller trenching a yellow wake that rolled among the flooded canebrakes and gumtrees, the sun dissolving into clouds that were red and purple, like smoke reaching from the horizon to the top of the sky. Ciro cut the engine and let us drift into the reeds where the body bag rested. It was black, the surface crinkling in places, bent in others, like a slug someone had stepped on. An iridescent shimmer hovered over the split in the plastic.

An ambulance was supposed to meet us at the dock. But right now we had to take care of things on our own. All of us put on latex. Ciro picked up a boat hook. His helper was probably eighteen or nineteen.

"The hook is gonna tear up the plastic, Ciro," I said.

"Whoa," Dave said.

"I've got a rope and tennis shoes," I said. "Plus, I'm responsible for the guy in this bag. If it hadn't been for me, he wouldn't be in the bag."

"Clete, you stop it!" Dave said.

"Oh, jeez, big deal," I said. "Get out of the way, noble mon."

I went over the gunwale. Right up to my hips, my weight driving my feet into the silt up to my calves. I felt like I was standing in fresh cement. Water was seeping into my pants. I grabbed the end of the bag and pulled it toward the boat's bow. The body was probably waterlogged, and the bag was heavy with mud that had gotten through the rip. Ciro and Dave leaned over the gunwale and pulled on the points of the bag while I pushed. The bag fell on the deck with a wet slap. I went up a ladder that Ciro hooked on the gunwale.

"What y'all wanna do, Miss Helen?" he asked.

The zipper on the bag was broken in a spot above the face and coated with soggy organic matter. Regardless, I didn't want to open it. I don't think anyone did. Helen looked at Dave and then me. "We've been highjacked once," she said. "The guys in the plane will probably be back or the Feds will. If we want to learn anything, we'd better learn it here."

"The guys in the plane and the Feds may be the same," I said.

"Lose the doodah, Clete," she said.

I shrugged. "What do I know? Lee Harvey Oswald killed John Kennedy without any help. Then got killed himself. That happens a lot."

She gave me a sour look.

"What do you think, Dave?" she asked.

"Your choice," he said.

"Oh, man," Ciro said. He was bent over, staring down at the body bag. "Oh man-oh-man-oh-man, I ain't never seen nuttin' like dat."

"What is it?" Helen said.

"A tarantula," Ciro said. "It's crawling out of the guy's mout'."

We all stepped back. I had seen tarantulas on the docks in New Orleans when my father and I unloaded bananas after he was fired from his milk route, and once when Dave and I saw a stream of them run like dismembered fingers across the two-lane highway south of Huntsville Pen in Texas, just before an electrocution.

"Let's get this done," Dave said. He clicked open a switchblade stiletto and sliced the plastic from the corpse's chin down to his knees.

I couldn't call him Ink Man anymore. His skin looked like it had been cured and stretched on a rack; the tattoos had become colorless. I could have counted the bones in his skeleton with my ballpoint. His mouth had gone into rictus. One eye had popped out of his head. A stench like animal hair and offal rose from the bag. The young fireman vomited over the rail.

"Jesus Christ," Helen said.

Dave rubbed his forehead. Ciro and I looked at each other. There are moments that have no name and no content, like a whisper you can't acknowledge. This was one of them.

I dragged a tarp over the bag. "Take us out of here, Ciro," I said.

"You got it, podna," he replied.

All the way back to the dock I kept my face in the wind, my gaze on the beauty of the evening, my head empty. The vibration and roar of the engine like a narcotic or the silly sound of a song like "Sleepy Lagoon." Dave always said there were moments when the world is too much and too soon. I never understood that. Now I did.

CHAPTER SEVENTEEN

In the morning at 0800 I went down to the locker at Iberia Parish Hospital where we had parked Ink Man. Helen was just leaving the emergency entrance. One look at her face and I knew what had happened.

"The Feds got the body?" I said.

"Ten minutes ago," she said. Her hands were on her hips. She wore a starched short-sleeve shirt and blue slacks. She looked up and down the highway, the moss straightening in the oak trees, her mouth tight. "I feel like kicking the shit out of those guys."

I glanced at the emergency entrance. "You might have a chance."

Samuel Hawthorne, the FBI agent, had just come out the door. I could see Helen biting her lip and knew she was about to make a choice. She wasn't afraid of anyone. But Louisiana has a core of political corruption that few other states can equal. Florida and Jersey are our only real contenders. Many rotten politicians would have liked to bury Helen in an anthill. Think that's a metaphor? I knew a guard in Angola who put convicts on anthills if they fell out from heat exhaustion, and for a long time if they didn't get up.

The point is, I knew Helen would make the right decision. She might screw up, and she might lose friendships, but when it came to principle, she would not budge, no matter what it cost her. "I need a word with you," she said to Hawthorne.

"Yes, ma'am, that's why I'm here," he said.

"Call me Sheriff, call me Helen, or call me Sheriff Soileau, but do not call me ma'am. I am not a 'ma'am.' Got it?"

"Copy that, Sheriff," he said.

"Now who told you guys you could wipe your feet on us?"

He was wearing a white shirt and tie with no coat. He pressed his hands together, like a pair of pancakes, and rubbed them in a crisscross fashion, then looked over his shoulder and raised his eyebrows.

"What in the fuck are you doing?" she said.

"I have a rental in the parking lot," he said. "Can we talk there?"

"No, we can talk right where we are," Helen said.

"Okay," he said, looking again over his shoulder. "I'm not the most popular person among some of my colleagues. Yes, they respect me on a professional level, but they think my background is an influence on my professional perspective. Follow me?"

He should have left out the last two words.

"Oh, gee! White man use big words me no understand," Helen said. "Where do you get off talking to people like that?"

"Okay, again," he said. "I'm from Mississippi. Others think I grew up next door to Fred Flintstone. They think I have primitive ideas."

"Like what?" she said.

"That something terrible is taking place in our midst. Something we never thought about before."

"Say, Agent Hawthorne, how about spitting it out?" I said.

All the light went out of his face. His eyes misted, then he looked back at us as though he had gone away somewhere. "I think it's something like the plague. Like the fourteenth century. It was the darkest time in history, and it began with rats on a Florentine boat. I think it's out there."

"What is?" I said.

"I don't know. I'm sorry about my comparison with the fourteenth century," he replied. "I have no evidence about what's occurring here and shouldn't frighten you. I think you're good people. I'll help you any way I can."

He seemed lost, unsure of his bearings. Then he walked into the parking lot and got into his rental and drove out on the Old Spanish Trail, a canopy of moss and oak limbs above his head, his skin checkered with sunlight.

Helen and I looked at each other.

"What happened?" she said.

"I don't know," I said. "I think he's a lonely man. Can I buy you a cup of coffee?"

# # #

Dave and I ate lunch together in his screened-in back porch, along with Buggs and Snuggs and a pet coon who was house-trained, at least most of the time. We were about to finish and wash the dishes so Dave could get back to work. Then I heard the sound of leaves crunching under a great weight moving along the side of the house. I thought I had finally cut the string on my balloon and was about to float into another hemisphere, somewhere that has a yellow brick road.

It wasn't just me, either. Dave stopped eating and so did the coon and the cats. Dave wiped his mouth and stood up from the table. "What in the—"

He didn't even try to finish. An NOPD squad car rolled into the backyard, its flasher rippling silently. Guess who got out?

"I want to talk to both y'all right now," Banner said.

"You just drove into my backyard," Dave said.

"If you don't like it, answer your fucking doorbell," Banner said. He walked to the steps and looked up through the screen door.

I lowered my voice. "Take it easy, Streak."

"You made a deal with the Feds, didn't you?" Banner said.

Neither Dave nor I said anything.

"You got wax in your ears?" Banner said.

"Get off my property," Dave said. "And don't use profanity on it, either."

"Fuck you, Robicheaux. Everybody is tired of your holier-than-thou dog shit. Now get your asses out here."

I stood up next to Dave and spoke out of the side of my mouth. "It's a setup, Dave," I said.

Dave made no reply. That was a warning sign, one that Banner gave no heed.

"Did you hear me, big mon?" I said. "Eighty-six what you're thinking."

"What are you guys whispering about?" Banner said.

"Nothing," I said.

"Hey, Purcel, I hear they call you the Fuckster in the Quarter now. I hate to admit this, but I'm impressed."

He was wearing a sports coat and silver tie. Banner was a bad cop, but he was not to be underestimated. He was a light heavyweight Golden Gloves champion back in high school and had to be cautioned by the referee for hitting after the bell.

"You guys just gonna look at me?" he said.

I stepped in front of Dave. "What's your beef, Earl? What did we ever do to you?" I said.

"Dishonored the entirety of the NOPD," he replied.

"Okay, we got the message. What do you want?" I said.

"What's the gen on the disappearing body bag?"

"If you're talking about the dead guy who tried to kill me, we don't have any gen," I said. "Join the club."

"How about that bitch living in your house in the Quarter?" he said.

"What did you say?"

"Gracie Lamar. She's dirty. I told you. If you didn't have your head up your fat ass, you would have caught on by now."

I felt Dave start to move behind me.

"Hey, Earl, I'm begging you," I said. "Get out of here. We'll work this out. We go back, we got commonalities."

"My commonality with you is I pulled you in on a DUI, with puke all over your suit."

Dave brushed past me and went down the steps. He didn't say a word. He hooked Banner in the face and knocked him into the flower bed. Banner's face was stunned, white with shock. Then Dave got into the squad car and drove it down the slope and through the trees until he reached the bayou, then he opened the door and stepped out of the car and watched it drive itself into the water, steam immediately rising from the engine.

Dave walked back up the slope and went inside without speaking, and sat down at the table and resumed eating while reading the *Daily Iberian*.

# # #

Sound improbable? Wrong. Banner had driven into the backyard. How was he going to explain that to his superiors? He called for a wrecker that hoisted the squad car from the mud and dragged it up the slope, water gushing out the doors. Dave and I drove away in my Caddy.

"Hey, Earl," I said. "Dave's got a six-pack of diet Docs on the back porch. Get you one."

# # #

The rest of the afternoon I visited Miss Sally and saw clients, one of whom came into the office armed, and had to dime a hysterical wife who was terrified of her husband. I hated my job. And I had another problem, too. Banner was butt crust, but he wasn't stupid. Gracie Lamar was getting to him. She got to me. In my case, I was thirty years too old for her, although she didn't seem to mind Dave's age, which hurt me a little bit. Banner was different. He was about power. When it was denied him, he'd break bones.

Hey, to tell you the truth, I couldn't take it anymore. I felt like a dartboard. People were beating me up, tearing apart my Eldorado Caddy, and trying to kill me in Henderson Swamp. What did I get for it? Maybe a free wax job at Eddy's Car Wash? I packed my overnight bag and threw it in the back seat of my Caddy and barreled butt on down to the Big Sleazy without notifying Gracie or Chen or Miss Dorothy.

The sun was just setting as I parked my Caddy in the courtyard and walked up the back stairs. The bricks were a dull red in the shade, the elephant ears and banana fronds dripping with humidity, the sky pink and blue directly overhead. I tapped on the French doors so I wouldn't frighten anyone, then unlocked the door and went inside. "Hello!" I called.

No answer. I walked through each room making sure no one was asleep or using the bathroom. Everything was tidy and neat, the bedspreads stretched tight, the tabletops wiped, the kitchen sparkling.

It was nine o'clock now. I didn't know if Gracie Lamar was still dancing at the club on Bourbon or not. I didn't like the work she did, but who was I to judge? A girl who knew how to play the customers on the stools could make two to three hundred dollars a night. Most of the men on the stools were dimwits. I never knew a dancer who didn't have total contempt for them.

I should talk. Gracie was really put together. And yeah, I know, money is money. But anyone that beautiful shouldn't be curling and swinging around on a chromed pole for a bunch of guys who never got out of puberty or were genuine piranhas.

Anyway, I was standing in the hallway wondering where the women might have gone, when I glanced through the doorway into the bedroom Gracie was using and saw a dull strip of metal and what looked like a chunk of rubber sticking out from under a pillow. I didn't want to violate Gracie's privacy, but I had a hard time believing what I thought I was seeing. So I went in and picked up the pillow, and there it was, an S&W titanium five-round .38 Special that was as light as air and as deadly as a .45 auto. Under the handles was a leather badge holder with a Birmingham police ID card inside, not a badge.

Had Gracie stolen this? Or had I really been taken?

I flipped out the cylinder. Four chambers were loaded; one was not. The hammer rested upon the empty chamber. Whoever owned it was old-school. I flipped the gun and the badge on the bedspread, then headed for the dump where she danced on Bourbon Street.

CHAPTER EIGHTEEN

I t was packed, too, the girls up on the stage and the runway, the geeks at the stools and tables or standing, all the way to the men's room. You have to forgive me. I was in the Crotch, meaning the Corps. I've been in every slop chute from Tijuana to Saigon and Cherry Alley in Tokyo. The girls in those joints had to be there; but couldn't we do a little better than that in New Orleans?

Gracie was on the pole, with the kind of spangled strips of clothing that girls wear in those situations. I couldn't look at her. I wanted to climb up on the runway and put her over my shoulder and kick the teeth out of every lascivious toad on those stools. There are times when I fear myself. My hands tingle, like they're filling with blood, like I have lead inside them. I could break a glass inside my palm and not feel it.

I was about to turn around and walk outside and find a Dixieland joint and get swacked on Jack and crawl home at four in the morning. Then I saw Lauren Bow at the runway, surrounded by other men, all of them with smiles that looked like wounds. Hey, I haven't told you something. Sometimes my wiring starts crackling and sparking and defaults to Shitsville. I'd been having a lot of that lately, particularly when I had visions of the lady who saved me in

Henderson Swamp and who promised she would always be with me. What I'm saying is I had all this noise and the bodies of these geeks wrapping around me like a wool blanket in July, and Lauren Bow with his muttonchop whiskers and car-grille face standing right below Gracie on the pole, grinning at me like a house of mirrors, grinning at Gracie, too, yelling something, his mouth a black hole.

Someone knocked into me and knifed me in the back with an elbow; another guy stepped on my foot; another was breathing his halitosis on the side of my face.

I didn't come here for this, I told myself. Let them drown in their own cesspool. Then I saw Gracie's eyes fix on me, and I saw the alarm and sadness and embarrassment she felt and I wanted to leave before I brought her more pain. No, that's not true. I wanted to wipe out the place, like bowling pins exploding throughout the entire room.

"Have a drink, laddie!" Bow yelled. "The best in the house for you!"

I pretended I didn't hear him and began pushing my way toward the front of the building, where the French doors were, where clouds of cigarette smoke were rolling into the street, because there was no smoking ban back then.

Bow grabbed me by the arm and held on. "Be a good lad!" he yelled, his fingers biting into my muscle, crimping to the bone.

"Get your hand off me," I said.

"Boy, you've got a fuckin' fireplug for a bicep, haven't you? I bet you could rip some serious ass! Come on, let's you and me raise a little hell!"

Then I was suddenly outside, the noise stripped away from my ears, the neon reflections on the sidewalks and the jazz music in the air like a blessing. But Lauren Bow was still with me, breathing hard, his face full of triumph, as though we were a pair of Brits who had just fought our way up the Khyber Pass.

"What are you doing with Gracie?" I said.

"Who?" he said.

"Gracie Lamar. Up on the runway."

"I don't know her. Is that your girlie? She looks like a fine one."

"It's coincidence that you're here?" I said.

"Coincidence about what?" He looked genuinely puzzled.

"Nothing," I said. "A man who was on your property tried to kill me."

"I'm not following you at all, lad." He rested his hand on my shoulder in a fatherly way. "I think maybe you got on the grog a little early today. How about we go to the Napoleon House and sit outside and have some shrimp and grits."

"This guy was a walking tattoo," I said.

"We've had a bunch of those around," he replied. "Soldiers of fortune, oil drillers in the Sahara, a few fuckers from the Golden Triangle. You know who those laddies are, don't you?"

"CIA guys?"

"Sometimes, sometimes not."

"You're with the CIA?"

He shook his head. "Of course not. You remember their hallmark? If the bomb killed everyone except the target of the bomb, everyone knew it was a CIA job."

"I don't think that's funny," I said.

"I didn't mean to be. Tell you what, come to the house. Talk to any of the personnel you wish. Bring the girl up there on the stage with you."

A bunch of college boys walked around us, stepping into the gutter, laughing, spilling beer out of their paper cups, with no awareness of the world Bow and I were talking about. I hoped they would retain their innocence until they died.

"Can I ask you a personal question?" I said.

"Have at it."

"All those people who went bankrupt investing in your soap business? Do you think about them?"

"I've compensated many of them. Right now I'm in bankruptcy. At some point I hope to give back, with interest, every dollar I can to the remaining claimants."

Bourbon Street was a crowded pedestrian street because trucks and cars were banned during the night hours. Bow kept talking, but I was no longer listening. There were people of every kind on the street—Midwestern tourists peeping through the doors of the skin joints, foreign sailors, frat boys, Black kids dancing with clamp-on taps, Black kids shining shoes, Black kids saying, "Bet you five dol'ars where you got your shoes." When you take the bet, they say, "You got your shoes on your feet, and your feet are on Bourbon Street."

They were all on Bourbon Street that night, but I no longer saw them, just as I no longer heard Lauren Bow. At the end of the block a solitary figure had made eye contact with me, as though a magnet and a piece of metal had suddenly met. It was Baylor Hemmings, one of the three men who tore up my Caddy, the man who wore a T-shirt calling for a greater extermination of Jews, a man who had locks of hair coated with grease, a man who wore lace-up, steel-toed hobnail boots, a man who knew how to inflict pain when the arithmetic was three to one.

I started walking fast, my porkpie hat tilted on my forehead. But I was pretty sure he had already made me. I looked from under the brim of my hat just as he started running. I took off after him.

I chased him for five blocks. Fortunately, both vehicular and pedestrian traffic proved a greater problem for him than for me. On the edge of the Quarter, up by Canal, he ran into an alley behind an empty building that was being remodeled. I came huffing up the alley just as he slipped through an emergency door and went inside. I went in after him.

Even though I had a permit to carry a concealed firearm, I'd left my .38 snub at the apartment, because I never carried a gun into a bar lest I should have to use it. I was now standing in an unlighted hallway strewn with paint cans and tarps and calking material. The glow of the streetlamps outside leaked dimly through the windows. I could hear myself breathing, my heart thudding. The stairs were made of steel. I put my hand on the rail, then pressed it flat on the steps. I could feel the vibration from above.

I climbed the steps as quietly as I could. On the second landing I touched the floor and the wall and the railing again. The St. Charles streetcar was making its turnaround for its trip uptown to Tulane and Loyola and the Garden District, so the whole building was quivering. I waited until the streetcar was gone, then went to the third landing but heard nothing at all. I wondered if Baylor Hemmings had found another staircase and doubled back on me. Then I heard a bucket fall from the fourth floor, *bang, bang, bang,* one step at a time.

I looked around for a tool, a bottle, or even a broom. My only weapon was a penknife. What an occasion to be an idealist.

The building was not ventilated, and the heat and dust were stifling. I had sweated through my shirt, and my armpits smelled like soiled kitty litter and my saliva tasted like pennies—you know that taste, it's like blood.

I took a deep breath, then called out, "What's the haps, Baylor?"

No answer. And I had expected none. I've got to admit something here. I was tired of messing with these guys. They were recidivists, and had no redeeming virtues and no decency, the kind of people Dave believes come from a different tree. These are the kind who take their secrets to the grave, even the location where they buried their victims, when they could give the families a degree of peace.

"Hey, podjo," I said. "I think you're political rather than criminal. That means you know better than to come into the Quarter packing. So walk toward my voice and put your hands on your head, and we'll work things out."

"Oh, it's Louisiana Fats," he answered. "I thought you might have sent a cop in here."

"I'm coming up, podjo. If your hands aren't on your head, I'm gonna rip off your arms and beat you to death with them."

"Sure," he said. "I'm at your service."

I left the stairs and walked down a hallway where he was silhouetted against a window. "That's far enough," he said.

"I'd like to show you a picture," I said.

"Kiddy porn?"

"It was taken at Auschwitz. It's of a mother and her three children."

"It's boo-hoo time?"

"I need you to turn around and lean against the wall."

He made a sound that was like a half laugh. I had already said too much. Wyatt Earp or Wild Bill Hickok said, "Don't blink. Don't speak. And don't miss."

But I had nothing to miss with. Maybe I was fifteen feet from him. What do you do in that kind of situation? You brass it out. I started walking toward him. I could see the gray, paperlike deadness in his skin, the pits in his cheeks, the lack of humanity, even the lack of anger in his eyes, as though he were incapable of emotion.

Then he brought a taser from his back pocket and set my chest on fire. No, it was far worse than that. My chest was not only electrified; it felt as though someone had driven a cargo hook into the muscle and was pulling it from the bone, twisting it, wrapping the pain around my armpits while urine seeped down my thighs.

Then I made a grinding sound and drove him into the wall, knocking the taser from his hand, jabbing my elbow in his eye, then grabbing his shirt and smashing him over and over against an ancient radiator, then swinging him in a circle, faster and faster, like winding up a bag of trash to throw on the garbage truck.

Then I let go. I thought there was a fire escape outside the window. He crashed through it, glass and frame. There was no fire escape. I stuck my head out the window and looked four stories down into an alley. A dumpster was pushed snugly against the wall, the lid open, and Baylor Hemmings was looking up at me like a crucified man upon a soft pad of garbage. He climbed over the side and ran into the dark, howling at the sky, glass sparkling in his hair. I had the feeling I would see him again.

CHAPTER NINETEEN

I walked back to the apartment and unintentionally woke up Chen. "What happen, Mr. Clete? You look like you fall down in sewer."

"Thank you, Chen," I said. "I'll take a shower now."

"You look beat up, Mr. Clete. What somebody did to you?"

"You should see the other guy. I threw him out of a fourth-story window."

"Oh, that good. I hope a car run over him. Maybe we can go make sure."

"Have you been feeling okay, Chen?"

"You worry about I use the hypodermic again?" she asked.

"No, I'm sure you won't do that."

"That because I go to a meeting every day with the Work the Steps or Die Motherfucker group. The Motherfuckers are very nice."

"Out in public, you might cool it on the use of that word, Chen."

"What 'cool it' mean?"

"I'm gonna take a shower now," I said. "I'll see you in the morning."

"Goodnight, Mr. Clete," she said. "The cats like to see you back. I like to see you back. You such good man. You leave lid off the toilet so the cats can drink."

Her laugh sounded like "tee-hee-hee," then she ran into her bedroom and shut the door. She reminded me so much of the girl I loved in Shitsville, the one who died. Tell me women are not the most beautiful creatures in the world. Tell me they are not the most loving, also.

I took a shower and put on a robe and waited for Gracie Lamar, like a father waiting for his overdue teenage daughter. She came in at 4:13 a.m. Before I could speak, she said, "Why did you come to the club, Clete?"

"To ask you why you've got a .38 and a Birmingham police ID under your pillow."

"I'm tired," she replied. "Can we talk later?"

"No, we'll talk now. Lauren Bow was standing five feet below your pole. Or do you not know who that is?"

"Oh, I know who he is, all right. Now lose the attitude. I've got to go to the bathroom." Then she stopped and looked at the open top of my robe. "What happened to your chest?"

"Go to the bathroom," I said. "I'll tell you when you get back."

"No, give it to me now," she replied.

So I did.

# # #

After she came back from the bathroom, she fixed herself a ham sand-wich and ate it standing at the counter, her eyes crossed with fatigue.

"Here's my history with the Birmingham Police Department," she said. "I was there two years, then quit when my partner was set up and murdered. I swore I would get the people who did it. End of story."

"What about Lauren Bow?"

"I think he was part of it. I think he recruits for the Klan. He's partial to people with military backgrounds."

"Bow is gonna refight the Civil War?"

"No, worse. He wants to control the Earth."

"The king of soap is gonna do that?"

She didn't answer.

"Did you hear me?" I said.

"I think he wants to turn the Earth into a cinder heap." She put a piece of sandwich in her mouth and chewed, wiping off the mayonnaise and tomato juice with the back of her wrist.

I don't like to say this, but strange things were happening to me. I felt like I was seeing someone else, maybe from another century.

"Why are you looking at me like that?" she said.

"I think that taser damaged my batteries."

"Get some sleep," she said. "I'll clean up in here."

"I gotta say something," I said. "I saw a woman outside my cottage in New Iberia. She looked like you."

"You're accusing me of being a voyeur?"

"No, she was from the Middle Ages."

I thought she might mock me, but she didn't. "You've been under a lot of stress."

"I know what I saw."

"Come here."

"What?"

"Come here."

I stepped closer to her. She put her hand on the top of my chest. I could feel her pulling the heat out of my skin. "You're a good guy, but you're gonna get yourself killed. Stay right here."

She went into the bathroom and came back with a jar of Vaseline and rubbed it on my chest. "Do you trust me?"

"Sure."

"Lauren Bow makes examples. Protect Dave Robicheaux. I think he's on a list."

"How do you know this?"

"My partner at Birmingham PD was also my boyfriend. Snipers took him down. They weren't gangbangers with boom boxes for brains."

"Why won't Bow come after me?"

"Because he knows you won't break. You'll die instead."

"Streak will spit in their faces. I've seen him do it."

"You want him to prove it?" she said. "You still don't have any idea what you're dealing with."

I felt a sensation like water draining through my viscera.

# # #

I took Gracie and Chen and Dorothy to an early lunch that same morning, and pretended that everything was right with the world. But it wasn't, at least not for me. My wiring was shutting down on me in ways that I recognized from the past. It's called agitated or clinical depression, or the Dark Night of the Soul. It's a son of a bitch. I don't like to talk about it, because I'll end up heaping a pile of hot ashes on my brain before I can address the problem. That's how it works. If you try to think your way out of it, you go deeper into it. If you don't try to think your way out of it, you start running from your own thoughts. By sunset you'll be in an iron box, one with spikes.

After the ladies went back to the apartment, I rode the streetcar up St. Charles to the public library and began reading about Joan of Arc. There were many paintings of her in the illustrations, but none that were authentic, at least that I could find. Oddly, there was a supposed photograph of her with the date 1913 on the bottom, which made no sense. The young woman, or girl, was wearing armor, without a helmet, her sheathed foot pointed forward, her face defiant, her dark hair cropped. Everything about her resembled Gracie Lamar, except her hair.

I closed the book and walked out of the library into a grand day, the live oaks full of robins, the red and yellow four-o'clocks blooming in the shade, the 1910 streetcar clanging and rattling down the neutral ground, a Black man selling snowballs from his cart. For just a second I believed I was ten years old and in short pants, my father holding my hand, the two of us walking toward the cart.

Then the cart and my father and the green neutral ground and even the St. Charles were gone, replaced by sunlight that broke through the canopy like an acetylene flame.

# # #

I couldn't remember the days of the week. I went back to New Iberia on a Monday and wrote the word "Monday" on a pad and placed the pad on the dashboard of my Eldorado Caddy and met Dave behind his house, where he was barbecuing some chicken with some sauce piquante, his eyes squinting in the smoke. His house was shaped like a boxcar and had a peaked tin roof stained with orange-and-purple rust and lichen and damp moss that stayed on it year-round. I sat on the steps and drank a diet Doc and watched him fork the chicken on the grill. It's funny how a simple situation like that can mean so much—you know, with the animals abroad and having fun, flipping their tails, the bayou swelling with the tide in the late sun, the bream dimpling the shallows between the

Japanese hyacinths, a blue heron standing in the water, pecking its feathers.

That's Louisiana. And it's free, I told myself.

"Something wrong?" Dave said.

I had already told him about throwing Hemmings out a window and about Gracie Lamar having been an Alabama cop. But that was all.

"I'm seeing things," I said.

"What kind of things?" he replied, looking into the smoke.

"The woman who saved my life in Henderson Swamp."

"You saw her again?"

"Yeah, outside my cottage. I did some digging in the library up St. Charles. There was a photo just like her. The photo looks like Gracie, too, except for her hair. This stuff is kind of driving me crazy."

He closed the lid on the grill and wiped the smoke from his eyes, then opened a diet Doc and sat down beside me. "Don't argue with the world, Clete. Or the universe or all the great mysteries. The thing to understand is that the mysteries exist. The denial of them is an absurdity."

"How did Joan of Arc get into my life?"

"I used to talk to John Bell Hood."

"Yeah, because somebody dropped LSD in your drink."

"He told me where to find a revolver left behind in a firefight in 1863."

"Yeah, and that's why people think you're a little strange, noble mon."

He put his arm over my shoulder. "There's something else bothering you, Clete. Neither of us ever had problems with the dead. What's really got you down?"

"Gracie thinks you're on a list. You're gonna be tortured."

"And not you?" he said.

"Yeah, they want me alive."

"She's a smart lady," he said. "But that doesn't mean she's right."

"If only we knew what these guys were after," I said. "Gracie thinks they might want to start a plague."

I picked up Snuggs, Dave's big white warrior cat, and put him on my head, his feet slipping all over my face. Dave was smiling.

"Did you hear any more from Earl Banner?" I said.

"About his squad car sinking in the bayou? No."

"I think he's onto something," I said. "Something that has to do with Ink Man. Something that can make Banner a hero."

Dave was silent a long time. "I wish I hadn't put his car in the bayou."

"Why?"

"He's a cockroach," he replied. "That's all he is. You don't get in the ring with cockroaches. Come on, let's eat, then walk over to the park and watch the softball game."

# # #

I had trouble sleeping that night. Not because of apparitions, either. The world of law enforcement has many shadows in it, all of them bad. Don't let anybody tell you different. Here's the deal, though. There are things that no human beings should ever see or hear or know about. If they do, they are never the same. You cannot undo knowledge. Crime newspaper reporters know this, so do caseworkers, and so do flatfoots, in plainclothes or uniform. That's why a lot of them drink, and drink only among themselves.

The day that one of them does not shudder at certain kinds of crimes, and the day that one laughs at the sexual degrading of a woman, or of any defenseless person, is the day he has become pathological, unless he had been a sociopath all his life.

I called NOPD and asked that someone patch me in to Banner or make sure he got my message. I didn't know the woman I was talking to. "What's the message?" she asked.

"To call me. You got my name, right? Clete Purcel?"

"Yeah, I think so," she said, dragging out her words.

"You're saying you know me?"

"No, I don't think personally. I will pass on your message, sir." Then she hung up.

At least she didn't call me Bozo or fathead. What a culture to belong to.

It wasn't funny, though. Banner didn't dime us about flooding his car because he had to protect himself, but at the same time he took a lot of heat. Plus he was a New Orleans street rat, like me, like many of my generation who grew up there. I figured the guy couldn't have turned out any other way than he did. Don't believe that "Irish eyes are smiling" crap.

I spent the rest of the day visiting Miss Sally, clanging iron at Red's Gym in Lafayette, running the jogging trail in City Park, then eating two dozen raw oysters at Bojangles. But I couldn't sweat out the gloom I carried with me. It was like trying to outrun my own shadow.

The next day Dave called me at my office at 1:03 p.m. "Hey," he said.

"Yeah, hey, big mon, what's the haps?" I said.

"No good haps on this one, partner. Helen wants you to go with us down to Thibodaux."

"What for?"

He blew out his breath. "You don't want to know."

CHAPTER TWENTY

It was a languid late-summer afternoon in Lafourche Parish, the kind when the heat will not die and the sky is like brass and the humidity hangs on your skin like a damp blanket, all of this southwest of New Orleans, deep in Cajun country. It was an antediluvian place that could have been formed on the first day of Creation and then forgotten, feral and threatening in calm fashion, the marshlands and swamps bleeding into the Gulf of Mexico, with no end in sight. Its beauty testifies to itself, like a vain and dangerous mistress. The miles of flooded cane and reeds and cattails and moss-hung live oaks, the pelicans flying in formation overhead, the rumbling in the clouds and the waterspouts on the horizon make you tremble. The sun does not go down; it dies, and its fire takes its red smoke with it.

Or that was the way I saw Bayou Lafourche and all its surroundings on that particular day. The parish seat is Thibodaux. We met the sheriff there and got on his airboat. The sheriff wore khakis and shades and a coned straw hat and had a profile like an Indian and hardly spoke. A helicopter from NOPD had already gone ahead of us. Helen had driven the car for the three of us and had been somber all the way. Helen was a pro. But you learn early as a first responder of any kind that an image is forever. You can tear up a photograph or break a camera, but the photo in your head is another matter. None of us wanted to see what we had come to see.

We ended up in a hummock that had a duck blind on it and a shack that at one time was probably a boathouse. The shack was gray and rotted, the door hanging halfway open, the inside dark. The hummock was surrounded by sandbars that looked like the backs of gnarled fingers jutting out of the water, the waves sliding across them. The hummock and its shack resembled a wound, one would not heal.

The sheriff cut the propeller on the airboat and let the bow scrape up on the hummock. The NOPD helicopter had made two circles but obviously didn't have adequate landing space without the propeller hitting the shack. The helicopter turned east and droned away. The sheriff took off his shades, leaving two dents in the bridge of his nose.

"Me and a deputy were chasing a drug runner through here when we hit a half-sunk oil barrel and had to pull in," he said. "Otherwise, the tide might have brought the gators in."

But we had no response and were obviously not interested in drug runners.

"Y'all ready?" he said.

"No," Helen said. "I want to get this straight. My name is on a note with Clete Purcel's?"

"Yeah, that's why I called y'all when I called New Orleans. We're gonna need the Feds on this, too. We ain't got the technology, and neither does the coroner. Some kind of sadistic experts had their way."

"Where's the note?" she said.

"On his chest."

We all walked in together. The light was weak, but I could see a heavy chair in the middle of the structure, maybe one made of oak. Earl Banner was sitting in it, looking straight ahead, his forehead buckled to the headpiece of the chair, his forearms and body strapped to it also. There was no odor. Nor any emotion in his eyes. Nor blood that we could see. His mouth hung open, as though he were thirsty.

"Okay, I'm gonna turn on my flashlight now," the sheriff said. "Ask any questions or leave when you want."

He held his flashlight over his head and clicked it on. I heard Helen clear her throat. Dave shifted his feet and dropped his eyes. I took off my hat for no reason and put it back on.

"Hold the light steady," Helen said, and read the penciled note pinned to Banner's shirt.

"What's it say?" I asked.

"It says, 'Sheriff Soileau and Mr. Purcel, give back what is not yours.'"

"Does that make any sense to y'all?" the Lafourche sheriff said.

"Yeah, he's gonna kill more people," I said.

"Why did he come into Lafourche to do this?" the sheriff asked.

"He wants to turn everybody against everybody else," I said. "His name is Baylor Hemmings."

"You know this bastard?" the sheriff asked.

"I threw him out of a fourth-story window," I said.

He looked at me blankly. The sheriff in Lafourche was a good guy, and I wished I hadn't added more to his load. But he wasn't looking at me now. "Hold on there, Sheriff Soileau," he said. "You don't need to go back there. The FBI needs to take a look at that first."

"Those are tools back there," she said.

"Yes, they are, and we don't wanna be messing with them."

"Pliers and screwdrivers."

"Damn it, this is my bailiwick, Miss Helen," the Lafourche sheriff said. "Come outside with me."

"Shut up," she said. "I'll come when I feel like it."

But she didn't mean it. And the Lafourche sheriff knew it, too. She walked past him and past Dave and me and through the door and into the orange glow upon the water, then rubbed the back of her neck and tilted up her chin. I saw her eyes close briefly and her lips move, as though she were praying. Then she said, "We've seen enough of this. Pack it up."

"We don't have anything to pack up," Dave said.

"It's a figure of speech," she said, her hands on her hips, her breasts as hard as softballs, blowing out her breath. "Fuck and fuck. There's some people here'bouts not like the rest of us."

# # #

I didn't say much to anyone for the next couple of days, primarily because for good or bad I don't think like other people and sometimes I scare them if I don't have a filter on. In the struggle between good and evil, individuals like Baylor Hemmings have the importance of cannon wadding. They're used and discarded. Like Dave says, they're adjectives, not nouns. Or maybe they're used in a clandestine chain of torture chambers the government will not acknowledge. These kinds of statements get people mad. So I try not to make them. The point is, slumlords don't stack time, even if one of their tenements burns down with the welfare occupants in it. Check out the stories of the *Titanic* or the Triangle Shirtwaist Factory. Who got blamed? It sure wasn't the guys who did it.

I'm sorry for proselytizing.

Hey, I got to own up on something. That note pinned to Earl Banner's shirt was written to confuse and mislead. Helen had nothing to do with the issue, but now the Feds and NOPD would think the opposite. Putting her name on the note would also make her resent me and by extension resent Dave. The three men who tore up my Caddy wanted their goods, but I did not know what their goods were. Neither did I know if Lauren Bow was a player or not. Or his former wife. Actually I didn't know anything. If I were in need of a private investigator, I would not hire myself.

As I was locking up the door on Thursday at 5:00 p.m., guess who pulled up to the curb in a plum-colored Corvette with a white rolled-leather interior. She was wearing dark shades, and her hair had just been clipped, and the sweetness in her face was enough to break your heart. She could have been the real Clara Bow's twin. "Jump in," she said.

"What for?" I said.

"You never can tell." She tapped the accelerator, still grinning.

"Did you hear about an NOPD cop named Earl Banner?"

"Sorry, I don't know who that is."

"What do you want, Miss Clara?"

She pulled off her shades. I have to say she was alluring. Her face seemed timeless in its innocence, like a girl you remember from down the block, or like a close-up on a silent screen during the 1920s, the cheeks pale, the eyes vulnerable and lustrous, the mouth aching to touch yours. "Do I offend you in some way?" she said. "Have I hurt you, Mr. Purcel? Please tell me what I've done wrong."

I looked up and down the street. It was 5:07 now. The sidewalk was warm, even in the shade. There were few cars in the street, which seemed strange. I felt detached in time. I've had those spells many times over the years. It feels as if the era in which I was born is about to end, and horns are blowing on an ancient hill, one nobody else can see. My mouth becomes dry, then I swallow and move on and say nothing to others about it, not even to Dave.

I wondered if the lady who saved my life at Henderson Swamp was on the street. But I did not see her.

"Miss Clara?" I said.

"Yes?"

"Why don't you park your car and let me treat you to dinner at Bon Creole?"

"I'd love that, Mr. Purcel," she said.

# # #

Bon Creole was down on the bayou, on St. Peter Street, and specialized in deep-fried fish and shrimp and oysters that are better than any in New Orleans, although I haven't eaten in all the cafés in New Orleans, I don't think. Look, forget about food. I knew I was getting in dangerous water. A PI shouldn't get involved with his client, particularly if the client is a woman and particularly if she's beautiful. And particularly if the PI is me. Look at my record. My wife was so desperate she dumped me for a Tibetan cult in Colorado run by a guy who made his followers take off their clothes. Doesn't everybody?

Anyway, I shouldn't have been with Miss Clara, and I was hoping the lady who saved my life, the one who I thought might be Joan of Arc, would tell me to get my head on straight and stop acting like an overweight idiot.

But she didn't, and now I was convincing myself that I had permission.

Oh, jeez, how do I get in all this trouble? At least I did one thing right. With our food I ordered a pitcher of iced tea.

"Mr. Purcel, I have to be honest," she said. "You don't look well. Did something happen to a friend of yours?"

"He wasn't a friend, Miss Clara. He was a bad cop, but he didn't deserve what happened to him."

Her eyes went away from me, then came back. I tried to see inside them but saw nothing there.

"You keep looking around," she said. "Are you expecting someone?"

"I had a little trouble in New Orleans," I said. "I ran into your ex-husband in a pole-dancer club, then got tased a few blocks away. The guy with the taser is named Baylor Hemmings. Know him?"

"No, I do not. And I don't like the way you're talking to me."

"Sorry," I replied. "What did you come to see me about?"

"I don't know if I should tell you."

"Suit yourself. If you want an update on your ex-husband's activities, I don't have a lot to offer," I said. "I've learned that he's a liar and hangs out with scum, and he tried to compromise me and probably employs a lizard named Baylor Hemmings. By the way, Hemmings took a four-story free fall off a building on Canal Street courtesy of me."

"I think what you're saying is gibberish, Mr. Purcel, and I'm about to leave this table unless you stop acting like a fabulist."

"People usually call me an idiot."

"*What?*"

"Nothing."

She looked out the window, somehow shorter than she'd been a few minutes before. She seemed like a little girl. A live oak tree grew beside the building, and the sun was red inside its branches, and a swing hung from one of its limbs. She looked like she wanted to climb on the swing. That's the kind of interpretations I have when I really get clinically messed up. It's a mindfuck. That's the only way I can describe it.

"Miss Clara, I apologize," I said. "I've had a few bad days, so please forgive me. That said, I'm gonna tear up our agreement and not charge you anything. You're a mighty nice lady, and it's been good knowing you."

The waitress came with our food. Miss Clara said nothing until the waitress was gone.

"Mr. Purcel, if you try to leave this table, I will pour this pitcher of iced tea over your head. Do you understand me?"

"Yeah, I think I got it," I said.

"I'm starting up a production company. The director and some investors are coming in next week. I want you to take a screen test. I guarantee you the director who tests you will hire you on the spot. You're made for this role."

"What kind of film?" I said.

"It's called *Flags on the Bayou*. It's about the Civil War in Louisiana."

"Are you in it?"

"You'd better believe it," she said.

She reached across the table and squeezed my hand. It felt warm and cool at the same time, and also hard and soft, and everything else I wanted a woman's hand to be. Then she let her eyes linger on mine, and I was absolutely sure she had just surprised and frightened herself, and the little girl was much more a presence than the adult.

# # #

After we left Bon Creole I visited Miss Sally, then drove in my Caddy to Red's Gym in Lafayette and went to work clanking iron, curling a forty-five-pound dumbbell in each hand, pounding the heavy bag, jogging the track, doing fifty push-ups with my feet elevated, the way we did it at Parris Island, then sweating off three pounds in the steam room. I also went into Walmart and stocked up on health food. Wow, I felt ten years younger driving back to New Iberia.

Does that sound like bipolar disorder? That's one name for it. I can think of a half dozen more. One way or another, they mean the same thing: duck when the "polar" shifts in the opposite direction.

CHAPTER TWENTY-ONE

O n Saturday morning Dave and I went fishing in his boat at Henderson Swamp outside Breaux Bridge. It was the season for sacalait, and it had rained before sunrise and the bays and channels were high, the waves from our boat slapping the tree trunks.

I told Dave about my prospects as an actor. We had anchored near an island and were casting into the lee of the trees. Dave put a fresh shiner on his hook and dripped his hand clean in the water and flipped his line next to some lily pads, all of them blooming with yellow flowers. "That sounds good, Clete," he said.

"Think so?" I replied.

"See if you can get me a role."

But I knew he wasn't serious. Nor was he happy about my relationship with my client Clara Bow.

"You think I'm crossing the wrong Rubicon, don't you?"

"Ms. Bow was with her husband a long time, Cletus."

"Yeah, I know," I said. "But people change. Plus, I'm just going through a screen test. Look, her ex is a monster. He burned her breast. Cut her some slack."

"Then why didn't she leave him?"

"Maybe she didn't like working in truck stops."

"We're talking about the m-word, Clete. The m-word is 'money.'"

"Okay, you're right. So what should I do now?"

Dave reeled his line back in and set the rod on the stern. The shiner, or minnow, was dangling in the air, just above the water. It made me feel sick, actually in pain, as though I were torturing it. This is part of depression. You can't think your way out of it, either.

"Answer me, Dave," I said.

"Go ahead with the movie project, Clete," he said. "You know more about movies than movie people do. It's a Civil War story?"

"Yeah," I said.

"Fire a cannon ball through Lauren Bow's house. Somebody should have pulled that guy's plug a long time ago."

Dave probably shouldn't have said that.

# # #

Sunday morning, Clara Bow was at my cottage door with a box of jelly doughnuts in her hand. She wore a white dress, and her hair was curled around her cheeks like a doll's.

"What's goin' on?" I said, standing in my bathrobe.

"I need to confess some things to you," she replied.

"Can it wait until tomorrow at my office."

"Please, Mr. Purcel. This really bothers me."

I stepped back and opened the door wider. "Come in," I said. "I'll get dressed in back."

Five minutes later I returned from the bedroom and picked up the coffeepot and two cups. She was sitting at the breakfast table, her eyes on the bayou, with the intensity of someone whose guilt is so bad they can neither live with it nor own up to it.

"Miss Clara, you don't have to be ashamed or feel afraid," I said. "I think you're a nice lady. Whatever difficulties you've had are on their way out. That's the way to think about it."

"I need to tell you about Lauren's finances," she said. "He's known for several years that the IRS was going to strip him of the fortune he made in his Ponzi scheme. So he decided to switch as much money as he could to the cartels. Are you hearing me?"

"You're talking about Colombia?"

"I'm talking about black tar heroin in Colombia, Asia, Mexico, and anywhere else he could get his hands on it. He's got money hidden all over the world. There's no way to know how many people have died from his drugs."

"Well, you're done with him now," I said.

She put her face in her hands and sobbed. What do you do in that kind of situation?

"Miss Clara, think about the motion picture you're going to make," I said. "Your ex is a bum, a piece of shit waiting to be sent to the septic tank. Don't let this guy rent any more space in your head."

She stopped crying and blew her nose on a paper napkin, then didn't know what to do with the napkin. I took it from her and dropped it in the wastebasket under the sink, then didn't know what to do with my hands.

"How about we take a drive?" I said.

"To where?"

"You said your film is a Civil War story?"

"Yes."

"I'll show you where twenty-two thousand bluecoats came down Loreauville Road trying to catch Colonel Mouton. Did you know the Episcopalian church on West Main was a Confederate field hospital? That's right. When the Yankees captured it, they pushed the pews together and turned them into feed troughs for their horses."

She was sniffling but had stopped crying. "How do you know all this?" she asked.

"I read books," I said.

# # #

But Miss Clara had wound up the alarm clock, along with Dave's help. At this point in the story I need to be a little discreet, know what I mean? I'll simply put a few events in the third person so we can move along without getting involved with a lot of minutiae that nobody cares about.

It was Monday evening, the day after Miss Clara had told me of her ex-husband's commitment to the deaths of street addicts all over the world, the ruined lives of children, the poverty and disease spread among entire cultures in the Third World, and here as well.

So just pretend now that a guy like me was sitting in City Park, reading a book, when he started thinking about all these things and put away his book and took a ride down Bayou Teche to Jeanerette, where he saw the classic thick-pillared antebellum home of Lauren Bow silhouetted against a sunset of clouds that were like fire and curds of black smoke consuming the entirely of the sky. In fact, the scene took the breath out of him.

The brass carriage lamps were lighted, the window glass as black as oil, with no movement inside. Then the guy looked at the cane fields where an unknown number of slaves were buried, dumped in holes, their skulls and teeth scattered by mechanized plows, their names and their suffering unrecorded.

Then the guy saw a grader and a concrete mixer where a tennis court was being constructed down by the bayou. There was no traffic on the two-lane; the sky was darkening, the flames in the clouds burning themselves out, a solitary pelican skimming the bayou, the cicadas droning.

Then the guy parked his vehicle behind a shed and strolled over to the concrete mixer and made a 360-degree turnaround, yawning, stretching, just a guy enjoying the evening or investigating the countryside. Probably a tourist.

As a teenager the guy probably had a history of hot-wiring vehicles of all kinds. But as it turned out, the keys to the concrete mixer were hanging out of the ignition. So the guy slipped on a pair of work gloves and climbed in and slammed the door and fired that baby up.

He reversed the mixer and backed it across the yard with the barrel spinning, crashing over birdbaths, flower beds, and a sundial. Then the guy made a complete circle, crushing the lawn furniture on the patio and destroying the greenhouse, then shifted gears again and backed through the French doors into the living room, where he parked the truck and left the engine running and the water system blasting and the concrete discharging and piling up like soft ice cream.

Then the guy got in his own vehicle and drove away, the alarm systems in the antebellum home shrieking at a trailer slum down the bayou, on the other side of the drawbridge. The trailer people popped beers and watched the firetrucks come from Jeanerette and New Iberia, and had no comment on who might have destroyed much of the plantation home, one they had never seen the inside of.

# # #

On Tuesday morning Dave walked into my office. "Got a minute out back?" he said.

"Sure," I said.

We went out on my back porch and sat down at my spool table under my beach umbrella. I could feel his eyes on the side of my face.

"What's up, big mon?" I said.

"I heard Lauren Bow's home was visited by an interior decorator last night."

"No kidding?"

"There's a concrete truck inside his house. The ceiling caved in on the truck."

"That's heartbreaking."

"Did the woman put you up to this?"

"Which woman?"

"She looks like she fell off a movie screen in 1925."

"Miss Clara?"

"Clete, what are you doing?"

"I don't know. When I find out, I'll tell you."

He drummed his fingers on the wood spool and stared at the glare on the surface of the bayou. Then he looked at my profile. Then he shook his head. "Not a word to anyone on this, got it? Particularly to a certain attractive, short, innocent-looking woman who will have you sticking your gun in your mouth."

"She has nothing to do with this."

"Oh, yes, she does. And eventually she'll put you in Crazy Ville."

"Maybe that's a cool place to be."

"Clete—"

"Okay, roger that. No problem."

Then he shook his head again and laughed. "Clete?" he said.

I waited for him to continue.

"Clete?"

"What?"

"Nothing," he said, and walked out the door.

Sometimes Dave can really act weird. As I told you earlier, I have to keep him under control. Did you know he went undercover with the New Orleans Mob? They dug him, particularly this Italian don who had been in Shitsville and was known as the Johnny Wadd of the Mafia. Even worse, Dave looked out for the guy and helped him get to Mexico with his crippled little boy and told the Feds, who he was working for, to bugger off.

CHAPTER TWENTY-TWO

Early Wednesday morning I got a phone call two minutes after I unlocked my office door, the kind of ring that for whatever reason seems to bode trouble, maybe because I was alone in the office, or maybe because the destruction of Lauren Bow's home was going to be a serious factor in my life.

The ID was blocked, the accent unrecognizable, as though the oily rasp in the voice was definition enough. "Remember me?" the voice said.

"No, who are you?" I replied.

"I watched some guys tear up your shit-mobile on your patio."

"Oh, yeah," I said. "You're the third guy, the one in cargo pants. You wear them below your navel."

"We need to work a deal."

"Really?"

"Yeah, let me line it out for you," he said. "I got no beef with you, you got no beef with me. I didn't touch your shit-mobile, and I didn't hit you, either. But you slugged me in the solar plexus. However, you had cause. Want to talk business or not?"

"Keep talking," I said. "I'm open."

"That's what I thought," he said. "You're a smart man. Except you're not aware of what you're sitting on."

"Yeah, I'd really like to learn about that. Did Earl Banner give you guys any help?"

"Hey, man, if you're talking about that vice cop and what happened in Lafourche Parish, I didn't have nothing to do with it. Look, there was some stash in your car, and now it's gone. You have no idea what the value of that stash is."

"You're talking about black tar?"

"We're talking about hundreds of thousands of people, man. You can get rich or you can get dead. And not just dead. With spiders crawling all over your face. Is that clear enough?"

"No," I said.

"Hey, man, you got a brain. The system screwed you. Why not get even? Why not buy your own paradise?"

"I'm glad to know that's within my grasp," I said. "Explain how I can make that happen."

"You're not trying to run a trace on me, are you?" he said.

"Not me. What's your name?"

"My name is Sandy Glover. I'm a pool hustler, not a bum, not a pimp, not a doper, and not an unteachable clod. Once you get your head out of your hole, have a good day."

He hung up. I'd blown it. I got up and started to walk down the street to have some coffee. Then the phone rang again. The ID was blocked. "Hello?" I said.

"I got a little heated up. You shoot pool?"

"Sometimes," I said.

"I gave you my name because I got no sheet. Also, I didn't commit a crime against your car or you. Also, I'm not hooked up with Hemmings. He's a nutcase. Do the smart thing, Purcel. You won't regret it."

He gave me the name of a dump in East Lafayette. "Be there tonight at nine o'clock," he said.

The line went dead again.

# # #

Crime is bad in Louisiana. There are all kinds of explanations for it, but for rapidity it's hard to equal narcotics. I don't know the cure for it, either, and neither does anyone else. The influence on the legal system is tremendous. Louisiana has the highest rate of incarceration in the country. There are over six thousand convicts in Angola, and over four thousand who are doing life without parole. What does this mean in our story? I'll tell you. Don't call 911 when your neighbor throws his garbage over his fence into your yard. The cops are a little busy.

The man who said his name was Sandy Glover was obviously more intelligent than Ink Man or Baylor Hemmings, whom I tossed out the window into a dumpster. So what does that mean? I'll explain. Mystify your enemy. Do the unexpected. When that doesn't work, don't do anything at all. Let silence be your weapon. The point is to confuse your enemy and make him turn his energies against himself. It's not hard. The best punch in boxing is the punch you slip.

I took the four-lane and cut through a backstreet to a tin warehouse that had been turned into a bar and dance floor and hookup joint, the kind where the music was deafening and people threw their trash all over the parking lot and copulated in the woods. If you wanted a fight, it could be as raw and dangerous as it gets.

The owner was an ex-chaser in a navy brig and used to manage dog and chicken fights in Breaux Bridge. You don't want to even think about a combo like that.

I got there at five minutes before nine and ordered a beer at the end of the bar, where I could see a pool table in an adjoining room. I went easy with the beer, though. Alcohol combined with depression leaves you in the morning like you're swimming in shit, sorry for the image. Then I saw Sandy Glover come in a side door and head straight for me. He was wearing starched khaki cargos, a see-through knit shirt, black Tony Lamas with a mirror shine, and a tablespoon of Vaseline in his hair. He had a matchstick in his teeth.

He raised a finger to the bartender. "Vodka rocks, Nick," he said.

"You're the man," the bartender said.

Then Glover looked at me. "You're a punctual man," he said.

"How do you know?" I replied. "You just got here."

"I was watching you from outside. In case you brought some company." He grinned around his matchstick. "I hear somebody did some remodeling on Lauren Bow's plantation house."

"They're making a movie there or something?" I said.

He grinned again. "Your beer's flat. I'll get us a booth in back."

"Before I do that, let's get something straight. I want some clarity about what you guys are after. *Diggez-vous?*"

"Oh, cross my heart," he said.

"Hey, this isn't funny, podjo."

"Podjo? That's cute. I couldn't agree with you more. I gotta take a piss. Meet me in the booth." He slapped me hard on the upper arm. "Wow, swollen as a fire hose. How old are you, anyway?"

I told him.

He shook his head. "I must be doing something wrong," he said.

# # #

I couldn't read this guy. But in the life, that's not unusual. There's a whole culture of people whose skin tissue looks the same as ours, but it's diseased. The residents of Jersey and Florida are good examples. They live in the suburbs; they go to PTA meetings; they're Little League coaches; and they're in the life and talk about it openly. In the United States hundreds of millions of dollars in storage containers are stolen from coastal wharfs every year. That's why I use the term "pathological." The guy I was talking to in this dump of a nightclub in East Lafayette was a perfect example. He could probably pass a lie detector with a Bible on his lap. But there was another possibility with this character. What if he asked me to walk out in the parking lot and have a smoke? I could end up in a car trunk. Or worse. Earl Banner had been outwitting Murphy artists, street dips, house creeps, money-washers, and firebugs for sale for almost three decades, and he ended up in a chair while a depraved man did things.

This depression situation was getting loose on me, like somebody filling a hypodermic needle with snake venom and injecting it into the back of my brain.

Then I realized I hadn't moved from the bar. I was standing there, staring at the dancers, wondering where Sandy Glover was. I ground the heel of my hand into one eye and looked at the dancers again. On the far end of the dance floor I thought I saw Baylor Hemmings, the man who had worked on me with the taser. I picked up my beer and drank it to the bottom, then looked again. But he was gone.

"Hey, mate," the bartender said. "It looks like you're weaving in the wind. Why don't you have a seat?"

"There's nothing wrong with me."

"Just checking," the bartender said. "Here's one on the house."

I put a twenty-dollar bill on the bar. "Thanks. Give me a double shot of Jack back and keep the change."

"You got it, bub," he said, bending into his work.

I dropped the shot glass into the mug and watched the whiskey rise in a brown cloud inside the foam, then lifted the mug to my mouth and started swallowing, the brassy taste of the beer sliding over my tongue and down my throat, the Jack as bright and smooth as a creek running across rocks in a forest. I went all the way to the bottom of the mug.

"Where the hell you been?" Sandy Glover said. "I told you I'd get us a booth."

"I think I saw your friend Baylor Hemmings," I said.

"Where?"

I was unsteady and had no idea what I was doing. "Hey, bartender," I said. "Hit me again with the same back in the booth. You copy that?"

"Roger that, big fella," he said.

I could see a worried look on Glover's face.

"Everything is copacetic," I said. "Where's our booth?"

"Follow me," he replied, looking past me at the dance floor. "You didn't really see Hemmings, did you?"

I looked again. "I don't know," I said.

But I saw someone else. It was my friend Joan, dressed in a white blouse with fluffy sleeves and a black dress that touched her shoes, with an Australian digger's hat on her head. She was staring straight at me and looked furious.

# # #

Our booth was in the back of the building, the cushions made of plastic and split with knives. The bartender brought me another beer and a shot, and went away.

"Okay, you want clarity? I'll give you clarity," Glover said. "A small number of people got hold of a substance that can change the human race, and not for the better."

"You're talking about germ warfare or something?"

"Worse."

"What's worse than that?" I said.

"It can think."

I lifted the shot glass, then put it back down. I could see the lady I called Joan by the bandstand. I know it was her. She looked like she was made of cardboard and was the only cutout in the building.

"What are you looking at, man?" Glover asked.

"Nothing. You said you don't have a sheet. How do you know what a sheet is if you never had a sheet?"

"I worked CID in the army. You want to hear what I got to say or not?"

I pushed the mug and the shot to the side. The first round had already started deconstructing the inside of my head. "Go ahead," I said.

"This substance can make whole nations change and do terrible things to themselves."

"And it's for sale?"

"What do you think?" he said.

"Sounds like some scary shit. If you were in CID, why not go to the government and be a hero?"

He leaned forward into my face, the flats of his arms pressed against the table. "Because I don't trust anybody. And I got the sense neither do you."

"What's the name of the substance?" I asked.

"The chemical name? That I don't know. The street name? Leprechaun."

"Leprechaun?" I repeated.

"Yeah, it lights up behind trees in the middle of the night. Certain people think you found it in your Caddy and hid it somewhere else. Do a good deed for yourself and the world. Where is it, Purcel? If the wrong guys get their hands on you or on your buddy Robicheaux—I don't want to talk about that, man. They got no mercy."

It felt like my entrails were sliding free of my body, like a smell was rising from my clothes and my gyroscope was wobbling off a cliff.

"You okay, man?" Glover said.

"What do you care?"

"Maybe I got some humanity."

I knew I was in some kind of psychological difficulty. I tried to get up but had to sit down again. Joan was walking toward me.

"What's wrong with you, man?" Glover said. "You gonna be sick?"

"I just need a little fresh air. Hey, I'll introduce you to a historical friend of mine. You dig stars from the Middle Ages? Here she is. The real deal."

Joan was standing four feet from us now.

"You're spooky, man," Glover said. "Forget everything I've told you. I wouldn't do business with you if you pointed a flamethrower at me. You belong on Mars."

Joan was right next to the table now. She touched my head, and all the heat in my face and the pain and sickness in my viscera went away, like snowflakes blowing in the sunlight.

"You're serious about your guys coming after Dave Robi-cheaux?" I said.

He jabbed his finger at my face. "One more word! Just one!"

I didn't have to say anything. Joan stared at the beer mug and the shot glass, which were still full to the brim. Then they exploded all over the table, drenching Glover.

He got up and wiped his face with his knit shirt, and I got escorted from the premises. I decided definitively this was not a good environment and I shouldn't visit it again.

But something more important than me was bothering me. Joan was helping me at every turn, but I wasn't doing anything for her. The guards in her prison tower or a shithead nobleman prob-ably molested her, and nobody cared at all. She was only nineteen when they burned her at the stake. And now she was taking care of me while I made trouble for her. That definitely was not cool. In fact, it sucked.

The state police pulled me over in Broussard, a tiny town midway between Lafayette and New Iberia. I had been drifting off the edge of the highway. I thought I was headed for the can. Instead, I passed both the Breathalyzer test and what they call the one-leg-stand test. How do you explain that? I wanted to go back to the fifteenth century and give Joan a big wagon of flowers.

CHAPTER TWENTY-THREE

I told all this to Dave in his office on the second floor of the Iberia sheriff's department. I know it might seem strange for me to hang out in a building full of cops after somebody crashed a concrete mixer into Lauren Bow's home, but sometimes high visibility has its merits. Want to disappear? Put on a cap, stick some ballpoints in your shirt pocket, and carry a clipboard.

Secondly, I didn't care what happened to me regarding Bow's plantation house. He bought it with money he cheated from other people. Thirdly, the images Sandy Glover created for me were eating a hole in my stomach. If I heard him correctly, he was talking about poisoning the entire Earth. Even saying those words sent weevil worms through my heart.

"Look, Dave, I don't care what happens to me," I said. "Glover thinks you're next, and there's no telling what'll happen to my guests in New Orleans or my animals or Miss Sally or maybe the whole world. Where'd Hawthorne go? Why would the Feds shut us out?"

Dave was sitting in his swivel chair behind his desk, one knee crossed over the other. Out the window I could see the oak trees puffing in City Park and the children on the seesaws and swing sets and the jungle gym, the way the world is supposed to be.

"I think you had a bad night, Clete," he said. "I don't mean the juice or the appearance of the lady who helped you, but the apocalyptic nature of what this guy was saying. It scares the hell out of you. We got within two hours of incinerating the Earth in the '62 Cuban Missile Crisis. You don't think he's just trying to put the slide on you?"

"No," I replied. "I think he's a cash-and-carry guy and just wants to come out on the winning side, which to me is worse than Baylor Hemmings, who'd jump at the chance to work at Buchenwald, like some others."

"I didn't catch that last part."

"You've met them, Dave. People we give badges and guns to. Don't pretend."

"You're right," he said. "I guess that's just the way it is."

He glanced out the window, his eyes veiled. I knew what he was thinking about. The wife who had betrayed him, the wife who had been murdered, the wife who had died from lupus, the wife who had been killed by a drunk driver, the mother who had abandoned him and been killed by her pimp. You know the expression "You got to hump your own pack"? I don't know how Dave made it.

But I knew he was thinking about Alafair, too. From the time he pulled her out of a sunken plane to the present, he had saved and stored her childhood things in the attic: her T-shirt stamped with a smiling whale and the words BABY ORCA, her pink tennis shoes embossed with the word LEFT on one toe and RIGHT on the other, and her Donald Duck cap with the quacking brim that he bought her at Disney World.

He turned around and looked at me. "Let's start with Hawthorne," he said.

"How do you even get in touch with the guy?" I said.

"Good question."

"You know what bothers me, Dave? What *really* bothers me?"

"Go ahead."

"We're bait," I said. "Just like those minnows quivering on the hook. That's what I think."

"I have to admit that occurred to me," he replied.

# # #

He always said I was the best cop he ever knew, but actually it was Dave who was best. What Dave had was improbability. He had a degree in English and a teacher's certificate from the University of Southwestern Louisiana, and he always thought of other people first, particularly people of color and people who didn't have any voice. Dave's troubles came from his lack of love for himself. He was dangerous when he was around the bad guys, and by "bad guys" I mean sadists and slumlords and misogynists and cartel dope kings and racists and politicians who steal from the poor and the bunch he really wanted to tear apart, those who profit off wars but never go to them. He would come out of a trance when I pulled him off one of these guys and he wouldn't know where the blood on his fists and the splatter on his shoes had come from.

Dave will tell you I do the same thing, but don't believe him. I don't have chemical problems or blackouts. Or maybe just a little. But who's perfect? Hey, dig this: How many people do you know who talk with regularity to the dead? That's Dave. That's why I love him. He knows there's another world, and he thinks the deniers are jerks but never says so. That's what I call class.

So I invited him for dinner that night at Clementine's, which had tables outside in back, with a view of the bayou and the drawbridge, and with all the green and red lights on and glass candleholders flickering on the tables, the wind balmy, wrinkling the water as the sun went down. Dave ordered iced tea. So did I.

"This afternoon I got through to Samuel Hawthorne," he said.

"No kidding?"

"I think he's wired up."

"You mean—"

"I could hear him breathing in the phone. He said something odd."

"What?" I asked.

"That maybe his ancestor was one of the judges at the Salem witch trials."

"Not the author, the judge?" I said.

"Or maybe both," Dave replied. "He said fear drives people crazy. Then they start believing things that can't be true."

"What's he talking about?"

"That's what I asked him. He said we may have a problem nobody will believe. The kind that's so bad that people will not allow themselves to examine the truth."

"Did you ask him about this Leprechaun stuff?"

"He never heard of it," Dave said.

"Maybe that's a good sign."

"No, he's got the heebie-jeebies," Dave said. "I asked him if I could help. He said he can't be helped."

He wiped his mouth with his hand. "Come on, let's order."

"Yeah, sure," I said.

"You're ready to eat, right?" Dave said.

"Yeah, that's what I said."

"Well, let's do it." He brushed at the back of his neck, as though a mosquito was on it.

Dave wasn't acting right. Or maybe it was my perception. I'll admit I wanted a drink. The full-tilt boogie, a skull-fuck pitcher of crushed ice and cherries and sliced oranges that I could drink with two hands, pardon the language again. Or maybe both of us wanted to go through a hole in the dimension. It's hard to be a drunk sometimes. Why? Because alcoholism is an incremental form of suicide.

Then I saw Joan walking down from Burke Street, wearing a plain long-sleeve gray jacket that may have been used as a liner for a knight's armor, her leather trousers a soft brownish gold, her hair clipped with an inverted bowl, her face expressionless, her eyes riveted on mine. She picked up a chair and sat in it. *Don't you dare*, she said.

I looked at Dave. He was reading the menu.

Did you hear me? she said.

"Yes," I said.

"Yes what?" Dave said, his gaze lifting from the menu.

"Nothing," I said.

Ask Dave if he feels well, Joan said.

"You okay, noble mon?" I said.

He looked up at me. "Yeah," he said.

"I was just checking."

"Clete, you're starting to worry me."

Joan put her hand on my arm.

"Everything is extremely copacetic, big mon."

"Good."

"Hey, Dave, I got to tell you something."

"What?" he said.

"Unless we get on it, we're not gonna make it."

"Make what?" he said.

"Five people have been killed since I took my Caddy to the car wash. Nobody is in custody, and nobody seems to be upset, except for Hawthorne. I had the same kind of feeling when I left Shitsville. The slick was piled with wounded, like pieces of beef. I could smell the feces and blood on all those guys, and I knew that none of it was gonna mean anything. The moon was up and we were flying over a rice paddy, and you could see the slick's shadow racing across the water and the hooches, and I knew that no matter what those fuckheads in Washington said, we were in the toilet and in a few years no one would care and or even remember why we were there."

"Yeah, but we cared, Clete, and that's all that counts."

I made a face, then shrugged.

"You're not going to say anything?" he asked.

"Yeah, we need some breadsticks."

# # #

The waiter brought them, and I started to offer one to Joan, but she shook her head and looked over her shoulder at the bayou and the red and green lights on the drawbridge and the cypress and live oak trees leaning over the water. But this was not the same environment I had been in just a few moments earlier. Instead of the bayou, I saw a huge horizontal tunnel of energy spinning for miles where the bayou had been. Instead of the drawbridge and the Shadows and the Victorian and antebellum homes along the bayou, there were tens of thousands of medieval soldiers, wearing armor, with spiked elbows, lifting their swords and spears and pikes above their silvery helmets, their flags flying above them in the afterglow of the sun.

But that wasn't all. They were chanting Joan's name, some clattering their swords on their shields and pounding their feet on the earth. In the distance were rolling hills and rivers and mountains and castles with moats and drawbridges and tiny villages that contained peasant huts made of straw, houses that reminded me of Shitsville.

"You see something on the bridge?" Dave asked.

"Dave, I don't know how to say this, but, uh, we have a visitor with us."

His eyes went sideways, then focused on me again.

"Yeah?"

"It's her."

He cleared his throat and scratched behind his neck. "Are you about to tell me your friend Joan is here?"

Joan was wagging a finger in my face.

"She doesn't want to talk right now, but, yeah, she's sitting right there, three feet from you."

Like I say, Dave thinks deniers are jerks, so he showed no reaction. "I would really like to meet her, Clete. I think she's one of the greatest and bravest women in history."

"To your left there are probably fifty thousand French infantry inside what looks like a giant snake about to drop off the edge of the Earth."

"Tell you what, Clete, why don't we save the supper until another night and instead take a walk down the bayou?"

"Sure, if you want."

Joan patted my hand and winked.

Dave got up and put some money on the table, because I had forgotten which of us had invited the other to supper. Then we walked down Burke Street in the cooling of evening. Joan and her army had gone away, and the moon and the stars had replaced the afterglow of the sun. I didn't consider that a blessing, though. I wanted to go with her and maybe save her from the fate that had consumed her in a giant envelope of flame.

"You don't think I'm losing it, huh?" I said.

"Not any worse than me."

"My ability to think is worse than when I came home from Nam."

"So what?" he said. "Easy does it."

"You don't get it, Dave. My problem isn't that I'm seeing apparitions. My problem is I believe they're there."

"So what, again? One day they'll go away."

"Think so?" I said.

"Yeah," he said.

We were almost to the Shadows. A tugboat was coming up the bayou, its running lights on. Below the bridge I could see cattails and elephant ears rocking on the current and a piece of metal protruding from the mud. I left Dave and skidded down the embankment and with my bare hands scooped up the piece of metal and washed it in the shallows, then labored back up the slope.

"What is it?" Dave asked.

"The guard and grip of a sword. The blade is broken off."

"We've had reenactors and movie people here, Clete."

I took my penlight from my pocket and clicked it on. Then I gave the grip and broken blade to him.

"Would they carry weapons stamped with the fleur-de-lis?"

"This has not been here for five hundred years," Dave said.

"I didn't say it has," I said.

He let out his breath and placed one hand on my shoulder and looked me straight in the face. "Don't chase after what you can't explain, Clete."

"Why not?"

This time he didn't have an answer.

CHAPTER TWENTY-FOUR

I slept pretty good that night, and in the morning I had a big breakfast and went to the office while it was still cool and the day fresh, the bayou swollen over the banks from a storm in the Gulf. Only one thing bothered me. Did you notice Dave scratching himself? He never did that before, particularly not in public. That made me a little uneasy.

At the office I checked in with Chen and Gracie Lamar by telephone. Nothing unusual had happened in the last few days. But the calm I should have felt wasn't there. Do you sometimes have a tightness in your chest, a whirring sound in your ears, a sense that just around the next corner a faceless figure is waiting for you?

I'll take it a little further here. I felt like a few people had been chosen to take on a drama that would influence the whole earth. I know that sounds arrogant. But if you look back through history, the actors are few and the spectators are many.

I poured myself another cup of coffee at my metal army-surplus desk and tried not to think too much. My clients came and went. They were a poor bunch on many levels, fraught with character defects, unwanted at birth, whipped as children, their lives tangled in welfare and jail. The most pitiful were the women.

Just a few blocks away there was a shelter where they hid from their husbands. Many of their children were addicts before they reached puberty.

I wanted to get out of my own head and go back to fifteenth-century France. Then a sixty-thousand-dollar automobile pulled out of the traffic on Main and parked in front of the office, in the yellow zone. Guess who was behind the steering wheel, in a tropical shirt and a Panama hat and purple slacks and black lace-up shoes a wrestler might wear? And guess who was in the passenger seat? Yeah, you got it: Clara Bow. That was enough to break my heart.

She stayed in the car, staring straight ahead, her expression dead, like she was stitched to the rolled leather. The bell tinkled over my door when her former husband walked in, the man whose home I had ruined. Seven of my clients were sitting on metal chairs, one reading yesterday's newspaper, one asleep with his head on his chest, one putting on her makeup, one just out of the can for throwing a brick through a car window on the four-lane, one who hung paper all over Morgan City, one who had bitten his social worker, and one stoned out of his mind and jerking his head at everything that moved.

Bow had his car-grille smile in place. "There's my laddie," he said.

I pulled my foot over my knee and took off my loafer and massaged my instep and toes. "How about leaving the nicknames for someone else?" I replied.

"Sure enough, I will. Wouldn't think of spoiling your day."

"What can I help you with?" I said.

"Maybe a touch-up or two at my house. Or maybe you haven't heard. Some fucker turned it into a gravel pit."

"Don't use profanity in my office, please."

He gazed at the people in the chairs. Then looked at me. "Sorry," he said. "I just wanted to close out Clara's account with you."

I looked through the front window and kept massaging my foot. Clara made me think of an abandoned rag doll. "Then let her come in and say that."

"She isn't feeling well," Bow replied.

"There's some coffee on the table. I'll be back."

"Suit yourself. Don't be long, though. We have an airplane of Hollywood characters coming in today."

I went outside. The car was in the shade, the wind out of the south, a balmy tinge of salt in the air. Her window was down. She made no effort to acknowledge me.

"What's going on, Clara?"

She didn't answer.

"You want to tear up our contract? Of your own volition?"

"Yes," she said.

"Look at me."

Instead she looked across the street at Victor's.

"Cut that out, Clara."

Zero response.

I walked to the front of the car and looked through the windshield. She gave up hiding and lifted her face into the light. I strained not to knot my fists and went back to her window. "You can stay where you are. Or you can walk down the street. Or you can call 911. But do not come in the office."

Then I went back inside and pointed my finger at Lauren Bow. "Come into my office, please," I said.

"Anything wrong?"

I put my hands together, as a preacher might. "Just a chat."

"Certainly, sir. I am at your service."

He walked ahead of me. When we were inside, I partially closed the door. I did not offer him a seat. "You hit her in the eye?"

"No, I think she was looking through a keyhole. She's very good at that."

"Any man who strikes a woman is a moral and physical coward. Lower than a pimp."

"Flinging around the insults, are we?"

"She's my client and she will remain my client until she tells me otherwise, and not in your presence."

"You're a sack of shite, did you know that?" he said.

I sniffed and rubbed at my nose. "You can leave now, partner."

"I'm not easily pushed around, fella."

"You don't have to convince me," I said.

"You like to show off in front of your assembly out there. That's why you left the door open. Am I correct?"

"No, I wanted them to know you are of no importance, that whatever you say has no value and doesn't need hiding."

"Well, you piece of Celtic trash. If I were not in such a hurry, I'd plunge your head in your own toilet."

He spat in the wastebasket and walked through the waiting area, his metallic smile back in place. "Good day to you, ladies and lads. My friend Mr. Purcel just told me a grand joke about you. Ask him. You'll love it. Ta-ta."

Then he was outside.

I walked to the front door and opened it, the bell ringing. Bow was standing on the sidewalk, talking to friends by his car, inches from his former wife's face, her right eye purple and as swollen as a duck's egg, her humiliation guaranteed.

"A word with you, Mr. Bow?" I said.

He turned around, still smiling. "Yes?" he said.

I caught him right in the mouth. It was a beaut. It burst like a tomato. He hit the concrete like a piano thrown from the roof. I picked him up and threw him through the door into the office, grabbing him by his pants and tropical shirt and driving him straight into the restroom, slamming his head into the toilet bowl, stiff-arming his neck, flushing his head as long as the tank water held out.

Then I let him go, like I had walked out of a dream, like Dave Robicheaux and I had exchanged personalities. I staggered out of the restroom, my hands in the air.

"Hey, everyone! Sorry for the commotion!" I said. "Either beer or pecan pie is on me at Bojangles!"

A big cheer went up.

"But make it fast," I added. "I think I hear a siren or two."

"Don't worry, Clete," the stoner said. "It was self-defense. Am I right, everyone?"

Another cheer, this one louder.

I was touched, even though I was going to the can.

# # #

I thought I would be put in a holding cell at the sheriff's department, but I was booked and taken to the parish prison. The process is not fun. Here, or in any can, the issue is not confinement; it's degradation. It's the instant loss of your identity and dignity. You do not make choices; you go where you are told; you shut your mouth; you drop your pants and shorts and bend over and spread your cheeks; maybe you feel a flashlight touch your skin. A hack wears latex because you're a germ; when he's finished, he pulls off his latex and throws it in the trash.

When you're photographed, the only words spoken to you are "left face" and "right face." A screw or deputy rolls your fingertips one at a time on the ink pad, then on a piece of paper. If the print is a good transfer, he's happy. But not about you. About himself. You're shit.

Want to go to the bathroom? You're told to hold it. You tell the screw you can't. He walks you to a cell that is in plain view. The bowl has no seat. A roll of toilet paper is on the floor. You tell the screw you've got to do a number two. "It's not the Four Seasons," he says.

I was given an orange jumpsuit and put in a cell with four other guys, the same kind of poor, dysfunctional guys I see every day in my service as their bondsman. It's a system unto itself, fueled by narcotics. These guys made me think of children with long hair and bearded faces who had never grown up and were waiting for someone to tell them what to do.

A deputy came down the corridor. "Let's go, Mr. Purcel," he said. "The rest of you stand back."

"What's the deal?" I asked.

"Follow me," he said. Screws do not answer inmates. I walked behind him in my jumpsuit to an office in the discharge area. He opened the door and left me standing there. Helen and the FBI agent Samuel Hawthorne were waiting inside.

# # #

Hawthorne was smiling; Helen was not.

"How'd y'all get me out?"

"Your clients say Mr. Bow started it," Hawthorne said.

"Really?" I said.

Helen was frowning.

"What?" I said to her.

"I heard Agent Hawthorne talking on his cell phone to somebody at the IRS," she said. "I don't like doing business that way."

I looked at Hawthorne.

"I have no influence with the IRS, Mr. Purcel," he said. "Nor do they interfere in our business."

"You two guys cut the bullshit," she said. "Clete, what you did was crazy. I'm getting you off the hook because you're too immature to take care of yourself."

"I appreciate it," I said.

"Why did you do it?" she said. "With your record, Lauren Bow can have you in Angola. How about the destruction of his house? Do you think that's going away?"

I definitely wanted this discussion closed down. "Well, not everyone is perfect," I said.

She made a sound that was like a hog grunting, way down in the throat. "I just don't know what to do with you," she said. "I just don't."

"I'm sorry."

"Yes, that's the right word for it," she replied.

Sometimes Helen could reach up and hurt you.

"We need to talk, Mr. Purcel," Hawthorne said. "We're finding out more about our enemy. By that I mean the handful of people in Eastern Europe who made Leprechaun. They made several variants. Then they sold it in this country. Its consequences are unthinkable."

I felt my stomach drop. Helen had been angry. Now her face had drained.

"You're talking about contagion?" I said.

"Yes, sir," he replied.

"What are the symptoms?" I said.

"You ever hear of hemochromatosis?"

"No," I said.

"Everything goes wrong with you. Your liver, your stomach, your brain, your skin."

"What happens to your skin?" I said.

"It can turn yellow or brown. All your body hair falls out. I suspect the level of depression is terrible."

I thought about Dave scratching himself, and doing it in public.

"Look, get your street clothes on, Mr. Purcel, and let's you and I and the sheriff have a bite to eat in the park."

"Is something wrong with my office?" Helen said.

Hawthorne smiled with his eyes.

"You think it's bugged?" she asked.

"Think about what's at stake," he replied.

# # #

In Louisiana, the third meal of the day is supper. The second meal is dinner. It was close to supper now, and I went to a café in the Black district and loaded up on deep-fried chicken and shrimp, dirty rice, Cajun fries, mashed potatoes with milk gravy, and a bucket of ice cream. I met Helen and Hawthorne at a picnic table by the bayou in City Park. Hawthorne ate like he hadn't eaten a decent meal in weeks.

"What's the average lifespan around here?" he asked.

"We don't keep records," Helen said.

She was in a better mood now, and it made me happy when she smiled instead of frowning. It's funny how you change when you get older, huh? You want to stay on the sunny side and not let anyone steal the day from you.

Hawthorne took out a notebook while he was eating and began reading it to himself. "Okay, here it is, y'all," he said. "The Europeans were politically and monetarily motivated. Two or three of them died making it. Spiders can be carriers. The greatest challenge in fighting the transmission is its lack of predictability. It transforms itself when it feels threatened, almost like it can think. The synthetic manufacture of it, the Leprechaun version, has already morphed into a deadlier form. The infected person can go berserk and start shooting or stabbing people on subways. This is a long way from hemochromatosis."

I was starting to feel my forehead sweat. "What's Lauren Bow's part in all this?" I said.

"The guy's in politics, and probably a sociopath and pervert on top of it, but we can't find any ties between him and Leprechaun or the New Rising."

"I saw the tattooed man on his property," I said.

"The tattooed man worked for rich people up and down Bayou Teche."

I thought Clara Bow would have a lot to say about her former husband's potential, but I said nothing, automatically sheltering a person who could have been a source of information, the kind the FBI takes seriously. What kind of source is that? As witnesses, battered wives spare nothing, no matter how much they injure themselves.

"You keep saying 'we,'" Helen said. "Who is 'we'?"

"A few agents here and there," Hawthorne replied. "I put in my vacation time on it."

"Excuse me?" I said.

"I interest anyone I can," he said.

Helen looked at me. Then at him. "You don't have a lot of support?" she said.

"Y'all are behind me," he replied.

She lowered her eyes then, and left them like that. Neither she nor I had any more to say. The moon was rising into a blue porcelain sky, the sun still aflame in the west. It was a strange way to end a conversation. But there was no point in talking. The words, the images, the players we knew about were so dark and disturbing I felt like I was reaching back into a barrel of bad dreams I had as a child. But those were only nightmares. Our ordeal was real, and we could do nothing about it, and our government seemed uninterested.

Our picnic table was close by the softball diamond. There were no children on it. I could see a large, black spider crawling its way across home plate, its many legs mechanically working, like bent wires, out of control. I got up and crushed it under my loafer, grinding it into an ugly smear.

CHAPTER TWENTY-FIVE

I did not rest well that night. At 12:42 a.m. I put a shaving kit and a few summer clothes in the back seat of my Caddy and headed for New Orleans. The night was absolutely black, as though the stars and the moon and even the heat lightning had been sucked inside the storm clouds. I crossed the Atchafalaya at Morgan City and could see waves flowing through the swamp, dashing against the tree trunks.

I had no plan, nor any motivation that I knew of. Instead, I heard a loud scream inside my skull, but I didn't know if it was me or the soul of someone in the past, or perhaps a contemporaneous creature longing for a savior who would break his chains and pull him from the darkness in which he was entrapped.

I honestly believed I was going mad, and I'll tell you why. Hawthorne and Helen and I were calmly talking about an apocalyptic situation that somehow we had gotten past. Oh, yeah, *that*. We got rid of *that*, didn't we? What's for dinner? I felt like I had a bowl of cancer in the middle of my stomach.

I was doing eighty, maybe ninety, when I was fifteen miles out of New Orleans. I think I blew right past a parked state police car. I didn't even glance in the rearview mirror. I suspect he was asleep. I couldn't have cared less. Oh, sorry, officer. Was I speeding? What's your feeling about this apocalypse thing?

I was wired, in a nonchemical blackout, except I could see and remember everything, the wind outside my Caddy tearing apart the buildings flying by, ripped power lines that popped sparks all along the highway.

When I got into the city, the sky looked covered with soot, but I didn't know where it had come from. I drove into the courtyard below my apartment and stepped out on the bricks. There was no sound from anywhere. The windmill palms and elephant ears and banana fronds were motionless. My watch said 4:41 a.m. I took my clothes and shaving kit from the back seat and went up the stairs.

Chen was sound asleep, but Gracie Lamar was not in her bedroom. Of course, she worked late hours. Hey, I know I said I had no motivation to be there. But that wasn't quite accurate. Not only did I have her on my mind, I had Joan of Arc on my mind, and I was starting to believe that I had made up Joan so I wouldn't seem like an old fool chasing after a beautiful young woman, and in this case, a young woman who was drawn for whatever reason to Dave Robicheaux.

I went into the kitchen and got a quart of chocolate milk from the icebox and drank it at the window and looked down on the street. Nobody was there. That made no sense. The French Quarter was like New York; it never slept. Derelicts and dealers and addicts and prostitutes stayed on the prowl. But not this morning. The outside of my building reminded me of a nineteenth-century painting of Arles, with only one streetlamp lit and one character in the street, a young woman leaning against the lamp's stanchion, wearing a beret and tight skirt, smoking a long cigarette, a hand propped on her hip.

She could not see me, but I could see her. It was Gracie Lamar. I knew why she was there, and I knew I was looking down at Arles. I wanted to freeze the past and the artistic world and the beauty of a young woman whom I could put on my arm and take out for coffee and pastry in an outdoor café. I wanted to leave the world of criminality and war and suffering; I wanted justice for the Jewish mother and her children whose picture was in my wallet, and I wanted to build a stone monument with their names on it and for the rest of my life put flowers on it, and do this with the girl whose arm would rest on mine.

I did not trust the era I lived in, nor did I want to live in it. The twentieth century had been the most violent in human history. The amount of killing had no precedent, and I had the feeling it was about to get started again, and once more by those who had never gone to war but gloated over the graves they spread through a neocolonial world. If I had to go to war again, I'd like to do it against those bastards.

I stepped closer to the window frame, my breath fogging the glass, tapping on it with one knuckle. There was still no light in the sky, which never happens in New Orleans. You can be across Lake Pontchartrain, twenty-four miles away, and see the city lights glowing in the clouds. But a lid as black as cast iron seemed to stretch from horizon to horizon. I tried to jerk the window loose, but it was jammed solid, like nails had been hammered in it. I hit the window with the flat of my fist, hard. Then I headed downstairs.

Not one person was in the street, except Gracie Lamar. She was still smoking her cigarette, then she dropped it on the sidewalk and stepped on it, breathing out the last of the smoke. Her beret was cut at a cute angle.

"What are you doing here, Gracie?" I said.

"Waiting for you," she replied.

"I never saw you smoke before."

"Might as well join the drips who stick bills in my shoes."

"That doesn't sound like you. In fact, none of this seems real. In fact, I think Van Gogh or Gauguin should be hanging around here."

"You're a stand-up guy, Clete. Stay off the grog and get some help with that melancholia. It'll fuck you proper."

"Enough with that kind of language, Gracie."

"Listen to who's talking. Why are you in town?"

"I don't know. I think I've splashed my grits. I think you might be Joan of Arc."

"It's as you say; I'm not real."

I nodded.

"But Joan is," she said.

"Then why am I seeing you?"

"You've put me inside a painting. That way I can always be yours. Come here."

"What for?"

"Give me your hand."

"What are you gonna do?"

She picked up my right hand and turned up my palm and felt the calluses on it, then turned up the back side and ran her fingers across the scars. "Did you get those in Vietnam?"

"No, in the Iberville projects."

She pressed the back of my hand to her cheek, as though she were warming a cat, then blew on it, then turned my palm up again and kissed it and softly bit one of my fingers.

"It's Dave Robicheaux you want, though, isn't it?"

"I'm a wraith, Clete. Just a strip of fog."

She stood on the tops of my shoes and kissed me on both eyes, then on the mouth.

"You did that before," I said. "Please. You're her, aren't you? You're Joan."

"Bye, Clete," she said. "I'll be around."

"No, no, don't do this to me. I was never with a woman like you. Please stay. I'll do anything."

"I know. And that's why you're going to be killed." Her voice was breaking and fading away. She began running down the street, her feet clopping on the asphalt like wooden shoes.

When I woke up in the morning, I was face down on the couch in pajamas, a pillow over my head, the sunlight's glare like a sliver of glass.

# # #

She was standing over me in jeans and an Alabama Crimson Tide T-shirt and sandals, with a frying pan in her hands. "Want some eggs?" she said.

"How did I get on the couch?" I asked.

"I guess you put yourself there. Were you drinking?"

"No. You were under the streetlamp."

"You must have had a dream," she said. "You want sausage?"

"Yeah," I said. "Where's Chen?"

"At a meeting."

"You held my hand. You kissed it."

"Better get in the shower, big fella. You must have really tied one on. I'll be in the kitchen."

# # #

She was wrong. I wasn't drunk when I arrived in New Orleans, and I didn't get drunk out in the streets. Maybe I saw illusions. Or I had nightmares. Or what Dave calls nonchemical blackouts. Hey, I'll tell you a story. I got caught in a marching barrage of 105s. My soul left my body. I don't care what anybody says. I was floating right above three dead Marines I had just been sharing C-rats with. I don't talk about it because no one would believe me. So I dummy up. What else can you do when your best efforts are no good at all and no one believes you?

Gracie put a nice breakfast on the table, then sat down and looked at me, then seemed to go inside herself.

"Something on your mind?" I said.

"Yeah," she said. "I came to New Orleans to catch the people who killed my partner in Birmingham. I'm not getting anywhere. I think Lauren Bow is part of it, but he and others are metastasizing faster than any police force can contain them. I think maybe I should head back to Alabama."

"Who are they?" I asked, ignoring her last sentence.

"That's the point. They're everywhere, because they've always been here. They're just waiting for a leader. They'll put on their blinders and walk off the cliff if they need to."

"You're talking about political stuff?"

"No, it's not political," she said. "It's a state of mind. They're like fascists. There's no mystery to them. At the core they're bullies and they're cruel."

"What do you think of Clara Bow?" I asked.

"I hear you're gonna be in a film she's producing."

"We talked about it," I said, my throat catching.

"What's that say?"

"It says I've lost my appetite."

She looked down at her plate. "You've been very good to me, Clete. I apologize."

"That's all right," I said. I picked up a big fat tabby cat named Dumpster and set him down on the table, his tail switching all over the plates and coffee cups and juice glasses. "Gonna work in Birmingham, huh?"

"Okay, I didn't want to say this, but now I have to," she replied. "I spent some time over in New Iberia and Jeanerette without telling you. I saw Clara Bow going in and out of Lauren Bow's plantation home, the one undoubtedly you turned into a cement factory. She was with the kinds of assholes that like to beat up gays and lesbians and Blacks and Jews."

"How do you know that?"

"Because I photographed them with a telescopic camera and got Samuel Hawthorne to run them for me."

"You know him?"

"We had a thing for a while."

"I feel like a dope."

"No, you're a nice guy," she said. "But wake up. Sam Hawthorne is a loner and has little support. If he can bring down an attempt to destroy the nation, he'll be head of Fart, Barf, and Itch."

"Where did you hear that expression?"

"He quoted it from you," she replied.

Dumpster walked back and forth across my food, rubbing his head on my chest, his fur and feet all over my toast and eggs. "I think I'll take a walk through the Quarter. No, don't get up. You and Dumpster read the newspaper."

I put on my shades and my porkpie hat and spent the rest of the morning playing a pinball machine in a drugstore on Canal. People always wondered why Streak and I were a team and trusted virtually no one, with the exception of Helen, who would rip the butt out of a rhino for either one of us. I suspect you *diggez-vous* on this now.

# # #

Chen was back at my building when I returned. She was smiling, and I knew her twelve-step program was working and would probably stay with her. She had gained a little weight, but in a healthy way, because Sperm-O Sellers, aka the Octopus, had been not only mainlining her but turning her into the town pump. I don't like to use that kind of language about her, but that's the reality of the world she had been living in. Anybody who thinks otherwise has no clue. One cartel piece of shit said his dope was his atomic bomb for America. I think he got it wrong. We've dropped it on ourselves.

"How you do?" Chen said when I walked in.

"Really well, Chen," I replied. "You look very nice."

"I look nice because you make me look nice. You always smiley-guy."

"Uh, Chen, that doesn't sound too good. See, a smiley-guy is sort of a greasy guy, like a fat worm or a slug."

"There are worms that smile?"

"Don't worry about this," I said.

"What is slug?"

"Never mind, Chen. It's not a problem."

"I ride the streetcar up St. Charles to the library with Gracie. It beautiful there. You make life so good for me, Mr. Clete."

"You don't have to call me mister. Please."

"People in Louisiana polite, Mr. Clete."

"That's the way people talked on the plantations. I'm not a fan of plantation life. The people who owned everything were deadbeats."

"They were dead and the Union soldiers beat them up?"

"Hey, there's some soda in the icebox," I said, clasping my hands, looking out the window at the bugle vine hanging from the balcony.

"You always like to play jokes. But you sad sometimes."

"No, no, I'm fine," I said.

"You pay hard price for the man you are. My father would like you. But he dead now."

This was the first time she had spoken of her family.

"If you don't mind telling me, how did he die?"

"Pay to smuggle into Thailand. Drown with most. Only me from my family survive. My mother and sisters and brothers all die."

I tried to keep my face empty. Again I thought about the Jewish mother and her three children at Auschwitz. I had to sit down. Then I got back up. "Hey, Chen, I'm gonna fix us a couple of root beer floats."

"I no want you sad for me, Mr. Clete. Your job is protect people. Like angel with big wings. You Clete Purcel."

I went into the bathroom and stayed there ten minutes, tingling all over. When I came out, she was gone. I have to admit this. I went into a panic. She was nowhere in the house or the courtyard or the downstairs office. I walked hurriedly down the street toward Jackson Square and accidentally knocked a cop in uniform off the curb. Fortunately he was a young guy and told me to forget it when I explained my situation.

Then I crossed the Square and walked down Decatur and plowed into her as she was coming out of a blue-collar café renowned for the ninety-weight tractor oil they cooked their food in, not counting the crust on every surface in the beloved dump that it was. She was loaded with cartons of takeout.

"Gee whiz!" I said. "Why don't you give me a heart attack?"

"See?" she replied. "You say 'gee whiz.' You no use bad words when women there. That why you good man and why I will always love Mr. Clete Purcel."

I wanted to cry.

# # #

I had to get back to New Iberia, because I had to keep Dave out of trouble and also I had to be close by Miss Sally, plus the amount of drugs in New Orleans was like a giant insect devouring the city, particularly in the projects, where crank and guns were a way of life. Put it this way. You didn't want to wander into Louis Armstrong Park or the cemeteries.

There's a lot of nostalgia about New Orleans, and I dearly miss it. I don't like progress. I tell people that Fred Flintstone used to be my next-door neighbor. Anyway, I had dinner with Gracie and Chen and Miss Dorothy, the food all bought from the lube joint by Chen, just as a storm broke over the city, the lightning forking in the clouds, the claps of thunder like locomotives blowing up.

The power went out, but we lit candles and kept eating the Creole food Chen had bought. It was like New Orleans of years ago, the city that would never change, that would never go below the waves, no matter how many hurricanes and tidal surges washed over the levees. This was New Orleans, unlike any other city in the world.

I hugged each lady, put on a raincoat and my porkpie hat, and went down the back stairs to my Caddy, the rain as hard as bird shot, balls of light flaring in the thunderheads, so bright you believed the sun had broken loose from its fastenings. Then I fired up my engine and drove slowly down the street, my headlights tunneling into the dark.

CHAPTER TWENTY-SIX

I woke up late Saturday morning and could hear rain dripping off the oak trees and see sunlight edging the window shades, and knew it was going to be a good day. At least I hoped. I've learned that in depression you should not ask for things or start to plan or try to analyze. If you do, you're asking for it. You have to be quiet inside your mind. Music helps. But your own noise can rip out your insides, particularly in the early morning hours. Remember the lyrics "light my fire" from the 1960s? Do. Not. Even. Think. Those. Words.

Hey, guess who was at my door. I pulled it open, still wearing my bathrobe. "Hello, Miss Clara. No matter what you have, I don't want it—no insult intended. You're a great woman, but great women don't hang out with losers like me. I'd better say goodbye now."

"You beat the daylights out of my ex-husband and you did it for me. No one ever did that. He would have had their skin peeled off."

When people are in depression? Don't use painful or ugly images. They're like drops of acid on the soul.

"How about cooling down the rhetoric, Miss Clara?"

She dabbed at the black eye her ex had given her, like she had a lash in it. There was always something photographic about her, as though once again she had taken over the entirety of a silent movie screen. "My director is here. I want him to meet you."

"I'm sorry, I have to go."

"May I use your bathroom?" she said.

"Keep going downtown. There're plenty of them."

"I'm about to wet my pants."

I stepped out on the porch. I couldn't believe this was happening. People on the driveway were looking at us. "Go inside, Miss Clara. I'll stay out here."

"Suit yourself," she replied.

A few minutes later I heard her flush, then she walked back out, wiping her hands with a paper towel, then looking for a place to throw it. What's the term for that? High maintenance? No end to it? Yeah, that's it.

"I want to do something for you," she said. "But I'm also going to prove to you that you're a natural talent. It's all over you. You don't have to work for it. You know what my friend Burt Reynolds said? 'Why grow up when you can make movies?' You know what your secret is, Mr. Purcel? You love movies with a passion, and you think people who don't love them are nerds."

"Nope, I don't call people nerds and my only talent is falling down stairs and things like that. You've got class, no doubt about it. But I gotta go."

Then I closed and bolted the door and turned on the television set and showered and shaved and dressed and drove to Dave's house on East Main, hoping not to see her car in my rearview mirror.

"You got the Furies behind you?" Dave said when he opened his front door.

"Nope, just Clara Bow," I said, getting inside his house as fast as I could.

# # #

I told him about my conversation with her and about my trip to New Orleans. We were in the kitchen, with me at the table, wired to the eyes, my hands knotted in my lap.

"You saw Gracie Lamar leaning against a lamppost on a street that looked like Arles?" he said.

"Yeah," I replied.

"Maybe you had a dream. Or maybe she was actually there."

"She said she wasn't."

"That's what *she* said. How much do we know about her, anyway? You just found out that she and Samuel Hawthorne used to be close."

Notice the care in Dave's word choice. That was Dave, always looking out for my feelings.

"I'm more worried about Clara Bow's overture," he went on. "She seems not to understand what the word 'no' means. You're done with her, right?"

"Yeah, that's what I told her."

He was sitting across from me, relaxed, his hand on his coffee cup, staring out the window at the pecan and oak trees in the backyard, the sun winking on the bayou. "I think she'll have another run at you."

"Let her."

He scratched the back of his neck.

"Will you stop that?" I said.

"Come on, Clete. You've got a big heart. But you keep getting hurt."

"Well, maybe I've learned."

He nodded again. "That could be."

"You're not convinced?"

"What can I say, Cletus? You're the best," he said. He made a quiet groan under his breath. "It's Saturday," he said. "Let's catch some fish."

# # #

On Sunday night I got a call from Gracie Lamar. I was on a hard-line in my cottage, and another storm had just hit the area. "I can hardly hear you," I said.

She said something, but it was eaten by the static.

"Sorry, Gracie. Maybe you should call back later," I said.

"No," she said. "Can't take it anymore."

"What?"

Then I got another earful of static.

"Repeat what you said, Gracie. Can't take what?"

". . . don't know how long . . ."

If she wanted to scare me to death, she was about to do it.

"I can't hear you!" I shouted. "But whatever you're doing, stop it!"

The line went dead. Is there anything worse than half of an emergency call? Why didn't I use my cell phone, you ask? Many times they didn't work in the wetlands. I often wanted to run over them with a truck. I went out on the four-lane and used the pay phone at a gas station. Gracie picked up.

"Tell me what this is about!" I yelled.

"I couldn't take my job anymore! I feel like a piece of meat hanging on a hook! Yuck! I kicked the owner in the crotch to make sure I couldn't go back."

"Well, I guess that's one way to handle things."

The thunder had reduced to a rumble; the static was gone from the line.

"But I'm fucked on money," she said. "I want to pay you what I owe."

"That's no problem. And would you watch your language? You're better than that."

"I know you're paying for the hospitalization of your temp, what's-her-name."

"Miss Sally."

"I know you don't have that kind of money. So I'm taking a really good job, actually quite an upgrade for me."

I was starting to have bad intuitions. "What are you talking about, kiddo?"

"Call me kiddo again and I'll kick you in the same place I did my recent employer."

"Who is giving you this new job?"

"Clara Bow. She's making a picture. She said you might be in it."

The wind outside the filling station was probably blowing over sixty miles an hour. A garbage can was skidding and bouncing down the asphalt on the highway. The lanes were empty, the sugarcane in the fields flattening, the sky black.

"You're taking Chen with you, aren't you?" I said.

"I'm not taking anybody anywhere. She thought you'd be happy about it."

"What about Miss Dorothy? Did she get an offer, too?"

"Yes, she did. She turned it down. She didn't want to leave New Orleans."

"Why didn't you talk to me first?" I said.

"I don't have to consult with you about my employment, Clete."

"I guess you make a point. But maybe Clara Bow isn't what you think she is."

"She's not a criminal."

"The IRS might disagree," I said.

"Okay, I'll restate that. She's not a killer."

"Yeah, but what *is* she? If you find out, let me know."

She started to say something, then I heard the receiver clatter in the phone cradle and the connection go dead.

Things were not working out.

# # #

At 7:15 Monday morning I asked Dave to meet me at Victor's. The street was bright and damp and strewn with twigs from the storm. He was there in ten minutes, silhouetted against the glare inside the front door. He walked toward my table, a question mark in the middle of his face. He sat down and looked around, not speaking.

"You're not having any coffee?" he said.

"I was waiting on you."

"When did you start doing that?"

"Today," I replied.

"What's goin' on, Cletus?"

"I got the dry shakes. My teeth are clicking."

"You have anything to drink last night?"

"No, I did not."

"Something happened though, didn't it?"

"Clara Bow gave jobs to Gracie Lamar and Chen."

Dave looked at the people eating at other tables. His face was tan; there was no light in it, nor any in his eyes. It made me feel funny.

"What kind of jobs?" he said.

"She didn't say. She said the money was good."

"Does that sound like Chen?"

"No, it sounds like shit," I said.

"Let's get something to eat, then talk."

"Why did Gracie do this?" I asked.

"Maybe this is the best and worst of times and she's trying things out."

"Meaning what?" I asked.

"Maybe half the population shouldn't be allowed to vote," he said.

Dave can be a little unoptimistic on occasion.

# # #

After breakfast I visited Miss Sally. Her doctor believed she might go home in eight or ten days. The doctor said the visits of a young Frenchwoman seemed to work wonders in Miss Sally's recovery. "Do you have this woman's name, Doc?" I asked.

"I don't remember," he said. "You might check at the nurses' station."

"What does she look like?" I asked.

"Nineteen or twenty. Attractive. Hair like it was cut with a bowl. Anyone you know?"

"Yeah, Joan of Arc."

"Is that supposed to be cute?" he said.

"You can't ever tell, Doc. What kind of day care is Miss Sally gonna need?"

"I hope she has Medicaid."

On the way out, I stopped at the nurses' station and asked about the young Frenchwoman. The nurse had no memory of anyone who fit her description. "What was her name?"

"Don't worry about it," I said. "Thanks."

# # #

I know I was acting crazy. I couldn't help it, though. What really bothered me was my belief that Joan had saved my life when she took out Ink Man at Henderson Swamp. Joan never killed anyone, even though she carried a sword and a flag and was in the midst of all the battles she fought. Nothing made sense anymore. I felt I was coming to pieces. That night, long after I fell asleep, I got a phone call of a kind I had never received before. It flat tore me up.

CHAPTER TWENTY-SEVEN

The call was from Chen. She left a voicemail message, and this is what she said:

"I must go with Gracie, Mr. Clete. I know you want me stay, but I cannot live on your charity. I clean of drugs now and nothing can make me put them in my body again. Someday I maybe can do great thing to repay you, not with just money but the love we should show all people who in need. I never know a man like you. You strong but kind at same time. But you give yourself no credit for that, and it make you hurt yourself for things you haven't done.

"I love you, Mr. Clete. If I have my choice, I would stay with you until you told me to go. But I not like other woman. I cannot have baby because pirates captured me and when they let me go, I was not same.

"I know sometime we will see each other again. Miss Clara said you can play Confederate colonel in movie story. That would be fun if that true. You always fun, Mr. Clete. I have to go now.

"I feel sad. You are like the sunshine in my life. You did not know this, but each morning I sketched you with my pencil and pad while you sleep. It made me feel good because your face look like little boy's. You don't belong in any wars. You the man to stop them before they start."

I sat on the side of my bed and listened to her message three times, then beat my fists on my thighs and flung an empty beer mug into the wall and became possessed by the same sick feeling I had when I learned my grandniece had died from a fentanyl overdose, like my soul had the flu and I would never get rid of it.

# # #

I called the Louisiana Film Commission and got all the information I could about the production of a film titled *Flags on the Bayou*. It was set in the year 1863 and involved a story about two slave women and a Confederate soldier who had the same name as the bishop who sent Joan of Arc to the stake. His name was Pierre Cauchon. That sent me a chill. I couldn't keep history separate from the present. Reality felt like wet tissue in my hands. I felt the same way when I got back from Southeast Asia. I stayed stoned and zoned at the navy hospital, and sat all day in a wheelchair on a sunny porch that overlooked a bay where I swore I saw laughing baby whales playing with their mother.

The guys in the other chairs said there were no whales in the bay. In fact, they said the "bay" I watched each day was a parking lot. So I told my nurse to ease up on the flack juice, and she kindly explained to me that my drugs had been reduced to nothing three weeks previously. She also squeezed my hand and tried to smile, but I saw the pity in her eyes.

A friend at the film commission told me of three places where I might find the movie crew that particular day. Louisiana, like Georgia, wised up and gave big tax breaks and incentives to Hollywood productions and brought lots of production money and tourism to the state. The problem in Louisiana, however, was the weather and the tropical environment. Being in New Orleans is like walking around on a wet sponge. If you stand or sit outside too long, you will sink into the ground or be eaten alive by the mosquitoes. The humidity makes you feel like you're wearing sackcloth. A waterspout can skip onto the land and leave the set a wreck.

Anyway, I asked my friend at the Louisiana Film Commission if he knew Clara Bow personally.

"Yeah," he said.

I waited for him to go on. But he didn't.

"What's the deal?" I said.

"Takes all kinds to make a world," he replied. "Have a good one, Clete, and watch your butt."

# # #

I drove to three different locations. Another storm was brewing in the Gulf, and nobody from the film industry was there. All of this was costing me. I don't mean to sound mercenary, but I was broke. No, that's not the word. I was busted. I knew that Dave would give me everything he had, but he was not a rich man. No honest cop is. If you were rich, would you work on a garbage truck?

At the end of the day I was worn out and went over to Dave's place and got in the hammock in his backyard and went to sleep. His cat named Snuggs slept on my stomach. For whatever reason, he decided to sharpen his claws by digging them into my privates. I spun out of the hammock and landed on my face. I woke up not knowing where or who I was.

Thanks for the memory, Snuggs, I thought.

But what was my real problem? I'll tell you. I knew something bad was coming down the track. There's an emotion that therapists don't have a name for, at least not exactly. The closest they get is "psychoneurotic anxiety." That means you're sweating ball bearings and are about to blow your gaskets, except there's no actual danger at hand. The kind of anxiety I'm talking about is warranted. Imagine yourself on a night trail, one that's strewn with Chinese toe-poppers and booby-trapped 105 duds, or the real trickster, a Bouncing Betty, one that's engineered to take you off at the waist.

Every leaf, every root, every water-dripping frond is your enemy. With each breath you take, you are convinced the next one will come with a *klatch* that will end your life. You hold your rifle so tightly your knuckles glow like bones with streaks of blood in them.

That's what I felt in Dave's backyard. We were about to run out our string, and the people who would kill us would keep killing and killing and killing. Does this sound like a mania? It might have been. But look around you. How much madness do you see in the streets of America? Maybe you see none. Or maybe you see it aborning. But I see it everywhere. Maybe the problem is me.

I heard Dave's truck come into the driveway. I got up and walked up to greet him. I don't think I ever felt so glad to see him.

"Hey, Cletus, come have a diet Doc with me," he said.

I think that was the best diet Dr Pepper I ever drank.

# # #

We watched a baseball game in his living room that evening. I don't remember the teams. I just wanted to watch a game and see the excitement of the crowd and the players, who were more like boys than adults. A baseball stadium is always a happy place, with no anger among the spectators; it's a celebration of our country, the one that rebuilt the countries of its enemies, knowing if the Axis had won the war, searchlights and barbed wire and crematoriums would have been strung from sea to shining sea.

Enough.

Aside from my finances, here was my dilemma. We were dealing with a handful of people. Only one of them had real power, and that was Lauren Bow, and that was because he had money. But real power lies in government and politics. So far the only political move Lauren Bow had made was with a group called the New Rising. In my lifetime I had seen numerous groups come and go. Their names change, but their membership remains the same—people who feel they have been left out. They blame immigrants and women and gay people and Jews and Blacks and anyone else they can pick on. Needless to say, most of them are not bright and get chewed up and spat out by the rich people who exploit them.

Again, enough. My problem was my depression and the lowlifes who had been sicced on me and my friends. Somebody wanted to get his hands on a lethal chemical called Leprechaun in order to take over the world. And no one except a very small group of people seemed to care. When I thought about that, I felt I had a hole in my chest the size of a pie plate.

I guess the big question was simple. Who was leading these people? Lauren Bow was certainly a candidate. He was a militarist and a con man and a misogynist, the kind of guy who never lets you know what he's thinking. But he was also in the crosshairs of the IRS and would not like more publicity than he had already earned.

No, it had to be someone who was intelligent, devious, sociopathic, and cruel, someone you can't remember five minutes after he or she walks out of a room. Think about it. Have you ever seen photographs of Hitler before he bought a pair of elevated shoes and a coat with pads in the shoulders? How about Mussolini? His lips looked like a plumber's helper. Check out Lenin. He looked like a toilet brush slinging spit at his audience.

That was the way my head was thinking. It's the way suspicion and depression work. Everyone becomes an enemy. The most unlikely people seem to reconfigure their faces; yesterday's friends become sources of fear. As I write these words, I feel like someone has scratched a kitchen match on my soul.

Why had Gracie left the apartment, a place that had become a home for her and Chen and me? And what about Chen? She was hardly off the needle. That sounds coarse. But there's nothing polite about the skag culture. The people who run it are not human, and the bigger they are, the more they stay on the street.

I felt like I had a strand of piano wire wrapped around my head, with a stick in it that someone was twisting. It's called "hatband syndrome." You feel like you're wearing a hat canted on the side of your head all the time. The anxiety can be unbearable. In my case, I began to believe someone was out there on the bayou, aiming through a scope on a sniper's rifle, about to drill a hole in Dave's forehead or mine. That's how Bed Check Charlie kept us sleepless in Shitsville. It's very effective. You go crazy after a while and do things you shouldn't.

I slept on Dave's couch, with an electric fan blowing, then in the early dawn went to my motel and promised myself to do all I could for my country and myself and finally the world, and to try not to be bothered by the shadows of the heart, as Dave calls them. It's not that simple, though, and Dave knows it, but sometimes you got to fake it until you make it. In the meantime, you might find another wayfaring stranger on the pike who'll help you carry your load, although there are not many of them.

CHAPTER TWENTY-EIGHT

That night I went over to Dave's house again, this time with my own folding chair, and in the sunset sat down under a live oak on the edge of Bayou Teche. I didn't know where Dave was, but it didn't matter. I wanted to be there at that special moment when the sky lights with a special kind of flame, one that issues from the rim of the Earth and trails curds of purple-and-red smoke to the top of the heavens. It made me think of *Gone with the Wind*, when Tara is set afire and an era is burned to the ground.

It was a strange feeling to have. I felt something glorious was happening, but at the same time I was sickened by the cruelty of slavery and the arrogance of a class who slept under mosquito netting while Black people thirty yards away suffered in cabins with no window glass. I never understood how the rich lived with themselves, or why I still admired the boys in butternut who went up Cemetery Ridge.

Not five feet away from me was the gnarled head of a gator protruding through the Japanese water hyacinths, the lavender flowers in full bloom. Gators hang either in the current or under the hyacinths to catch turtles or raccoons. It's the latter that they hate, because out of every six eggs a gator lays, raccoons eat four. I can understand their dissatisfaction with raccoons, but nonetheless I threw a stick at the gator, and he dove deeper under the flowers, ripping them apart with his tail, splashing water on the bank.

Then I saw a pirogue that was sunken under the surface. It was old, green, and soft with lichen, bubbles rising from its bow and stern, as though it had just gone under. But I had never seen it before. Where did the air come from? I was wearing my slip-on half-tops, so I stepped down into the shallows, trying not to cloud the water with silt. A blue heron was watching me from ten feet away, then it suddenly lifted up and flew low across the water into the red brilliance of the sun.

My heart began to beat, but I didn't know why. Bayou Teche had a notorious history: disease and cannibalism among the Atakapa, slaves brought illegally up the bayou by Jean Lafitte and James Bowie, the invasion of Union gunboats in 1863, the public hanging of slaves, and a white man who tried to escape to the North.

Fireflies were lighting in the trees like flashes of burning string that sparked once and turned to ash. The wind came up and fluttered the water's surface and I felt a solitary raindrop strike my face. I reached down and touched the side of the pirogue, then lowered my hand and slid it down the furry lichen shell that seemed to cover the boat. I was up to my thighs in the water now, and clouds of silt were rising around me, so I could no longer see my arm. But I knew one thing. This was not a pirogue.

I stood up straight and felt my way along the boat's side, then went deeper into the current. My knee knocked something that was hard, not wood either, maybe metal that was rough or coated with rust. Was it an oarlock? I pulled on it, but it was secured to the bow, maybe a ring of some kind. Then I felt farther along the boat's side and counted three rings in a row. I jerked on each and got nowhere. I raised my hand to the surface. My palm was orange with a crusty stripe that looked layered on my skin. I knew what the rings were. They were not steel; they were iron. And the boat was not contemporary; it was from the Middle Ages, used by French sappers. I had seen them in a museum in France and in pictorial re-creations of battles on the Seine.

I waded back up the bank, my half-tops sloshing with mud and water. I sat down heavily on my folding chair, almost crushing it, and wondered what I had walked into. Had I finally found the door in the dimension I had secretly sought all these years with booze and weed? That boat was not there before today, and I was not imagining the objects I had just touched. Objects exist or they don't exist. Or maybe they can exist in a different medium. I didn't know then, and I don't know now.

The shadows in the trees were purple now, the sky still aflame. I saw someone beckon me. No, that's not right. I *felt something* beckon me, a puff of warm air, a rivulet of sweat running out of my hair, a whisper tickling the inside of my ear. A mist or fog settled on the bayou. Then I heard a voice.

Don't be afraid. It's not your time.

I got up from my chair, stumbling, ready to fight.

She was standing on the water, chains wrapped around her body. *I was betrayed and died at the stake. Nothing is worse. Others will turn against you, too. So you must beware and you must be brave. You must also act now.*

"Act where?"

Wherever you hear their crooked tongues talk to you. Your vulnerability lies in your willingness to believe people who take what is best in you and turn it against you. You're a dreamer, Clete, and your friend David is a poet. The consequence is that you may end up face down on your shield, a symbol for the ages but of no value to your cause.

"What is my cause?"

The same as that of the true knight-errant—justice and charity and a voice for those who have none.

"Miss Joan?"

She smiled. *No one has ever called me that.*

"I get real sad when I think about what was done to you."

I'm with you now, so let's not think about the past.

"I don't know where to start, Miss Joan. I feel like somebody has got a gun aimed at me all day, and I have no idea where my enemies are or who's leading them."

Stay silent when they expect you to speak. Yawn at their rages. Turn yourself into a mystery. Never bargain or argue. Smile if one of them strikes you. His anger will turn upon him.

"You carried only a flag, not a sword?"

Yes, but don't you try that.

"You make me smile, even in the midst of all this trouble."

Then maybe I did something right. I have to go now. Don't trust everything you see or the words of Occidentals who speak like swamis.

"Say again?"

Goodbye, Sir Clete.

"Sir Clete? That makes all my bells ring. Don't go away, Miss Joan. It wasn't you who killed that guy in Henderson Swamp and saved my life, was it?"

She said no, moving her lips without sound, then was gone in a blink, the fog and the mist as well.

# # #

Normally I'd get drunk after an experience like this, but I didn't. Neither did I tell Dave or Helen about the apparition out on the bayou behind Dave's backyard. Nor did I tell them about the disappearance of the boat, either. Because that's what happened. The following day I stood on the bank and looked at my own boot tracks and poked a boat oar beneath the water all around the area where the ancient boat had been submerged. It wasn't there.

Several days went by, and early on Tuesday I borrowed money from the bank and moved Miss Sally back to her home and hired a couple of Black ladies to help care for her. There are real weirded-out attitudes about whites and people of color in the American South. The worst bigots will not hire white people to care for their children, or clean their houses, or care for their family members. Ask them why, and they will say something like this, and I mean again and again: "White people will steal from you. They ain't no good with old folks or sick people, either. Where the hell you been, boy?"

In the meantime I had heard nothing from Gracie Lamar or Chen. I went into my file drawer and dug out Clara Bow's cell phone number and dialed it. She picked it up on the first ring.

"Hello, Miss Clara," I said. "This is Clete. I wondered how your film production was getting along."

"Why should you care?" she said.

"I could use an extra job."

"You could also use a heart," she replied. "You certainly did enough damage to mine. You barely let me use your bathroom. What did I do to deserve that?"

I remembered Joan's warning about crooked tongues. "I haven't heard much from Gracie and Chen. Are they actually going to get roles?"

"Who?"

"Gracie Lamar and an Asian lady named Chen."

"I never heard of them."

I felt an icicle slide through my insides. "You hired them."

"I most certainly did not. Are you drunk? You should go to church or something."

She hung up.

# # #

I drove straight to the Iberia Parish Sheriff's Department and parked a few yards from the reflecting pond. It was a grand day, with a hint of fall in the air, the sun shining through all the live oaks and the Spanish moss, the grotto dedicated to the mother of Jesus in shadow, the wind rattling the bamboo along the driveway. Two plainclothes detectives came out on the porch of the department. One stopped to light a cigarette with a book of matches, the smoke rising from his cupped hands. One of my Black female clients claimed he sexually extorted her. He was also the same guy Dave hooked in the face, which caused Dave a temporary suspension.

"Your pimpmobile is in the red zone, Purcel," he said.

"No kidding?" I said, and snapped a forefinger in the air. "Remind me of that the next time I come here. Hey, you still rolling crippled newsies?"

"One of these days, Purcel."

"Yeah, I know," I replied. "In the meantime, eat shit."

I walked past them into the building and went upstairs and tapped on Dave's door. He was on the phone and waved me in. I stood by the window and watched a steel boat on its way to the Gulf of Mexico. I wondered what these guys would think about all the people who had preceded them. My guess was they would not be too interested.

Dave got off the phone. "Glad you came in," he said. "That was my neighbor."

"Yeah?"

"She had left a note under my door I hadn't seen."

"So?"

"She said a few nights ago you were wading in the bayou behind my house, and talking to somebody. She was a little worried, because she likes you."

"Yeah, I talked to the lady from fifteenth-century France," I said.

He pressed his thumb and his fingers on his temples. "You've got to get out of this, Clete."

"I came here because I called Clara Bow and asked how Gracie Lamar and Chen were getting along," I said. "She denied knowing them."

Dave stiffened his arms on his knees. "Oh, boy," he said.

"It's a crock, all right. But I think it's gonna get worse."

"Why?"

"I don't know. It's eating me alive. The things Joan told me are eating me alive."

"Let's keep the last part of that out, okay? No more pronouncements from medieval times."

Before I could answer, Dave's private line lit up. It was Wally, the candy-bar-addict dispatcher. Dave listened, nodded, then hung up. "Dooley LeMay called the wrecker service on your vehicle."

Dooley was the plainclothes who called my Caddy a pimp-mobile and who Dave punched in the face.

"I'd better get rolling," I said. "Meet you at noon at your house, okay?"

"You got it."

Dave never let me down. You've heard the "November Song," right? About the days dwindling down to a precious few? That song makes you think about your family and your friends. They're the only valuable things we own. The rest of it is like the ashes and the blackened pillars at Tara; they're worth nothing. Right or wrong?

CHAPTER TWENTY-NINE

When I arrived at Dave's house at 12:03, his truck was gone and the house was locked. A box of food was on the small front porch, a receipt from Victor's taped on the cardboard. I put my hand on one of the sacks and felt the greasy heat in the paper. Dave had ordered ham and onion sandwiches, a special treat he had taught the cook at Victor's to make. If there is a better sandwich on the planet, I've yet to eat it. Ask anybody.

I waited twenty-five minutes, then gave up. I picked up the box and carried it to the backyard and stuck it inside the rabbit hutch, The door on the hutch was never latched, unless for an emergency, like one of Snuggs's brawls with the cat next door. I started to leave, then smelled those sandwiches. I couldn't resist. I unwrapped one and sat on the back step and bit into the French bread and the sliced onions and ham and tomatoes and mayonnaise and sauce piquante, and almost fainted at how good it was. Let's face it. We're talking about food that some people consider orgasmic.

But where was Dave? I folded the paper around the sandwich and put it back in the box. Then I stood up. I felt like one leg was two feet shorter than the other one. I fell sideways into Dave's caladiums. The trees had turned red and orange, the colors themselves pulsing, and an aluminum tunnel had opened up through the trees, across the bayou, and into City Park. I saw hundreds of people sliding down the tunnel, children and women and men, crying out for help, their fingernails scratching across the aluminum. At the bottom of the tunnel was the worst place in the history of the world, a chain of extermination camps.

I didn't want to see it. I dug at my eyes; I crawled on my hands and knees; I pounded on the ground with my fists. I had seen the Jews in their agony. The cruelty of it was beyond comprehension. I felt that my brain was bleeding.

I rolled up in a ball and was weeping when Dave Robicheaux found me. He knocked me down when I tried to get up, and threw water on me with a bucket and hose, then fought me up the steps and into the kitchen and pinned me to the floor and leaned into my face, yelling, "It's me, Clete! You're on acid! Listen up, gunny! Nothing you're seeing is real! You're on a trip! We'll nail the guys who did this! We're the Bobbsey Twins from Homicide."

Suddenly it all went away, as though as I were waking from a dream, the kind you have when the days dwindle down to a precious few.

"Hey, Streak," I said, my voice as weak as water. "What's the haps, noble mon?"

# # #

Whoever put the doped sandwiches on Dave's porch was slick. The receipt was probably stolen from an order pad or off the glass counter at Victor's, the sandwiches made somewhere else. But let's face it. I acted pretty dumb. If I had eaten any more, I probably would have fried my grits for good. I couldn't get rid of the images I saw in the aluminum tunnel. I guess in some ways I've always been in denial about my fellow man. There's a whole lot about the human family I don't want to know or see. Who does? Oh well, I got a break on this one, and I was determined not to let it happen again.

Dave made me go to Iberia General, and after I got checked out, he said he'd meet me at my cottage at 7:00 p.m. I said that was swell; we'd relax and go to a movie or something. But the big mon was getting into excesses about my judgment and psychological welfare. As you know, it's Dave who has gotten the Bobbsey Twins from Homicide into the most trouble. Yeah, once I dropped a pimp and some porn guys off a tenement roof, but there was a tree down below that broke the fall, and yeah, I poured the liquid-soap dispenser down a guy's throat in the men's room at the casino and fire-hosed him down the hallway, but this is what I call cosmetic stuff. It was nothing like Dave going apeshit in a blackout.

Anyway, at 6:28 p.m. I heard an outboard engine whining down the bayou, like a dentist drill, then making a wide turn, circling into the shallows and reeds that were not far from my window. Dooley LeMay had just cut his engine and was letting his boat slide up on the mudflat, the waves lapping against the trees; then he stepped off the bow onto dry ground.

The clouds were bright red, but in some places full of darkness. Like Tara again. I wondered if this was an omen. Dooley was wearing unironed slacks and blue tennis shoes and a Hawaiian shirt, what we used to call a "goon shirt" in the Corps, and aviator glasses. Actually, Dooley had been in the Crotch. He had a big chest and big arms and was a simpleton on the surface but dangerous when crowded. The kind of guy who should never be given power over people.

A six-pack was hanging from his left hand. Dooley was right-handed. One of those things you don't ignore. I beat him to the door. "What do you want, Dooley?"

"To make amends," he said. He lifted the six-pack so I could see it.

"That's not necessary."

"Maybe not for you."

"No, Dooley. You don't owe me anything."

"Come on, Purcel. I need a break here."

"Break for what? You tried to impound my car."

"I was pissed."

"For what?"

"You treat me like shit."

"That's too bad."

"What'd I do?"

I knew if I told him my Black female client had dimed him, he'd be breaking down her door. "You voted for David Duke."

"You and me go back, Purcel. Maybe not in the best way, but we're both old-school. I got a lot of bills to pay. I need help."

"Sorry, Dooley. I gotta go."

"Clara Bow?" he said. "The broad who's running that movie picture?"

I stopped, my hand resting on the doorknob. I bit down on my lip. It was one of those moments when you cross or don't cross a line. "What about her?"

"She's your client, right? I thought maybe you could get me a what-do-you-call-it—a screen test."

He tried to smile. His mouth reminded me of a glob of discarded chewing gum that had been stepped on.

"She's no longer my client."

"What happened?" he asked.

"None of your business."

"Have a beer with me."

"I quit."

"When?"

"Five minutes ago."

"You know how to hurt a guy, Purcel."

I had never wanted so hard to close the door on a guy. But I had a feeling he knew more about Clara Bow than he let on. Dooley LeMay was a scavenger. Anytime money came to town, Dooley was on it. He and another corrupt cop extorted some local nuns who held a race with plastic ducks on the Teche to raise funds for local hurricane victims. What a guy.

"Dooley, there's a lady who's a friend of Ms. Bow. Her name is Gracie Lamar. Know her?"

The light was dying in the trees, and I couldn't see his eyes well. But they looked like marbles, unblinking, completely dead, and I knew that whatever he said next would be a lie.

"No," he said. "Who is she?"

"A lady I thought could open a door for you."

He shook his head. "Nope, I haven't had the pleasure."

"She travels with an Asian woman named Chen."

"Double zeros on that."

"Good luck to you."

"Yeah, see you around, Purcel. You're a piece of work. I'll leave you my beer. Enjoy."

From behind my window curtain I watched him walk halfway down to the bayou, then stop at a small dock and light a cigarette with a match from a matchbook, then flip the matchbook and the burnt match in the water and unzip his fly and urinate on the lily pads.

I dropped the curtain and tried to get the previous images out of my mind. Dave would be here in a few minutes, I thought, and we'd go to a movie. But I felt responsible for bringing a man like Dooley LeMay onto the property. I got an old, throwaway broom and walked down to the dock and dipped the match cover and burnt match out of the water lilies and carried them to a trash barrel on the driveway. The light was much better here than down in the trees, but I wasn't thinking about the trash; I just wanted to get rid of it, just like I wanted to get rid of a gutter rat of a plainclothes like Dooley LeMay. I tapped the broom handle on the rim of the barrel and watched the paper match and matchbook drop inside. Then I saw the name that was printed on the matchbook just as Dave's pickup turned onto the driveway. Dave stuck his head out the window. "You ready for a movie?" he said.

"Take a look at this," I said.

"What?"

"No, get out of your truck. I think some of that acid is still in my brain."

He pulled off on the lawn and walked to the trash barrel. "What?"

"Dooley LeMay just left. Don't put your hand on that matchbook. After he lit his cigarette, he pissed on it."

Dave looked down into the barrel. The tan went out of his face. "Eddy's Car Wash," he said.

"The one and only. Where every bit of this started."

"Dooley's in on it?"

"Earlier he tried to get my Caddy towed because I parked in the red zone at the department. At least that's what I thought."

Dave's eyes had not blinked, but I knew his thoughts were on overdrive.

"Are you thinking what I'm thinking?" I said.

"Maybe the stash, or Leprechaun or whatever it is, has been in your Caddy all this time?"

"That's a possibility," I said.

There was no doubt Dave knew what I was thinking: I didn't want to gut my Eldorado just because I was suspicious of a throwback like Dooley LeMay.

"Instead of vandalizing your own car, which has already been done by Ink Man and his friends, why don't we turn things around on these guys?" he said.

"What if the stash or whatever is in there?" I said.

"You haven't gotten sick so far, have you?"

"Yeah, but how about you? You're always scratching yourself."

"I've got some poison ivy," he said.

I put a stick of gum in my mouth. "How do you want to play it?"

"First we need some help. I don't think many people take us serious."

"When did they ever?"

"Let's go to a movie and start over in the morning," he said.

Then that's what we did. At the Evangeline, remodeled as a theater in 1929. Then we went to an ice cream parlor and then we took a drive. There was a big orange moon above the oaks on the bayou; it looked like it was hovering right over the Earth. Soon the sugarcane would be harvested, nubbed down to the ground, the stubble set on fire, and tractors would pull big steel wagons full of it to the mill, lining the asphalt with strips of gumbo mud that would harden into concrete, the air filled with smoke and threadlike black ash and a smell that was like syrup spilled on a woodstove.

For whatever reason, these moments under the orange moon and the thought of creaking loads of heaped cane and the shadowy faces of the tractor drivers made me uncomfortable, but I did not know why. I think the clinical depression that got into my head was holding on for the long haul.

# # #

Dave and I had an early breakfast at Victor's, then went to his office at 7:56. He told me to take a seat, then punched in a number on his landline. "Detective Dave Robicheaux for Federal Agent Samuel Hawthorne," he said.

In three minutes Hawthorne was on the phone. Dave hit a button and turned on the speaker phone. "Clete Purcel is with me, Agent Hawthorne," he said.

"Good! How you doing, Clete?" Hawthorne said.

"Okay," I said. "But as Dave will tell you, we've run into some real dog shit down here and we need some backup."

"I understand," he said.

"I don't think you do," I said. I didn't mean to get out ahead of Streak, but I was still a little fried from the acid and I was tired of being everybody's punch. "We need some technology here. We also need access to information we think you guys are not sharing."

"Sorry you feel that way, Clete," Hawthorne said.

"My feelings are not relevant," I replied. "Having somebody spike my food with LSD is. You know where Gracie Lamar is?"

"No, why?"

"She's gone missing," Dave interrupted. He was obviously trying to make me slow down.

"Is Gracie in trouble?" Hawthorne asked.

"Maybe," I said. "Why didn't you tell us you had a relationship?"

"You're over the line, bub," Hawthorne said.

"Too bad," I said. "What did you guys do with Ink Man's remains?"

"Up the stack, and that's all I'll say," he replied.

I looked at Dave and shook my head.

"Agent Hawthorne, we have a couple of leads," Dave said. "We'll get back to you."

"What leads?" Hawthorne said.

"I think you'll find them interesting," Dave said. "We'll call you later."

"Now, hold on a minute."

Dave eased the phone into the cradle.

"You know how to do it, Streak," I said.

"Who, me?" he said.

# # #

Dooley owned half a poolroom on the edge of the Black district in St. Martinville, ten miles up the Teche. I think he enjoyed being a star, a plainclothes floating around the tables, cuing up himself, squeaking the chalk, loaning money, being on a first-name basis with badass Blacks who had done heavy time in Angola, and earning what he called "reciprocity" with them.

That evening I put the top down on the Eldorado, and Dave and I cruised on into sleepy St. Martinville and parked at the curb in front of the poolroom and went inside. Not one person stopped what he was doing or even glanced at us, but every one of them saw us. Dave went to the bar and put one foot on the rail and one hand on the counter and said to the Black bartender, "How you doin'? Tell Mr. Dooley Dave and Clete would like to see him, please."

"They ain't no 'misters' in here, but I'll get him," he said.

That's what real animosity is about.

Dooley came out from the back wearing shades, with a plastic straw in the corner of his mouth. I didn't look at his right ankle, but I knew a throw-down was strapped under the cuff of his trousers. He looked at Dave first, then at me, then back at Dave. "What's happening, Robo?" he said. "You, too, Purcel. I got no grief with you guys. Wanna shoot some pool? It's on the house. Drinks, too."

"Thanks," Dave said. "We're just cruising around."

"Yeah, in my Eldorado," I said. "Wanna take a spin?"

"I got obligations," Dooley replied.

"So relax," I said. "You can get behind the wheel if you want. Bring along your girlfriends."

"You kidding? I'm too old."

He wasn't, though. He was powerful and smelled of masculinity. He twisted a crick out of his neck.

"Did you know somebody tried to poison Clete?" Dave asked.

"Poison?" Dooley replied. "No."

"I can't figure who would do that," I said.

"You destroy houses like other people crush potato chips," he said.

"Clete had his Caddy detailed at Eddy's Car Wash, across from New Orleans in Algiers," Dave said.

"And?" Dooley said.

"You ever go there?" Dave said.

"Yeah, once or twice, when I was in New Orleans. What about it?"

Dooley was a good actor. He should have applied for a job with Clara Bow. Or maybe he already had.

"Ride with me in my Caddy, Dooley," I said. "We'll leave Streak here. He doesn't mind."

"Why you got this obsession about me and your car?"

"That's what I want to explain to you," I said.

"All right, I got it. We'll go down to the Square. But you ought to look into some therapy or health club kind of shit."

I dropped my keys in his palm. It was hard to do that. But as the greaseballs say, what are you gonna do?

# # #

We motored on up to the Square, with Dooley behind the wheel, his plastic straw still in his mouth. He pulled into the small cemetery by the Evangeline Oak, supposedly the place where every day she mourned for the loss of her lover. The moon's reflection was wobbling on the bayou, the elephant ears like a long green carpet floating on the current. Dooley cut the engine. "So what's the gig?" he said.

"You were in the Corps, right?"

"Yeah."

"Did Lauren Bow try to sign you up with his militia group?"

"Maybe."

"The one called the New Rising?"

"Maybe."

"So what'd you tell him?"

"I told him they were shitbirds."

I knew he was lying. He never offended a power figure in his life, particularly a power figure racist. "Good for you. You nervous about something?" I said.

"What are you talking about?"

"Your foot is jiggering, like it's gonna come off your ankle," I replied.

"It's a habit I got."

"Your throw-down is showing."

"I'm getting kind of tired of this, Purcel."

"You like my wheels?"

"Why you giving me all this shit about cars?"

"Somebody tried to scramble my eggs with LSD, Dooley. Whoever did it probably killed thousands of brain cells in my head. The thought of that is hard to deal with."

His right hand was opening and closing on the steering wheel. A black pickup truck had pulled into an alcove where there was a picnic table and benches. The driver cut his engine and headlights. No one got out of the truck. Dooley took the plastic straw out of his mouth and wiped his nose with the back of his wrist.

"Why do you carry a straw around?" I said. "You're not doing lines, are you?"

"No. What's the matter with you?" he said. "It's because of that movie *Bonnie and Clyde*. Clyde was always twitching that matchstick up and down in his mouth. I thought that was pretty cool."

"Yeah," I said. "I remember you always liked movies."

"Let's call it quits on all this, huh?"

"On all this what?" I said.

"You know, go back to the old days. Guys drinking beer and watching baseball and barbecuing and stuff like that. Meeting a broad here and there."

I nodded. "Why are you rattling, Dooley?"

"What do you mean, 'rattling'? I don't rattle."

"Sorry, I misread you," I said. "Let's beat feet. Want me to drive?"

"What, I don't look like I can drive your car now?"

"Be my guest," I said.

I thought he was going to have a nervous breakdown.

CHAPTER THIRTY

Samuel Hawthorne was in New Iberia the following day. I wanted to believe more Feds were with him, but I doubted it. He talked with Dave and me about Dave's "leads," and discovered Dave's leads were close to zero. But he didn't seem to mind. I think he was a pretty good guy and maybe humping a ninety-pound pack for a whole bunch of other guys.

The worst of all this was the disappearance of Chen and Gracie. Thinking about them in the hands of the New Rising group gave me the flip-flops. I've worked PI cases with parents whose children were stolen by strangers in a store or playground, and for years they never learned what happened to them. I've never seen so much agony in human beings. My pain wasn't as much as theirs, but I think it might have been close, particularly when it came to poor Chen, who was so innocent in her ways, even though she was an intravenous addict.

Hey, I've been thinking about something regarding the people who believed we were dealing with something of an apocalyptic nature, if that's not too strong a term. The group was Samuel Hawthorne, Dave Robicheaux, Gracie Lamar, Helen Soileau, and me. I put Helen in there because she kept covering up for Dave and me, instead of having us sent to Angola, which a lot of people wanted to happen.

Know what we had in common?

We descended from people who had left their mark on the innocent. Hawthorne's ancestor hanged witches and piled stones on their chests; Dave's great-grandfather was at Chambersburg, where Lee let the graybacks kidnap freeborn colored people and send them to the auction block in Richmond; Gracie told me she was related to Mirabeau B. Lamar, the president of the Texas Republic who exterminated the Indians; and me, whose Irish family came over on the coffin ships and who drowned hundreds of colored people in their basement homes in 1863 in protest against the draft.

Helen Soileau?

Her ancestral family didn't seem connected with anything that was wrong. Maybe that's why she had several people living inside of her, all of them good. You got me?

Okay, back to the problem with Dooley LeMay and my Caddy and LeMay shaking to pieces when he drove the Caddy to St. Martinville. Was Leprechaun or whatever inside my car or inside the black pickup truck parked by the Evangeline Oak the cause of his bones shaking?

I talked it over with Dave, then we met in City Park with Hawthorne by the playground. "I think I gotta rip it up," I said.

"Your Eldorado?" Hawthorne said.

"Yeah, if that stuff is in there and I don't get it out, I won't be able to live with myself."

"I don't think it's worth it," he said.

"You don't?" Dave said.

"The guys who initially tore it up knew what they were looking for," Hawthorne said. "They didn't find it. Maybe someone else already got it. Or maybe it was never there and they had bad information."

"That's kind of a relaxed attitude on the subject, don't you think?" I said to him.

"There's another way of looking at it, Mr. Purcel," he said. "If it's still in your vehicle, you're probably already dosed."

"Thanks for telling me that," I said. "That really fills out my day."

"Have y'all got anything on Dooley LeMay?" Dave asked.

"Nothing," Hawthorne said.

Hawthorne was sitting in a swing, and kept fidgeting, like his mind was somewhere else.

"You want to tell us something?" I asked.

"Yeah, I think they've got Gracie and the Asian woman."

"The 'Asian woman' is named Chen," I said.

"Yes, sorry," he said. "I'm sure Gracie and Ms. Chen would not leave us in the lurch and with no knowledge of their whereabouts. Right now I would like to shoot the Bow couple."

This was the first time he had personalized the investigation, if I could call it that. For a Fed, who are known as hard-nosed sons of bitches, he was a decent guy.

"What's your perception of Clara Bow?" Dave said.

"She's in love with Hollywood mythology while the real world burns down," Hawthorne said. "She will believe any lie if it fits into her dreams about 1935. She seems to forget that twenty-two million people were out of work back then."

He seemed to have spent a lot of time thinking about Clara Bow.

I heard Dave's cell phone hum in his pocket. He took it out and put it to his ear. "Robicheaux here," he said.

He was looking straight at me as he listened to the caller. "We're on our way," he said, then closed the cell.

I waited for him to speak, but he didn't.

"LeMay?" I said

"Yep," he replied.

# # #

The shooting took place in the back room of an expensive brick home where he lived by himself near the old sugar mill. There were no other houses close by. Soot was everywhere. The offices of his employees were always closed at 5:00 p.m., a solitary bulb burning until dawn over the front door. LeMay seemed to have found the environment that suited his soul.

It took us six and a half minutes to get there. The ambulance was just arriving. A FedEx woman had glanced through the glass in the back door and called 911. She was trembling in the backyard when we pulled into the drive. Her FedEx package was from a fishing shop in Shasta, California, and obviously she did not know what to do with it. She kept walking in circles with it. She seemed to know Dave. I'm glad she did, because whatever she had seen had done its damage.

"I didn't know if I should go in or not," she said when she saw him.

"You did the right thing," Dave said.

"I couldn't have he'ped or nothing, huh?" she asked.

Dave was putting on latex gloves. He looked through the window. "No, you could not have helped, Irma. I give you my word."

He opened the door and went inside. Hawthorne followed. I didn't have legal access, but I went in anyway. A medic with a gurney was behind us. Dave told him to hold it up.

The back room was obviously LeMay's hangout. There was fishing gear stacked in a corner, beat-up shotguns and pistols with taped grips hanging from nails or pegs, all of them one step above junk, weapons that were probably taken during busts and never turned in. A square of tinfoil was spread on his desk, three lines of coke barely disturbed on it, a plastic straw lying next to the foil. LeMay was on his back on the floor. He had been hit three times in the chest, once in the palm, once through the throat, and once through the chin. His blood had already congealed. Ordinarily I would say he went out quickly, but I didn't think that was the case with LeMay.

The coke was undisturbed, which meant he was probably standing when he took the first round. The hole in the palm was defensive, with no angle in it; blood was slung on the side of his desk and on his trousers, and his right trouser leg was pulled up on his throwdown, the grips splattered probably with blood from his hand. I think LeMay went out the hard way. I also think he knew his killer.

Here were my other thoughts, although I didn't say them out loud, because I had no authority in the case. For certain six rounds had been fired, but there was no brass. Under the circumstances, and considering the environment, the shooter would not hunt around for his brass; hence, there was little doubt the murder weapon was a revolver, maybe a .22, since LeMay with his strength and power was able to make a good fight of it.

If I had to make a guess right there, I would have said the shooter was a woman. Why? Don't get mad at me for saying this, but when long-abused women decide to pull the string, which I do not recommend, they do it on the walls.

Dave squatted down next to the body. "What do you think, Clete?" he said.

He forgot to include Hawthorne's name. But we'd worked so long together at NOPD homicide, it was just a natural thing to do. I told him what I just told you.

Dave stood up and blew out his breath but didn't say anything.

"You got a woman in mind, Dave?" Hawthorne said.

"Considering who the victim is, too many to count," Dave replied.

"Why does that sound pretty disingenuous?" Hawthorne said.

"You know I hate polysyllabic words," Dave said.

"Sorry," Hawthorne said. "Does that Post-it on that smear of blood on his shirt mean anything? I think I can make out the word 'union.' Oh, look, there's a ballpoint under the desk. I wonder if he wrote that before or after he was shot. What do y'all think?"

Dave and I looked at each other. We looked dumb. But not really. There was no break-in. The victim knew his killer. However, if LeMay wrote on the Post-it before he died, he chose to write the word "union" rather than the killer's name. Was "union" connected to Leprechaun? LeMay was not a magnanimous man. Was he trying to save his soul rather than lead us to his killer?

"Tell you what, Agent Hawthorne," I said. "Call up your boss and ask him to send a shitload of agents like yourself down here before a few thousand people die."

"You make a point, Mr. Purcel," he said.

I saw a tiny spider crawl across the back of LeMay's hand.

# # #

Dave bagged up every item that would be considered critical evidence and secured the crime scene. Neither of us was ever keen on crime scenes, except for prints and DNA. The truth is most crimes are solved by informers and guesswork and dumb luck. Plus, most criminals are stupid and break into jails rather than out of them. If you wait around long enough, they'll find you, because mostly nobody else wants them.

That said, I couldn't sleep that night because of the Post-it and the word "union." The first thought I had was the Civil War. But what did the War Between the States have to do with a plot to spread a virus, one that has no geographic boundaries? The second thought I had was the labor movement. But today only 12 percent of the work force is union, and most of them are up North, because in the South we like working cheap.

I rolled and tumbled in my bed and thumped my pillow, then sat on the side of the mattress and stared out the window. The moon was behind clouds, but its light somehow was subsumed under the bayou and in the Spanish moss that hung in the live oaks along the bank. The Teche seemed to turn to pewter, some of it tarnished, some as bright as moonlight. I saw Joan standing on the dock, her chains still crisscrossed around her body, their links sunken into the white fabric she was allowed to die in.

I believed the acid had taken on a second life. But acid or not, I wanted to talk to Joan. I wanted to free her from her bonds and ride by her side; I wanted to be as brave as she was, a nineteen-year-old girl who struck fear in the most powerful men in Europe. I put on my robe and my rabbit-ear slippers and stumbled out the door and down the porch steps into the warm night air and the croaking of thousands of tree frogs.

But Joan was gone and another figure had taken her place at the dead end of the driveway. I could not tell if it was a man or a woman. The figure walked over to a boxlike 1930s four-door sedan, stepped up on the running board by the front window, a fedora shadowing its face, and hooked one arm inside. The sedan crept along the asphalt, its headlights on, blinding my eyes.

Somebody behind me hit me with a stun gun, and I went down on my knees like a sack of gravel. The car continued past me as though in slow motion. Chen was in the back seat. A man behind her shoved her against the open window so I could get a clear look at her, then drove a hypodermic into the base of her neck and depressed the plunger.

That's when I blacked out, either from another treatment with the stun gun or from the acid that was still in my brain. As I lay face down on the asphalt, I heard the Sunset Limited blowing down the line, headed for the Grand Canyon and sunny California and palm trees and giant waves crashing on coral caves, where the salt spray looks like a rainbow and is as cool as a woman's fingers on your brow.

# # #

The next day was Saturday, and I was back in the ER. The owner of the motel had found me curled up in a ball and called for an ambulance. Someone had poured liquor in my hair and on my robe and pajamas. A rookie cop in uniform wrote up a report on me and was polite and nodded each time I answered one of his questions. I told him I had either been sapped or hit with a stun gun and was booze-free. I also told him about the 1930s car and the forced injection of what was probably heroin in Chen's neck to get her back on the needle. He was a nice kid, and I don't think he believed one word I said.

I was assigned a room and fell fast asleep. Dave came into my room at 9:17 a.m.

"Sorry to get you out on Saturday," I said.

"I read the patrolman's report," he said. "You're sure the car was from the thirties?"

"Yeah."

"Like you'd find on a movie set?"

"Yeah, with George Raft or one of those guys," I replied.

Most people would discount everything I said, but Dave is one of the few people who, like me, believe there is more craziness in the world than rationality. Dave is kind to normal people, but he thinks they're squares and tries to get away from them as soon as possible. As a kid he always dug Harpo Marx and listened to Baby Snooks and Colonel Stoopnagle on the radio, just before *The Lone Ranger* came on.

"You couldn't see anyone's face?" he said.

"Nope."

Then he asked the question that hurt him most. "How about Chen?"

"They made sure I would remember every detail."

He knew what I was talking about. But he kept at it. He had to. He was a good cop. If you get lazy with a detail, you can blow a whole investigation. "Now is not the time to hold back, Cletus."

"They pulled her head back by her hair. Her blouse was torn off her shoulder. The guy with the hype held it like an ice pick."

"You didn't have your camera?"

"I thought I was going outside to see Joan."

Dave hadn't quite accepted my relationship with Joan of Arc. Know why? He believes I think I don't deserve a good woman so I make them up. Dave has got it all wrong. It's him who has the problem. You should have seen his first wife, the one from Martinique. She was the kind who makes guys put their brains on the ceiling. She could have been the Antichrist. I could go on.

Hey, kick me in the knee, will you? I want to avoid talking about what happened to Chen. Even though these events were long ago, I can't get them out of my mind. For me, I guess it was like when a father loses a daughter. There's a Louisiana writer named Andre Dubus who said God had a Son, but He never had a daughter. I don't know about those things, but I knew the feelings I had toward Chen and also toward those who had hurt her.

"Hey, podna," Dave said. "You're slipping away from me."

"I got to get out of here, Dave."

"Out of where?"

"The hospital," I replied, my voice rising.

"And do what?"

"Get my Caddy's undercarriage torn up. Go after Clara Bow. Chain-drag her husband. Find out what 'union' means on the Post-it. Get my hands on the New Rising crowd and dump them on an ice floe in the Aleutians."

It was doodah and he knew it. But Dave always let me pretend. He rose from his chair and folded his hand inside mine and pinned it back on the pillow, like men do when they arm-wrestle, except he didn't squeeze it. "We're backing your action, Jackson," he said.

"Who's 'we'?"

"I don't know."

"They're gonna do something to Chen, Dave. Then Gracie."

"Yeah," he said. He looked into space. "Yeah, they are."

CHAPTER THIRTY-ONE

A day later I got out of the hospital and drove down to Morgan City and dropped the Eldorado with the man who had done repairs on it when I first bought it. His name was Albert Guilbeaux, and he wore old-time grease-monkey overalls no matter how hot it got. He had a small unshaved face and wore Coke-bottle glasses and breathed through his mouth like he was thinking about something. But he wasn't.

"You want me to pull off everything?" he said.

"Except what you already repaired."

"Okay, my man. How you gonna get home?"

"I was wondering if I could borrow some wheels."

"Can you live with a hippy camper, 'cause that's all I got right now?" he said.

"I've always wanted to drive one of those," I said.

In minutes I was on my way over the huge arching bridge above the Atchafalaya, the engine straining, the butterfly-stamped cheesecloth curtains whipping in the wind, a Peter, Paul and Mary tape blaring, and me wondering what the life of a flower child might be like.

# # #

Hawthorne was staying at the hotel out by the four-lane. On my cell I had told him everything I had told Dave, except for the material about Joan of Arc, which would probably impress him as strange. Look, this is the way I see it. You don't learn anything from people whose central purpose now and forever is to obey other people. You learn from the crazoids. It's the same way with history, right? It's the little people who come out of nowhere and usually disappear again, after maybe inventing the wheel. In civil rights? Claudette Colvin and Rosa Parks wouldn't give up their seats in Montgomery. How about the status of feminism in 1952 before Kitty Wells sang her song "It Wasn't God Who Made Honky Tonk Angels"? It was banned by the National Broadcasting Company, which of course created even more demand. Way to go, NBC guys.

Anyway, I motored into the circular driveway of Hawthorne's hotel and saw him waiting for me outside, which I thought was a good sign. I still couldn't read that guy. Yeah, he was smart and not an elitist, like some of the Feds. But there was something hanging loose in him, something he couldn't deal with. Trying to figure it out was messing me up, because, let's face it, Gracie had said they'd had a thing, and I wasn't sure what a "thing" was, or "seeing each other" or "dating," you dig, because what do those words mean? If I'd had my choices, I would have loved to go out together and have dinner and dance and do all the things young people used to do, know what I mean? Probably not, but that's okay.

Hey, put it this way: When you're older, it's not about getting it on. It's about music and flowers and boxes of candy, the stuff you did when you were a kid.

Okay, it was none of these things that was bothering me. It was something different. Remember, Gracie said something not exactly nice about Hawthorne, something about his getting snubbed and maybe wanting to run the FBI. But when you hear someone dis an ex-lover, you can be assured there's a ready reply from the other party, hot and smoking. What would bother a straight shooter like Hawthorne? There are guys in the military who go crazy because there's a blade of grass on their spit shine. Why are they like that? Supposedly it's a potty problem. Have you ever known a slightly deranged drill instructor? It's not the f-word you'll hear; it's the s-word. Think "fecal."

That was it, I told myself as I pulled into the shade of the hotel in my borrowed camper. Samuel Hawthorne was a descendant of Puritans, with starch in his soul and the rigidity of conscience on his brow.

He walked toward my passenger door, wearing yellow-tinted aviator glasses, grinning at my hippy throwback. "Where'd you get it?" he asked in a merry way, pulling open the door.

"A friend is peeling down my Caddy and gave me this to drive. It's pretty cool."

He stopped, not quite inside. "A mechanic is tearing down your vehicle again?"

"If you want to put it that way."

He finished climbing into the seat and closed the door with his elbow. He took off his glasses and stared into my face. "You're a patriot, Mr. Purcel."

"Call me Clete."

"I'll call you whatever bloody thing I want," he replied. His door was loose. He freed, then slammed it. All the humor had gone out of his face. "We've got to find Gracie and Miss Chen," he said. "You know what a 'dungaree shore leave' is, don't you?"

"The port of call gets wrecked?"

He drummed his fingers on the dashboard. But it was show. Puritans might burn Indian villages and hang witches, but they don't break rules.

# # #

I had gotten Clara Bow's production schedule from one of my clients who was an extra. They were shooting outside St. Martinville, not far from the site of an old plantation known as Lady of the Lake. To the south was a chain of lakes and swamps and bayous that eventually bled into the Gulf. The sun had tilted into the clouds and turned reddish brown from either a mill or a pasture that was burning. Actors and extras in gray uniforms were spaced out between lines of cannon, the Stars and Bars flapping on their staffs. A hundred yards away, the boys in blue were about to charge, the American flags swelling and curling, filling with gusts of wind, undaunted, as though the outcome of the battle had already been determined, no matter how many farm boys lay face down and dead, their eyes staring into the grass.

I had parked about two hundred yards away. A number of people had gathered at the back of my camper. I watched them in the rearview mirror.

"What's going on back there?" Hawthorne said.

I shook my head.

"Why are they laughing?" he asked.

"Search me. Maybe they're toking up."

Hawthorne got out of the passenger seat and went to the back of the camper, then walked back to the passenger door and looked through the window. "Did you put that bumper sticker on?"

I scratched an eyelid. "Which one? I think there're a couple on there."

"Caution! Heavily armed badass leftist motherfucker on board."

"Oh yeah, that's mine."

"Let's find Clara Bow before the state police arrest us," he said. "Good Lord, man, I'd heard stories, but—"

"But what?"

"Nothing," he said. He sniffed at the air. "You weren't kidding. They're smoking weed on the job."

"*Laissez les bons temps rouler.*"

"What's that mean?"

"The Louisiana version of the national anthem. 'Let the good times roll.'"

"What a place," he said.

I told you he was a Puritan.

# # #

Clara Bow was behind the cameras talking to a half dozen people, wearing her jodhpurs and a white short-sleeve shirt, her hair tinged by the sun, her heart-shaped face right out of a candy box. I may be a fool, but she made me think of Amelia Earhart, confident she could live on the clouds forever. I hate to admit this, but she was the kind who could call a man back again and again, no matter how much she had hurt him, and each time successfully promise this time it would be different.

I walked into the circle she was addressing, with Hawthorne behind me. I made no attempt to ask her pardon. It didn't matter. I honestly believe she did not see me, as though she were in the past and I was in the present.

"How do you do, Miss Clara?" I said, touching the brim on my hat.

"What?" she said, seemingly confused, and not acting.

"It's Clete Purcel."

"Yes, I know. What are you doing here?" she replied. "You didn't show up for your tryout. We have cast someone else. You'll have to go now."

I wasn't looking at her now. I could see the pastureland and the Johnny Rebs and Billy Yanks and the rows of silent cannon and could hear the drummer boys rolling their sticks on their drums, the infantry forming up, gray and blue and butternut, the noncoms counting cadence—*your left, your left, your left, right, left*—all of them about to risk eternity, all too real. It made me swallow.

But I did not see the boxlike car in which Chen had been injected before my eyes.

"You'll have to leave, Mr. Purcel," Miss Clara said.

Hawthorne pushed past me and dropped open his badge holder. "I'm Special Agent Samuel Hawthorne, Ms. Bow," he said. "We have reason to believe criminal parties known to you are in the vicinity. These particular parties kidnapped a dancer named Gracie Lamar and an Asian woman known only as Chen. Do you have a vintage vehicle in your possession?"

"Sir, are you crazy?" Miss Clara said.

I had to admit Hawthorne was a little stiff.

"Madam, do you know the penalty for aiding and abetting a kidnapping?" he said.

"Yes, probably spending a lifetime under the control of people such as yourself," she said.

What was I thinking while all this was going on? I'll tell you. *Why did she have to get mixed up with a geek like Lauren Bow?*

"Do you know the penalty for lying to a federal agent?" Hawthorne asked.

"I don't care what it is. That's because I didn't lie. I can also say in the present tense I do not lie." Then she began spacing out her words. "Do. You. Understand. The. Words. I. Say?"

Hawthorne's cheeks were coloring. Let's face it, the guy was from Mississippi, probably reared in a fundamentalist church that taught him to respect women or get a slap upside the head.

"Lay off it, Miss Clara," I said. "Agent Hawthorne is trying to save the lives of two women who may be in the hands of your former husband, a guy who has the morals of a commode."

Her eyes went away from me. When they came back, the whites were shiny and pink. "I know nothing about these ladies," she said. "I hate what my ex-husband has done to the people he has cheated and the lives he has ruined. I also hate what I have done to the same people. I have nothing else to say."

Was she acting? I couldn't tell. Most of the actors I've known have turned out to be chameleons, re-creating themselves at first light. Their eyelids stay stitched to their brows, but behind them there's probably an antediluvian world with pterodactyls flying around in it. But flying monsters or not, the main subject is themselves. Absolutely. Without exception. To the last drop of your blood.

Hawthorne cleared his throat. "What does the word 'Leprechaun' mean to you, Ms. Bow?"

"Dancing little Irishmen with red noses and peaked green hats," she said.

"That's not clever, madam," he said.

Out on the field, the soldiers were in place, all of the flags unfurled, a stray dog running through the grass between the two armies, as though it knew it was in peril for reasons that had no bearing on its life.

"Call me 'madam' and I will slap your face, sir, even though you may put me in one of your prisons."

I had to hand it to her. What a performance. But I had to hand it to Hawthorne, also. "I meant no offense, Ms. Bow."

Then I saw their eyes meet. I couldn't believe it. Bingo. The ways of this world.

"Hey, the Civil War is waiting for you guys," I said.

"What?" Miss Clara said. She had just gone back into dreamland again, with Hawthorne right behind her.

I pointed at the field.

"Yes," she said. "Thank you for coming here. Come back anytime."

Then she and her circle went back to work, the cannons firing, the drums rolling, hundreds of bayonets pointed by Christians and Americans and brothers and sons and fathers at one another, their knees rising in the air as they marched through the grass, a blood-red sun reflecting on the buckles of their bandoliers, proud to undo Eden as their bayonets pinned each other to the ground.

# # #

"Are you all right, Mr. Purcel?" Hawthorne said.

"Call me Clete," I replied. "And yes, sir, I'm all right."

My cell phone throbbed in my pocket. It was Dave. "What's the haps?" I said.

"I'm at my house. Dooley LeMay's remains are turning black," he replied. "He must have been dosed with that stuff."

"Oh, jeez, he could have strung it all over the parish."

"Here's the rest of it. I just talked to the chief of police in Birmingham. He said this was off the record, but he believes Gracie Lamar dropped three guys in Lauren's militia group for killing her lover. He said it was all firefight stuff, but nonetheless she blew the shit out of them. What's going on with you at Lady of the Lake?"

Not much, I thought to myself. *I just figured out why Hawthorne isn't entirely comfortable on the subject of Gracie Lamar.*

"I'm with Agent Hawthorne," I said. "Can we ROA at your house?"

"Wait a minute," he said. "My landline is ringing."

I waited for him to get finished with the other call. But he didn't.

"Dave?" I said. "What's going on?"

"I should wait for you to get back to New Iberia. But, okay, here it is. Chen's alive. Whoever got hold of her sent a message and photos to Helen's office."

My ears seemed to go deaf.

"Clete? Are you there?"

"Tell me the rest of it."

"I should have waited for you to get here."

"Tell me what it is!"

"Most of the photos are not of Chen. They're of Gracie. Helen's on the way to the house now. You need to get here."

CHAPTER THIRTY-TWO

Hawthorne and I made it down the two-lane along the Teche in fourteen and a half minutes. Then we went across the drawbridge onto Main and turned into Dave's driveway. Helen's cruiser was already there. Hawthorne and I walked in without knocking or ringing the bell. Helen and Dave were in the living room. The photos were lined up on the coffee table. Helen was wearing latex.

"Y'all don't have a print man?" Hawthorne asked.

"It's Sunday," she said.

Way to win their hearts and minds, Hawthorne.

I started toward the photographs. Dave cupped his hand on my upper arm. "We're going to find her, Clete. We're going to pull out all the stops. We'll make this right on all levels. You got it, partner?"

"Yeah, what do you think? I'm gonna start shooting people?" I replied.

"I'm just saying."

"I got the message."

There were four Polaroids, each of them probably taken with an old camera. The light in the pictures was poor, the room probably the cinder-block substructure of a cheap house close to water.

Basements don't work in southern Louisiana. They quickly flood. Chen was curled on a dirty mattress, barefoot, stoned out, wearing oversize jeans and a sweatshirt. The other three photos were devoted to Gracie. I don't like to describe it, not even after all this time. She was tied to a chair and obviously had been beaten in the face, both of her eyes swollen shut; a man wearing a hood held an upside-down bucket above her, the water bright on her face; another hooded figure had just lit a cigarette with a BIC lighter and was blowing a stream of smoke in an upward angle.

"The envelope was delivered in the night drop," Helen said. "Nobody saw it until two hours ago. There was no letter."

"What'd the security camera show?" Dave said.

"A guy on a bicycle," she said. "I think he's homeless. But I'm not sure. We might find him at the shelter."

She was chewing on her lip, looking sideways at me. "You see anything that's recognizable in either of these guys or the room?"

"What's that in the corner?" I said.

Dave looked at me, then handed me a magnifying glass. "Here," he said. Then he looked at me again. Whatever he wanted to tell me, he was not going to do it in front of Helen and Hawthorne.

I passed the magnifying glass over the photos, the images swelling in size, wobbling, like bubbles, hard to take.

"You see something significant?" Helen said.

"I'm not sure. Here, you and Agent Hawthorne look," I said.

"Just junk, huh?" she said.

"Yeah, I guess," I said.

"What to do you think, Agent Hawthorne?" she said, handing him the glass.

"I need to call Washington," he said.

I blew out my breath. I had the feeling we were just about to have everything pulled out of our hands. "I need to sit down," I said.

"Yeah, you look a little tired, Clete," Helen said. "You've really had your hands full."

I knew that Helen was a friend, but I didn't like people talking to me in that way. "Could I use your bathroom, Dave?"

"Sure," he said.

I went inside the bathroom and turned on the water in the lavatory and washed my face. Then I opened the door and said, "Hey, Dave, you got a fresh towel?"

I knew very well where the clean towels were. He came to the door and leaned in. "You saw what I did?" he asked.

"Yeah, the broken grip and guard of a sword, like the French sword we saw near the drawbridge," I replied.

"You think it's coincidence?"

"No chance," I said. "There's more stuff in that pile. Three rusty iron rings, the kind I found on that sunken boat behind your house. They're from the Middle Ages. There are also links of chain that are exactly like the kind Joan had stretched across her gown."

"How can the material be in two places?"

"Who knows? We're looking through the dimension or something. Quit pretending we're not."

"Yeah, but how does this lead us to Gracie and Chen?"

"There's a rundown bar on the very bottom of Jefferson Parish that's got an attachment. The owner calls it a museum. He makes money by conducting tours for the schools. I've been there. The main building was made out of cypress for soldiers who came home with the thousand-yard stare after World War I. Guess what it's sitting on? A semibasement built of cinder blocks, with no windows."

"You don't want to share any of this?" Dave said.

"Can you imagine what Hawthorne would do with it? Or any of his FBI pals? We'll both be in straitjackets."

"I don't think the guy has any pals."

"You want to spread the news so we can get Chen or Gracie killed?" I said.

"No, of course not. What about Helen?"

"What about her?"

"She's the sheriff. I take my orders from her."

"It's your call, Streak."

"What about the locals?" Dave said. "Jefferson Parish has got the same attitude toward us as Orleans Parish. They'll take over."

"What you mean is they'll take *me* over."

"I'm bothered about this one, Cletus."

"We don't care what people say, rock and roll is here to stay."

"That's simpleminded and you know it," Dave said.

"So I'll go by myself."

"Clete, are you sure you saw all those things? We're risking lives on a message sent to us by Joan of Arc."

"Yeah, and you can trust it." I said.

He pressed the heel of his hand on his forehead, then took it away. "Okay," he said. "But if we need backup, we get it. Right?"

"Sure," I said, shrugging. "When did we ever do less?"

He gave me a look like I'd just gotten off a UFO. Then I realized he was thinking about something bigger than him or me. "What is it, Dave?"

"If we blow this, an awful lot of people might die. Maybe more than we ever thought."

I coughed, the way you do when you have a fishbone in your throat. I couldn't think of a response. He had just raised a possibility that made me want to hide in an ancient rainforest where the wheel had not yet been invented.

# # #

Dave and I said nothing to Helen and Hawthorne of our conversation, and we hit the road for Jefferson Parish in Dave's black pickup. By now you've probably gotten the feel of South Louisiana. It's a beautiful place, but it's also a place of endings, or change that's hard to witness. Many have a love affair with it, the way Dave loves it and almost destroys himself trying to save a lost cause. Then there are those who have no conscience and abuse its swamps and rivers and marshlands as though they were a trash dump, and that's no exaggeration.

Sometimes when I'm fishing way down on the Gulf at sunset, I'll see an old storage tank rusting into the water, or bamboo flooded with an iridescent reflection that shouldn't be there, or a man-made canal streaming saline into a freshwater forest of gum trees and cypress and tupelos. It makes me sad. It makes me feel that I am watching the end of something, maybe even time itself.

I wake in the morning and feel a sickness in the pit of my stomach I cannot understand. It seems to have no source. I feel like I'm walking around with buckets on my feet and a wool blanket wrapped tightly around my head. No one who has not experienced it can understand or talk about it. You feel you're inside a painting that is melting and running down the canvas. Talking about it now makes my head damp and cold at the same time.

It didn't take long for Dave and me to reach the little village on the rim of our beloved *Belle Louisiane*. That's what the Cajuns call it. The sky was aflame, the sun below the Gulf's rim, the air filled with storm clouds that could have risen from a rift in the earth.

Dave pulled to the side of the road and turned off the engine and looked at the lights coming on in the settlement where Chen and Gracie were probably being held at the mercy of guys who had the kindness of centipedes.

I waited for him to speak, but he didn't. Dave was heavy on recon. A long time ago, on a night trail, in a country I don't want to talk about anymore, a Bouncing Betty almost cut him in half.

"What's that remind you of?" I said.

"Nothing," he replied.

"How about John Ford's use of light and darkness in *My Darling Clementine*? In the night scenes only the brothels and saloons and pool halls are lit. He was telling his audience the early Republic was a dark place."

"Where's the bar and museum?" he asked.

"Three more blocks, then cross the railroad tracks and stop by the water tower. That way we can walk back to the bar and not draw attention. Get rid of your coat and mess up your hair and don't make eye contact."

"What if one of the shitheads is in the bar?" he asked.

"We slap him on the back and walk him into the shitter and cram him inside the rubber machine. What do you think?" I said. "Dave, you could make the invention of ice water a challenge. I mean it. You should do poster work for the Tylenol company."

Dave had a point, though. We could be kryptonite in the bar. Then we got a break; it started to rain, at first in small drops, then in a burst that swept clouds of mist and spray across the marshland and blew out the remaining light on the horizon. Dave dug out two hooded raincoats from behind the seat, then drove slowly through this tiny little town where a fatal decision might turn it into a charnel house.

Dave made a right turn and bumped across the tracks and parked in the lee of the water tower. He cut the engine and we got out fast and put on our coats and hooded our heads and dropped our weapons, which consisted of my .38 Special and Dave's 1911-model .45 semiauto, into our pockets.

That seemed inadequate considering what lay in the balance for us all, maybe even for the spirit Joan of Arc. But Dave had a steel box welded to the back and bed of the cab in which he kept solutions for many kinds of situations, including his cut-down Remington pump.

Hey, I got to stop here. Why? Because this story has what Dave always calls "one commonality" running through it. It's not what the story seems to be about. In this case the commonality is the kind that has no origin and leaps from group to group, like the great influenza epidemic in 1918, except the infection is moral and not in the glands.

It's like trying to explain the rise of Hitler, a guy who paid prostitutes to whip him. He convinced baptized Christians it was in everybody's interest to lock handicapped people in vans and fill them with carbon monoxide. That can't happen here? I mentioned this before, but I'll do it again. I knew a Klansman in Mississippi who stretched a Black man's neck backward with a chain while another man burned him to death with a blowtorch. You can find a photo of it if you don't believe me, although I do not encourage you to do this.

That's the insanity. We don't believe the things we actually do. See what napalm can do sliding through a village made of straw. What I'm trying to say is, we willingly give our children to the graveyard. How the fuck do you explain that?

We started walking toward the saloon, the raindrops blowing as hard as buckshot, steam rolling down the short strip of asphalt that served as a street, the lighted windows of the saloon radiating into the dark.

I mentioned that the boards of the building, once an asylum, were cypress. It's important. Cypress logs can reside on the bottom of a swamp for two hundred years, then be restored and be more resistant to storms than brick. The walls of the saloon were a blackish brown, shiny in the glow of the outside lights above a balcony. It could have been one of the places in *My Darling Clementine*. Behind the wooden portion of the building, on a slope, I could see rainwater guttering down toward the partial cinder-block basement that held up the rest of the building.

My heart was thudding, my nose running. This time we had indeed gone over the Rubicon.

I twisted the doorknob and went inside, leaving Dave on the porch, his back turned to me, his hands in his coat pockets, as though he were enjoying the night air.

A bell tinkled over my head, and every face at the bar and the tables looked at me. I went hood-down to the can and got as close to the urinal as I could and kept my forehead almost on the wall while I let go.

"Quite a night out," a guy down the line said.

"Yeah," I said, my eyes straight ahead.

"You look familiar. Aren't you from New Orleans?"

I made my voice as hoarse as I could. "I'm from Mobile."

"No shit? Where'bouts? I used to live there."

What a start.

CHAPTER THIRTY-THREE

He said his name was Billy Lee Wilkins and he sold frozen food out in the parishes, particularly ice cream and birthday cakes. He followed me out of the men's room, with no way I could get rid of him. He was either a talking machine or fried on crank.

"Want a beer?" he said. "I thought so. I like a raw egg in mine. I'll order up. What'd you say your name was again?"

"Look, partner—" I said.

He was talking before I got out a third word. I could see Dave at the end of the bar, his hood still on his head. I had to get rid of this guy. Then I thought, *Why?*

"You come in here often?" I asked. We were standing at the bar now, each with one foot on the rail.

"Sure, you bet. Great place for contacts. The owner's got all kinds of crap he digs up in the marsh. British junk from the War of 1812. A skull he turned into a flowerpot. The guy is a little nuts, but that's okay—who am I to judge, right?"

"Right," I replied, getting in a word as fast as I could.

"I like the way you talk. What's your name again? Hey, you haven't drunk your beer-and-egg float. Chug it. It's on me. What's your name again?"

"I'm fine, Billy Lee. Does the owner have some artifacts downstairs? I'm a collector myself."

"Yeah, I think so. You can hear a boom box playing while he works. He's a little weird, kind of hung up on race and civil rights and that jazz, don't get him started, it makes him cross-eyed."

"How do you get into his workshop area?" I asked.

"Go outside and circle around. I've never been inside."

"Can we go down there?"

"I don't know about that. Maybe we should talk about something else. You a Tiger fan?"

"Let me introduce you to my friend Dave. He's interested in history, too."

Billy Lee looked up and down the bar, then upended his beer and wiped his mouth. "I'm starting to get strange vibrations here."

"You're getting me wrong," I said. "You're a nice guy. I'm just doing a little research."

"I think I'm walking away from this."

"Billy Lee, I need you. I think you're a good guy and probably a patriot. Don't walk away. Stay with me. We can change history, right here."

"I think I made a wrong choice here, is what I think. I think I'll say good night."

I took out my PI badge holder and opened it under the lip of the bar. "My friend Dave is an Iberia Parish homicide detective. He used to be with NOPD. We just need you to walk us down to the back entrance of the basement."

The truth was I couldn't let the man named Billy Lee inform the owner that we were here.

"You lied to me," he said.

"You'll understand later."

"No, you lied."

Then I took a gamble. "You're right. It was a lousy thing to do. You're a stand-up guy, Billy Lee. Take off. We won't try to stop you. But dummy up for the next fifteen minutes, okay?"

His eyes wandered over my face. "What's it about?"

"You have children?" I asked.

"Sure."

"That's what it's about."

# # #

The rain had thinned. Dave and Billy Lee and I went out in the rain and walked behind the saloon and down the slope to the back of the basement. Billy Lee had on a raincoat and an aviator's hat with the flaps hanging over his ears. The air was dank, like soil in a garden that's full of white worms, and lightning was crawling all over the sky. I was getting to like Billy Lee. If you've been in emergencies, or disasters, you know the following is true: The heroes come out of nowhere; they're in grocery lines; they're bus drivers and street people. They pull old people off subway tracks with seconds to spare, swim into a river to save a cat, carry people twice their weight out of infernos, and are so nondescript you can't remember what they look like.

Yeah, Billy Lee was one of those guys. But I had something else chewing me up. All this was too easy. Even the weather was cooperating, the fog drifting around our ankles like wet cotton, the moon the color of ivory, with a purple bruise on its face, the rain warm, the kind that taps on a tent like a song and rocks you to sleep. There was no sound from the basement, no tire or foot tracks around it. The heavy wood door had a small lock, one you could buy for four dollars at Walmart.

It made me think of a night trail after the monsoons. It always looked too easy.

I had my .38 in the pocket of my slicker, and Dave had his .45 gripped with two hands and pointed at the basement door, but I could see the conflict in his face, wondering if we hadn't been played, because when you get played, you can also get dead.

There was a neat pile of wood on the ground, an axe snicked into a pine log. Suddenly an owl flapped from a tree and swam right over our heads, screeching like a tin roof being torn in half. Dave ducked, and so did I. Billy Lee jumped and cried out; the poor guy couldn't help it.

We froze, waiting for something to happen, but it didn't.

"Let's go in," Billy Lee whispered, his eyes dilated.

I put my index finger up against my lips to ask that he be quiet. Dave started walking back toward us, his piece pointed upward.

"Don't tell me to shut up," Billy Lee said, still whispering, his breath hot.

I patted him on the shoulder. "Cool it down," I said.

"Are you going in there or not?" Billy Lee said.

Dave looked at me and shook his head, meaning "Don't get this guy riled."

I started walking backward, trying to pull Billy Lee with me. It didn't work. He pulled the axe from the pine log and ran toward the basement and the wood door that had been carpentered into the cinder blocks, both Dave and me running after him, Dave lifting his hands, trying to say "no, no, no, no," without waking up the neighborhood, me catching part of Billy Lee's raincoat, then slipping on the clay.

I tried to get up but slipped again. In the corner of my eye, I saw Joan in her white gown and chains, her eyes downcast. Then she looked up at me, her eyes wet.

Billy Lee glanced back once, his face split with a grin, the axe lifted above his head, then he brought it down on the padlock, just as I shouted, "Don't do it!"

It was too late. I saw sparks fly from the padlock and the hasp, saw Dave cross his arms in front of his face, his .45 still in his hand, saw Billy Lee outlined in the brilliance of the explosion, and clamped my arms around my head when a solitary board hit my knee like a baseball bat and Billy Lee Wilkins dissolved into a pink mist.

CHAPTER THIRTY-FOUR

You know why people hang around a disaster area, like a gas main blowing up or a psychoceramic going apeshit on the street with military guns or a plane crashing into a high-rise? It's not because they're morbid; it's because they can't go home alone with the images that got tattooed on the backs of their eyeballs.

That's what happened down at the bottom of Louisiana the night that poor fellow gave his life for a cause he didn't have a name for. Cops, firetrucks, ambulances, and customers from the saloon were all over the property, but not for the reason you might think—namely, the burned bodies of Chen and Gracie Lamar. They were alive.

After the explosion, Dave and I choked our way through the smoke and powdered debris and the remains of Billy Lee into the interior of the basement. Both women were crouched in a hollowed-out, cave-like recess underneath the saloon, locked in ankle and waist chains, with the ankle chains locked to a D-ring anchored in the floor. They were dressed in orange coveralls, the kind that come from a jail. Two chemical toilets were propped against the far wall. There was no expression in Chen's face; her skin sagged on her bones; her hands seemed shrunken and clenched like claws. Gracie's hair was covered with dust, her eyes still puffed from a beating. I wanted to kill the guys who did this.

The local cops were not there yet, but in minutes a fireman with bolt cutters snipped the links of their chains. Chen fell into my arms. Gracie stood up, then fell down again. Dave picked her up, but she stepped away from him as soon as she got her balance and began pounding the dust from her coveralls. "Did you get that son of a bitch?" she said.

"Which son of a bitch?" he asked.

"Whoever it was. We never saw anybody's face. What's that above the doorway?"

"The guy who busted the lock and blew up the place," Dave said. "You never saw anybody?"

She didn't answer. I couldn't blame her. She was probably in shock. I think Dave was, too. The medics were bringing the gurneys in. I got Chen onto the first one and wiped her forehead and hair with my hand. Her eyes looked like the color had leached out of them, like the color of an oyster that's just been opened.

"You never saw anybody at all, or heard a name or recognized a voice?" Dave asked Gracie.

"No, I told you," she said.

"Did they mention a place?" I said.

"What did I just finish saying?" she said.

"Hey, bub," a medic said to me. "I got to get the lady in the wagon."

"*Bub?*" I said. "You know how old I am?"

I had forgotten how death works. We beat each other up.

"Sorry," the medic said. "We're taking them to New Orleans."

"You guys are doing a good job," I said.

Gracie put herself on the gurney. She looked angry rather than relieved.

"Was Clara Bow mixed up with this, Gracie?" I said.

"Clara Bow is a douchebag," she said. "Her husband is worse. But that's all I know. A producer picked us up, we had dinner, and then we woke up here."

"Why are you mad at us?" I said.

"Because a guy died who didn't have to," she said. "Where's Sam Hawthorne? Y'all decided to do it on your own, didn't you?"

I didn't try to explain why we left Hawthorne out. I believed then, and now, that she got into all this on her own, and she knew it. Chen was trusting and naïve; Gracie was an ex-cop and a dancer on Bourbon Street and may have popped three Klansmen in Birmingham. Gracie knew we did the best we could, and I could have taken her to task for her self-righteousness. But you don't hurt people when they're already hurting.

The medics were about to put her in the ambulance. I reached down and squeezed her hand and felt her squeeze mine in return.

In a few minutes everyone except Dave and me had left the basement area. The rain stopped. Pools of yellow lightning that made no sound rolled through the clouds and dropped off the edge of the Gulf. I tried to rethink what had just happened, but I couldn't. I knew my sleep would be difficult for a very long time. But the difficulties suffered by Billy Lee's family would be far more daunting.

# # #

Dave and I walked to the truck. Everyone was gone now. "How do you figure it, Dave?" I said.

"We got set up," he replied. "I wish . . ."

"Wish what?"

"Billy Lee, the guy who was going to help us," he said. "I wish we cuffed him to my truck. How many kids does he have?"

"He didn't say."

"What a crock," Dave said.

"Yeah," I said.

He looked into space, a sense of loss in his eyes that is hard to describe.

"I'll drive," I said.

This time he didn't argue.

# # #

On the way to New Orleans and my apartment and office in the Quarter, Dave put his phone on conference mode and checked in with Helen and Hawthorne. Both of them were furious. Dave waited until they were finished, then said, "Maybe everything y'all say is right, but we got the kidnap victims back. We're sorry about the man who helped us. We tried to stop him. Nonetheless, we should have cuffed him to my truck and gone in by ourselves. The thing that bothers me most is the fact he was a simple man just trying to do the right thing."

There was a long pause on the other end.

Then Helen said, "Roger that. Out."

But Hawthorne continued before she could hang up. "What's the level of damage on the victims?"

"How do we know?" Dave said.

"Did you ask someone?" Hawthorne said.

"No," Dave said. "We were dealing with emergency personnel. They don't do diagnosis."

"You know what I'm talking about," Hawthorne said.

"Yeah, we do," I interjected. "How would you like to be a rape victim and discuss it in front of ten people?"

"What's the saloon owner's name again?" Hawthorne said.

"Who cares?" I said. "He's probably swimming to Cuba with his hands tied and a bucket of concrete around his neck."

"What's the gen on Clara Bow?" Helen said, trying to dial it down.

"Gracie Lamar says she's a douchebag," I replied.

Either Hawthorne or Helen broke the connection. I could see the glow of New Orleans in the distance, the live oak trees on the sides of the highway flying past us.

"I guess we didn't win their hearts and minds," Dave said.

"I should have given Hawthorne the saloon owner's name."

"He can't get that from his own agency?"

"No, that's not it, Dave. I just feel rotten about Billy Lee."

He tapped me on the shoulder with the flat of his fist. "You're one of the best guys in the world, Clete," he said. "Don't let anybody tell you different. You'd give your life for that guy if you could."

# # #

We pulled into my courtyard and went upstairs and were overrun by my cats. Miss Dorothy had kept good care of them, and had swept and mopped around their litter boxes and their water and feed bowls. But cats are cats. Mine loved to pull books off my shelves and climb on the curtains and kick dry-feed bags off the top of the refrigerator so they would explode all over the kitchen floor; they also brought chameleons into the house and turned them loose under the beds, and then chased them across the rugs in the middle of the night.

I loved my cats. Isn't it funny? When you see real evil in the world, you want to see and do simple things, the way you did when you were a kid. Dave and I fixed ham and onion sandwiches and opened up a carton of chocolate milk. We still stunk from the explosion and our ears were still ringing, but we didn't care. We turned on the television in the kitchen and found a baseball game. It didn't matter who was playing; it was a baseball game. I knew Dave felt the same way I did about taking a civilian into a danger zone. I suspected he wanted to get a bottle of Jack down from my liquor cabinet and get wiped out. Dave had slips. Each one worse. I was doubtful that he could survive another. Or that he would want to.

I don't think I was ever so tired. I was watching the game, chewing on a mouthful of ham and onions and bread, when I felt my mouth stop moving and the food fall out on the table, my head slumped on my chest. I had never done that, even in Vietnam.

When I woke up, Dave was asleep on the couch and the cats were walking around on the table and I think the Red Sox were dancing on the diamond.

The next morning, I showered and shaved and brushed my teeth, and believed I would escape the nightmare we had walked into the previous night. I made coffee and poured a cup and lifted it to my mouth, but began shaking so violently I almost broke the saucer.

"Dave!" I shouted. "Where are you?"

He stepped inside from the balcony, the red and yellow flowers of the bugle vine and bougainvillea in full bloom behind him. "Right here," he said. "You okay?"

"Yeah, just fine," I said. "Copacetic in all ways, noble mon. I just wanted to know if you heard those 105s coming in short. Some fun, huh, boss?"

CHAPTER THIRTY-FIVE

Hey, you can't win on the game you pitched last week, can you? At least that's what Dave always said. He pitched American Legion when he was a kid. He used to say being a good detective was like being a good pitcher. He used to say, "Hide the ball behind your hip and don't let the batter see your fingers on the stitches." He also said the best pitch in baseball was the changeup.

And that's what I had to do. I didn't believe Samuel Hawthorne would ever find the people who were determined to destroy mankind if that's what it took to make them rich. I came to this conclusion not because I thought less of him as a person. He was a decent guy and a probably a straight shooter, but he did not understand people who were capable, with the flip of a switch, of soaking the earth and filling the oceans with blood for no other purpose than the gain of money.

Baylor Hemmings, the guy with the six-million-not-enough T-shirt, was not the exception. Probably he was the functionary for someone else. Regardless, mass murder was not committed by the few. It was done by the many.

Where did all this start? At a car wash where the owner, a kid I grew up with, was murdered, probably in the search for the

poisonous matter called Leprechaun. And who were the other players? Clara and Lauren Bow? The wife, no. The husband, maybe.
But who shot and killed Iberia Parish detective Dooley LeMay?
I was convinced the shooter was a woman. But who? I hated to
think this, but was Gracie Lamar perhaps a candidate? Her record
was intimidating and maybe just getting started. That's what happens to your mind when you're a cop too long. The whole world
becomes a toilet.

Then my cellphone vibrated. It was Albert Guilbeaux, my
grease-monkey friend I had told to rip the bottom out of my Eldorado. "Hey, Albert, what's the haps?" I said.

"There ain't no haps," he replied. "Your Caddy is clean. There
ain't no dope in it. There ain't no laundered money in it. There ain't
no weapons or stolen jewelry or explosives in it. In other words, you
ain't got shit."

"I can't believe that, Albert."

"I thought you'd be happy. Your beautiful car would not be
evidence in a trial that lasts five years."

"Thanks for your time, Albert. How much do I owe you?"

"Just bring back my hippy camper. It brings me fond memories
of my youth. By the way, I owe you an apology."

"For what?" I said.

"When you brought in the Caddy the first time, I cleaned out
the glove box and put everything in a manila envelope."

"What was in there?" I asked.

"Hang on," he said. He set down the phone, then scraped it
up again. "Tire and lube and oil receipts and road maps and a key."

"What kind of key?"

"It's like a locker or old-time hotel key. The number is 109.
Wait a minute, there's something here on the bottom. Let me get

my glasses . . . Okay, it says, 'Union Station, LA.' I guess that's Los Angeles. You been out there lately?"

I felt like a boil had just formed on the lining of my stomach.

"You still there?" he said.

I had to sit down. "Listen, Albert. Don't tell anybody about this. Do not use my name. Do not mention the Eldorado. You copy that?"

"Yeah, but you're scaring me a little bit here."

"I'll be there as soon as I can."

"Now you're really scaring me."

"I'm on my way," I said.

I hung up and went looking for Dave.

# # #

Dave had gone to the little grocery on the next block and was walking back to the building with a brown sack propped on his chest, two loaves of French bread sticking out the top. My heart was beating, and I wasn't sure I could get my words straight as I approached him. He smiled at me in a curious way, as though he wanted to tell me that everything was all right, although in truth it was not.

"Hey, Cletus," he said. "You want to come over here and sit down a minute?"

"Sure," I said, clearing my throat.

We sat on a steel bench in the shade, in the lee of the building, in the cool, dank odor of the storm sewer.

"I can't get my head ironed out, noble mon," I said. "I just talked to Albert Guilbeaux in Morgan City. He pulled some junk out of the glove box when he first worked on my Eldorado and forgot to give it to me. In the junk was a key for a locker at Union Station in LA."

It took three or four seconds before Dave's face stopped remolding itself. Then he set down the bag of groceries on the concrete and took a big breath. "What better place for the nucleus of a plague? Did you get on the phone to Hawthorne?"

"I just found out."

He waited for me to pull out my phone.

"Are you going to call or do you want me to?" he said.

I didn't move. My hands were shaking. I felt the blood drain from my face.

"What's wrong, Clete? Are you sick? You want me to call 911?"

"She's in the middle of the street," I said.

"Who?"

"Joan. She's on fire. She's burning to death. Right here."

He pulled me up from the steel bench and got my arm over his shoulder and tried to walk me to the house. I shoved him away.

"I see it all now," I said. "All of it. Give me your truck keys."

"You're losing it, Clete," he said, raising his hands at me.

"Look at Joan, Dave. She wants you to go with me."

Dave stared at the street and obviously saw nothing. Then he wet his lips and paused and wiped his mouth and looked again at the street and back at me. "Ask Joan what my mother's favorite hobby was."

The answer came into my head; I don't care if anyone believes that or not. "She didn't have time for a hobby. When she was a little girl, her father treated her on her birthday to a game of miniature golf in Lafayette. That was a big thing back then."

Dave's face looked like somebody had just eaten his heart.

# # #

We walked together up the stairs to my apartment and went inside. I called Hawthorne and told him everything that had happened. He couldn't believe my words. "Your friend in Morgan City has the locker key now?" he said.

"Yeah, that's correct," I said. I looked down from the window onto the street where I had seen Joan in flames. Now she was gone. Not even pedestrians were there.

"You told him we would be picking it up?" Hawthorne said.

"No, I did not."

"Why didn't you?" he said.

"Because I had to think it through. I didn't want an innocent person killed." I guess that sounded foolish considering what had happened to Billy Lee Wilkins.

"We're not in the habit of killing innocent people," he said.

I started to stay something about botched shootings by the FBI from John Dillinger to the present, but let it go. "The mechanic in Morgan City is a good guy named Albert Guilbeaux," I said.

"He'll be treated right, Mr. Purcel. I promise. But you gentlemen need to step back now."

I didn't answer.

"Did you hear me?" he said.

"My grandniece died of fentanyl. That's where all this started. Why don't you guys get that stuff off the street before you lecture the rest of us?"

"Where is Detective Robicheaux?"

"Right here."

"Both of you stay there, please."

I quietly replaced the receiver in the phone cradle. Dave looked up at me, his face empty. "What's going on, Clete?"

"Nothing is going on," I said. "At least not with us. It's the world that's got the problem."

"I'd like to believe that," he replied.

# # #

I told Dave I would be back and walked down the courtyard stairs and into the street. There was no trace of Joan, no scorch marks where she had been swallowed by flame. Why had she appeared in the way she had? I believed it was a reminder to us, a warning that the human race has a great capacity for both charity and cruelty. With that thought in mind, I went back upstairs.

"Listen up now, okay?" I said to Dave. "We've been looking at the wrong people and the wrong places from the jump. Dooley LeMay was a dirty cop. You knew that when you punched him out in the department restroom. I should have known that because my grandniece died of a fentanyl overdose."

"I'm not following you, Clete?"

"My niece used to take my Caddy to Eddy's Car Wash for me. It's probably where she got her drugs. And one of the stupes at the car wash put the Union Station key in the glove box."

"Yeah, go on," he said.

"Dooley was probably piecing off the action. Then he got into it a whole lot deeper than he wanted to," I said. "He went out to California on his fishing vacation and put the toxic goods in the locker and gave the key to somebody in the car wash."

"Yeah, maybe," Dave said. "But who's running the game, Clete?"

"Whoever popped Dooley," I said.

"A woman, you believe?"

"Who knows?" I said. "This is one gig we've been wrong about at every turn."

"What do you want to do now?" Dave asked.

"Go to the hospital."

"I thought you might say that," he said.

# # #

I called Albert Guilbeaux and told him the Feds were coming to his shop, but not to be alarmed and to give them whatever they wanted.

"When you gonna bring back my hippy camper?" he said.

"Soon as I can," I said.

"Clete, I ain't dumb. If the Feds are in on this, it's big, ain't it?"

"Yeah, it is, Albert."

There was a pause, then he said, "You drug me into some dirty stuff. Don't do this to me again."

"I'm sorry," I said.

"Yeah, I hear you, but 'sorry' don't pay the bills."

Who could blame him for his feelings? Fear is no fun. The fascists knew it. The Mob knew it. And guys like Ink Man and Baylor Hemmings and Lauren Bow knew it. And guys who owned a big broadcasting company knew it. You ever hear a hack or a chaser in a navy prison walk down a row of cells dragging his nightstick across the bars. That's the kind of fear I'm talking about. The little people, like Albert Guilbeaux, know when push comes to shove, they don't count.

# # #

The hospital was in the Garden District, probably one of the loveliest places in the world. Both sides of St. Charles were lined with antebellum and Victorian homes, the autumn sun spangling the live oaks and verandahs and flower beds and balconies, the leaves tumbling across the lawns, the dull-green iron streetcar lumbering down the neutral ground, a golden light trapped inside a tunneled arbor that ran for miles.

This was my father's milk-delivery route. One time a rich lady invited me to an ice cream party in the backyard. When I arrived, the yard was filled with raggedy Black children. That night I broke out all the glass in her greenhouse. I had a lot of anger back then. That's why I got along with the Italians. They got a bum deal in New Orleans. In 1891 a mob broke into the city prison and lynched eleven of them from streetlamps. You ever deliver the newspaper? See who pays you at the end of the month, blue-collar people or the rich. Duh. Same with hitchhiking.

What am I talking about here? Keep people poor, keep them scared, and you can do anything you want with them. Tell me one exception.

Dave and I pulled into the hospital and went inside. Guess what? Chen was sedated and sleeping, and Gracie Lamar had checked herself out, destination unknown.

CHAPTER THIRTY-SIX

We were about to leave Chen's room when I heard her say, "You no want to see me no more?"

"Oh, goodness, Chen," I said. "It's swell to see you."

"That's right," Dave said. "You look real good."

"No, I no look good," she said. "The men who kidnap me filled me with dope again. Maybe they do other things to me, too."

"That last part is not true, Chen," I said. "The doctors have made sure on that."

"Clete is not trying to make you feel better, Chen," Dave said. "He's telling the truth. And it wouldn't matter anyway. You're you. That's all that counts."

The injections had been done sloppily, leaving the tissue around the punctures bruised or inflamed or infected. It was the kind of thing Baylor Hemmings would do.

"Did you see anyone's face, Chen?" Dave said.

"No, they have on rubber mask," she said.

"How about their voices?" I asked.

She stared at the ceiling. "Yes," she said. "One talk like child. But he not child. He say mean things."

"Like what?" Dave said.

"He laugh at my name 'Chen.' He say he fuck up man's chin. Then he laugh some more."

Dave and I looked at each other. Dooley LeMay had taken three rounds, one in the palm, one in the throat, and one in the chin, the last one splintering the bone.

"Can you tell us anything else, Chen?" I said.

"I need to go back to the Work the Steps or Die Motherfuckers."

"I'll bet they'll come here," I said. "In fact, I'll call them up."

"Why your eyes wet, Mr. Clete?"

"I got hay fever," I said.

"No, you no understand yourself, Mr. Clete. Somebody make you hate yourself when you little boy, and now you think you no good. You stop thinking like that ever again."

"Okay," I said, now pushing at my nose.

"You make him keep promise, Mr. Dave," she said.

"You bet, Miss Chen," he said. "Can I ask you a question?"

She turned her head so she could look Dave full in the face. "What question?"

"Where did Miss Gracie go?"

I could see her chest rising and falling, her eyes veiled.

"It's not a hard question," Dave said.

"I no see her go," Chen said. "In basement we had cake and ice cream. Maybe she go for some."

Then she looked straight at the ceiling and refused to look anywhere else.

# # #

We went out the side exit and walked through a grove of live oaks. The leaves were shredding, dry and brownish yellow, scudding along the lawn and the asphalt. We got in the truck but didn't start the engine.

"How do you read it, big mon?" I said.

"Hard to tell," Dave replied. "She wants to help us, but she doesn't want to get Gracie in trouble. But what the hell does ice cream have to do with anything?"

"What's the worst day of your life?" I said.

"It wasn't a day," he said. "It was the night Annie was murdered and I couldn't get to her."

"What are the images you remember?" I said.

"What do you think?"

"You remember the first things you saw at the scene. But later everything became mixed up. You went over and over it, but it was a waste of time."

"So?" he said.

"When my grandniece overdosed, I wanted to kill every dealer in New Orleans. But every dealer didn't kill her. She got the fentanyl at Eddy's Car Wash. Nothing else counts. We need to start over, Streak."

"Where would that be?"

"Where else? Eddy's."

"I'm not sure about that about, Clete. It's not going to be that simple. We might have to spend years on this one."

"So we'll spend years."

Dave rubbed the back of his neck. "All right," he said.

I thought I saw Joan step off the St. Charles streetcar and stand next to a snowball cart run by a Black man in a white coat, like the cart my father walked me to when I was ten and he bought each of us a cone dripping with green spearmint syrup, all the time holding my hand so I would be safe from the traffic.

I thought she was going to disappear, as she had before. But she didn't. She waved and smiled, and I knew somehow she would remain with me the rest of my life. The trouble was, I didn't know how much time I had.

# # #

We drove across the Mississippi into Algiers and turned into the block where my boyhood friend Eddy Durbin had built his car wash business after doing double nickels in Angola, which no one can appreciate until they hear one of the gunbulls laugh about the one hundred inmates buried in the levee. I never really figured out how Eddy let his business, one he loved, become a center for the drug trade. You might not know a couple of things about New Orleans and drugs. The dope hit the projects like an atom bomb in the 1980s. A CIA guy told me the dope came north and the guns went to Central America; he also said the AK-47s came from China. Anyway, unlike the projects in New York or Washington, DC, the projects in New Orleans are spread throughout the city. In a few months New Orleans became the murder capital of the United States.

I could see Eddy's Car Wash in the next block. "How do you want to play it?" I said.

Dave pulled up behind a deserted liquor store full of broken windows and covered with graffiti. He cut the engine and left the keys swinging from the ignition. His arms were folded on the steering wheel. He looked at the sky. "You think we might have rain?" he said.

"Yeah," I said. "Maybe a real frog-stringer."

Down South that means the clouds will rain frogs.

"I'll be right back," he said.

He opened the door and got out and unlocked the steel box welded to the bed of the truck, then closed the lid and got back in again and slammed the door tight. His cut-down Remington was hanging from one hand, the magazine opened and empty. He was also carrying a bandolier that was stitched with cloth loops inserted with double-aught buckshot. The Remington had been his duck gun until he quit hunting. I once asked him why he gave up hunting, but his only answer was "Felt like it." He was also holding another gun I'd never seen. It was a single-shot .410, the barrel sawed off, the stock sanded into a pistol grip.

"Where'd you get that?" I said.

"From a kid in the eighth grade," he replied.

He hadn't restarted the engine. He kept looking at the cars going by at about forty miles an hour. The difference between that kind of normalcy and the potential of the guns we carried was enormous. We were making a choice for all those automobiles and the people inside them, one that in seconds could change lives of whole families, children included. Understand what I'm saying? It's that fast. A flick of the eye, a twitch of the finger, then you hear a *pow* and your ears go deaf and the acrid smell of gun powder is inside your head, and your hands are jerking with the thing you just turned loose on other people.

Dave looked at me.

"*What?*" I said.

"Maybe one of those kids at the car wash took your niece's life, Cletus."

"The kid who sold her the fentanyl is probably dead himself. First things first. You think Gracie Lamar is around here?"

"Yeah, I do," Dave said.

He had caught the bitterness in my voice. "Listen, big mon, everything we're doing is guesswork. If we get through it, nobody

will care. It's like the Cuban Missile Crisis. We came within two
hours of incinerating the Earth, and nobody remembers, like they
went to a movie and then forgot the movie."

Dave started the engine. "We don't care what people say . . . ,"
he said.

And I finished it with "Rock and roll is here to stay."

# # #

We drove onto the car wash property but didn't line up for the
brushes and steam and flying soap inside the tunnel where the
customers went in and came out, their cars seemingly brand-new.
The irony was that Eddy Durbin died inside those brushes, and
I won't repeat in what fashion. Eddy did his own time, and his
brother Andy's, too, and never got a break of any kind. I guess
Eddy didn't like me anymore, because I was a cop, and a dirty one,
but I didn't hold it against him. His parents were Irish fanatics,
but the Brits had been hell on their ancestors, starving them to
death and such, so how could you blame the poor sods? Plus, did
you ever know a more pagan race? The Jersey Mob was scared
shitless of them.

We parked in the shade and got out casually on each side of
the truck, both of us in sports coats, no guns showing. But don't be
fooled. When two guys wearing sports coats step out of a vehicle
simultaneously, their faces blank as cardboard, they're cops, and they
want people to know they're cops and can handle whatever kind of
trouble the neighborhood wants to throw at them.

Remember the Rodney King riots? Know why the riots spread
through the city? LAPD blew Dodge. Goodbye, Los Angeles.

A bunch of Black and Hispanic kids were popping chamois
rags and wiping down the cars with them, rocking to a boom box,

getting tips as the cars left the conveyor, rapping with each other as though we were not there.

A tall Black kid with blue eyes and a haircut like a sponge glued to his scalp and arms and hands that made me think of seaweed seemed to be running things. I let Dave talk. He had a cop's badge, I didn't. He didn't take it out, though. If you can get by without your badge, you're always better off. The second you show your badge in a minority neighborhood, you've announced you're their enemy, or at least that's how they read it. You've also proved you can't hump your own pack; you've got to use fear.

"I've lost a friend of mine," Dave said. "A beautiful woman with reddish-gold hair."

The Black kid's eyes were as blue as an Easter egg. He lifted them to the sky. "Ain't seen nobody like that today," he said.

"How about on another day?" Dave said.

"Nope, don't ring no bells."

"Where's Andy?"

The kid scratched his head. "I don't keep no track on other people. So cain't he'p you too much, suh."

Dave smiled. "I'm not a 'suh.'"

The kid wrung out the chamois and twisted it into a rope and tapped it on his palm to the music. "We ain't done nothing, man. Ain't sling no dope, ain't pimp no girls, ain't done nothing y'all think."

"I believe you," Dave said.

"I gotta get back to work, okay?" the kid said.

"The fentanyl that killed my grandniece came from this place," I said. "Did you know that?"

"No, I'm sorry to hear that, man," the kid said. "My sister went out the same way. Yeah, that's right, same shit, man. Same fucking shit. But that don't mean I know anything."

He turned and walked away. What are you going to do? You can't beat people up because they don't tell you what you want to hear. And if you do, the information is usually no good.

I was about to get in the truck when I saw Joan point at the back of the Black kid who said he had lost his sister to fentanyl. I asked Dave to stay where he was and followed the kid into the conveyor, into the jets of steam and the hot, waxy iridescence in the air and the clanking of the chain, into the place where Eddy Durbin had been eviscerated. Yeah, that's the kind word. The people who killed him tore his guts out.

"Don't lie," I said, my clothes getting drenched. "Where are the people we're looking for? Don't betray your sister. This is your one chance to do something for her, to show that her life meant something, that she counted, that she's still with us."

The kid looked back and forth, not afraid of others, not afraid of me or Dave, but afraid of himself and the code he had always lived by. He pulled up his T-shirt and wiped his face with it. "Andy's at the bowling alley. The woman you're talking about was here a half hour before you come. That's all I got."

"That's it?"

"She's gonna rip some ass, man. Hope it ain't yours."

He threw his chamois rag into the conveyer and watched it disappear into the brushes.

CHAPTER THIRTY-SEVEN

W here was the bowling alley? There was only one that was close by, in a poor and treeless neighborhood similar to other neighborhoods in St. Bernard Parish. The parish was defenseless against hurricanes, and with regularity it was torn up and half rebuilt and blown down again. This particular building, or bowling alley, could have been a warehouse or a dollar store or a bar and pickup joint. Louisiana was becoming a Third World country. The Mob opened the door, dope of every kind flooded the projects and the streets, and Reagan cut government aid by half. The Democrats got blamed for it, and the pukes in the projects armed themselves with nine-millimeters and sold crack for ten dollars a bag. Welcome to the Big Sleazy.

But this isn't my point. The bowling alley was like the end of something. A cheesy urban monument to decay, an acknowledgment of collective failure. A place where you didn't have to make comparisons. Or just a dump where people who lived on the margin would be encouraged to stay in their neighborhoods. The neon bowling pin over the front door told it all. It was pink and buzzed constantly and electrocuted any birds that tried to nest on it. It stunk of death.

Hey, I'm still not making my point. A bowling alley can be something. Like in the radio days of *The Life of Riley*. Working men and women drinking beer and smacking down the pins, yelling at the top of their lungs. Even the Mafia could have been something. Like Machine Gun Jack McGurn, who got cooled out in a bowling alley in Chicago, wearing a beige vest and lavender shirt and shiny black shoes, a Valentine's Day card thrown down on his body. It was kind of romantic.

But this bowling alley, the one Dave and I were looking at, was the end of the line. Dave felt it when we pulled into the parking lot, the first drops of rain sliding down the windshield. There were only two or three cars in the lot; pieces of tar paper on the roof were rising in the wind, and the barometer was dropping, the sky darkening. "Wow, this place is queasy," he said.

"Why?"

"I don't know," he replied. "I think it's because people come here by choice."

We went inside. The interior was dark, a couple of pin racks and lanes lit up. The air was frigid and smelled like dust and cleaning oil and bathrooms; it could have been a mortuary.

Gathered up on the far end of the alley was a group of maybe a dozen people talking to each other; I couldn't see one other soul in the building. They didn't look at us or seem perturbed. Dave and I were both wearing our slickers. Dave's cut-down Remington was hanging from the stock on a cord under his coat; I had the .410 stuck through the back of my belt. I also had my .38 snub inside my coat pocket. I had never felt so strange. I felt our weapons had no application to our situation.

Clara Bow was there, and so was her husband, Lauren. And so was the anti-Semite Baylor Hemmings and Eddy Durbin's brother,

Andy. I didn't know the others. Their faces seemed withered, like parched gourds, like figures from the time of the plague. Dave and I began to walk toward them, our footfalls echoing through the building, as loud as hoofbeats.

They looked at us with curiosity but not alarm.

"How do you want to play this?" I said to Dave under my breath.

"Make them talk," he said.

I knew he'd say that. If it was good enough for Wyatt and Doc, it was good enough for us.

Except Wyatt and Doc were flesh-and-blood people, like the Clantons. I wasn't sure about the group now looking at us from the far end of the building. Not one of them had picked up a bowling ball. My nose itched, but I dared not scratch it. I wanted to speak, but I didn't.

"You want to talk to me?" Andy said. His eyes were pulsing with a brittle light, like hard candy.

"What's the haps, Andy?" Dave said.

"Those are stupid words, Mr. Robicheaux," Andy said. "The way stupid people talk."

But neither Dave nor I was worried about Andy Durbin. The one I figured was worth watching was Baylor Hemmings. Plus, I really wanted to cool him out."

"I'm glad you're here," Clara Bow said, as beautiful as ever.

I didn't answer her, nor did Dave. I thought then, and think now, that she was a deliberate distraction, a fog, a wraith. If we didn't make it out of this building, it would be because she got our attention.

The tension in my body was starting to hurt. My heart was swelling, and not in a good way. Then, out of the corner of my eye, back in one of the pits, I saw a woman. I dared not look, because I would give up her position, although I was not sure who she was.

I would have preferred to take on the Clantons rather than face this bunch.

# # #

I glanced up at a sag in the ceiling. "Looks like the water is about to come through," I said.

No answer.

"We weren't expecting to run into all y'all," Dave said. "My heavens, a big event must be taking place."

Lauren and Clara Bow's eyes drifted toward Andy. He picked up a bowl of ice cream and frozen cake, the same brand Billy Lee Wilkins had been delivering to the saloon basement at the bottom of Jefferson Parish. He put a spoonful of ice cream in his mouth. "Want some?"

"When did you hook up with Baylor Hemmings, Andy?" I said.

"He's a fwend," Andy replied.

"Baylor is a Nazi, Andy," I said. "I don't think your brother would like you hanging with a dude like this."

"We can make y'all rich," Andy said. "We need somebody in Iberia Parish, now that Dooley LeMay is gone."

"Yeah, I thought a woman popped him," I said. "But that was your work, wasn't it?"

"Don't talk any more to this fat fuck, Andy," Baylor Hemmings said. His hair was still curly and uncut and metallic in color and full of grease, his unshaved face thick with whiskers as course as steel filings, his trousers stiff with grime. This was the Aryan race at its greatest?

"I'm glad to see you here, Baylor," I said. "After I dropped you out of that window into a dumpster, I thought you might have gotten too fond of the garbage and stuffed yourself to death."

"We saw you pull in, asshole," he said. "You don't have any backup, and you don't got any warrants. In fact, you got nothing on nobody. Why don't you just beat it?"

Actually, we couldn't argue. I was the only witness to a crime committed by any of these people. My legal word in St. Bernard and Orleans Parish was worthless. Secondly, I was a suspect in the partial destruction of Lauren Bow's historic plantation in Jeanerette.

"Hey, why don't you introduce us to these other people?" I said. "I want to show everybody a magazine clipping in my wallet. It's a photo of this Jewish woman and her three children who are about to go into the showers at Auschwitz. Everybody here probably thinks the Jews killed Christ. That's a lie. Read the Book of Acts, chapter 4, verse 27. It's written by St. Luke. The Romans and Pontius Pilate and Herod and a handful of bums in the Sanhedrin and some loafers in the courtyard were the culprits. The main culprit was Pilate, a real shit."

"Don't reach behind you, Clete," Andy said.

"I'm just reaching for my wallet," I said. "Plus, you don't have permission to call me Clete."

I heard someone or something clank at the end of a lane, where the mechanical pinsetter was. Everyone else did, too. I moved my hand away from my wallet and kept it in full view. I knew we were on the edge. You have probably been there yourself, one way or another. You can feel your sphincter slip, just slightly; you breathe through your mouth a teaspoon at a time; you can taste pecans in your spit; there's a tremor on the back of your hand; the world has never seemed so quiet.

Then Dave dialed it down. "Miss Clara, you're a fine-looking woman," he said. "Will you slap your husband upside the head and tell him and his friends not to be foolish?"

"Why, yes," she said. "I certainly will, Mr. Robicheaux. I declare, you are such a concerned and thoughtful man."

Suddenly we had Scarlett O'Hara in our midst. I was glad. Maybe I wanted to turn Baylor Hemmings into wallpaper, but the people you dust have a way of showing up at your bedside. Anyway, screw it, I thought. It's only rock and roll. Everybody gets to the same barn. It's how you get there that counts.

What am I talking about? I'll tell you. Back when Dave was seeing the Confederate signal corps sending up hot-air balloons in his backyard, complete with telegraphic equipment hanging from the basket, he made his peace with the nature of reality, or at least *his* reality. He said he thinks everything in existence happens simultaneously; there is no past, present, or future; it's as though you're in a dream inside the mind of God. For Dave, that means you can change the past. I glow with neurosis? Try Dave's craziness.

But we still had a serious problem. Clara Bow was a rose with a canker in it; her former husband would have paid to A-bomb Hiroshima. None of them knew the Feds had probably already picked up the package of poison that Andy and Lauren Bow were willing to string across the American West. Maybe the worst people in the world were sitting with us in a bowling alley. Would they ever be tried? Would any of them be interviewed by a journalist? Ask Jack Ruby. Our government has a long history of keeping secrets.

There was another problem, too. Someone had located themselves at the end of a lane not far from us. My guess was Gracie Lamar. But it could have been Joan, too. Or just a janitor with a push broom.

Yeah, I know problems with depression and psychoneurotic anxiety had taken their toll on me, and, yeah, I should have gotten rid of them at the VA, but those kinds of sicknesses don't work that way. I believed Joan was out there. I knew she was standing on a waxed maple bowling lane, wrapped in a cone of yellow flame. I looked at Dave, then at Joan again, then back at Dave. It was obvious he didn't see anything.

To tell you the truth, I was coming apart. Why? I saw a little red dot of light slide across everybody standing or sitting at the tables or by the bowling ball rack, like Old Death with his scythe.

It was a laser beam. I went to a rodeo in Wyoming where a bunch of badass motorcycle outlaws took up the seats and scared the crap out of everybody and were having a great time until some state cops aimed laser dots at their crotches. It definitely created an unsettled state of mind in the bikers.

I heard Dave clear his throat, but no other reaction from anyone else. I think no one else there knew what the little dot meant. I suspect the laser sight was mounted on an AR-15 or a semiauto rifle similar to it—in other words, a real meatcutter, its fire rate souped up with a bump stock and a thirty- to fifty-bullet magazine that any maniac can buy with his credit card in a sporting goods store, unless he's drooling or wearing his jockstrap outside his slacks.

I couldn't be sure. I just knew the red dot was not on me or Dave now, and I can't tell you how good that made me feel.

"Hey, Baylor?" I said.

"Yeah, what?"

"You believe in prayer?"

He was wearing a denim shirt with a tie, like the working man's business suit. He started flicking his fingers at his shirt. "What are you talking about?" he said, now messing with his tie.

He didn't know what was going on. Or maybe he didn't care. I think it was probably the latter. I've known criminals who have gone past their psychopathic state of mind and entered a place that doesn't have a name. They never get out of lockdown. And here's the real kicker: They like it.

"You're under arrest, Hemmings," I said.

"You got no power over me," he said.

"Yeah, I do. I'm bigger than you." I slapped him across the face.

He was dumbfounded. I don't think that had ever happened to him. He began to tremble, like a child that had been whipped unfairly.

"Here, here, now," Lauren Bow said, getting up from his chair, his face flushed behind his muttonchop whiskers. "You have no right to pick upon the boy. His politics are his politics."

"Sit down, Mr. Bow," Dave said. "If you do not, you will be arrested for obstructing an officer of the law. Add 'resisting' and you will spend multiple years in jail."

"I'm standing up for the boy," Bow said. "I'm also exercising my First Amendment rights."

I love Nazis who claim their constitutional rights. He was breathing heavily, his nostrils swelling. I believed he saw the red dot and feared for his life. I also believed he wanted the red dot to remain on Baylor Hemmings.

Andy Durbin continued to eat his ice cream. Clara Bow's eyes rested on me, then on Dave. "I'll be a witness," she said.

"Pardon?" Dave said.

"I just wanted to make a picture, that's all," she said. "Lauren killed a Black man in Baton Rouge years ago. With his bare hands. Just to show he could do it. He told me about it when he was drunk."

The information was probably worthless. Dear Old Dixie had many a story of racial homicide, almost every little town does, and if we acknowledged them all, we could probably never look in the mirror again.

Then I saw the red dot disappear from Hemmings's shirt just as a bolt of lightning struck the building, shaking all the windows, knocking out all the lights.

The cone of flame around Joan had disappeared as well. The rain turned to hail and pounded on the roof as Dave and I stood stock-still, our hearts in our throats, our hands inching for our weapons, wondering what our enemies were about to do.

CHAPTER THIRTY-EIGHT

I knew Hawthorne and Helen and federal agents and cops from Orleans and St. Bernard Parishes would eventually be coming along, so why not just wait on them?

Because I didn't believe they would see the same thing Dave and I had seen. I believed then, and I believe now, that we saw and participated in an event that other people would never learn about. The players were unlikely figures—misfits and neurotics at best and demoniacs at worst. Their common denominator was their mediocrity. But that's the way it always is. Mussolini had a profile like a pig's snout and was hung upside down at a filling station with his mistress; Hermann Göring should have been the mayor of Las Vegas; and Huey Long died from a ricocheting bullet fired accidently by his bodyguard—in the state capitol building.

They all go down, but never see it coming. Who needs regular criminals when you've got characters like this around?

What's the point? One small fire can burn down Rome. Yeah, that's what we were playing around with, and I'm still not sure how we got out of it. But I'll try to explain it as best I can.

# # #

The hail was thundering on the roof, then the red dot went from person to person in the crowd at the far wall, touching their foreheads and throats and chests, sometimes moving on and sometimes returning. Lightning struck again, beyond the levee, out on the Gulf, the sky and water and cars on the highway quivering in its brilliance; then the darkness returned, as black as the inside of a woodstove.

The red dot stopped on Lauren Bow's forehead. He tried to wipe it off, then tried to wipe it off his hands, then his forearms, then one eye. He was mewing and looking at his feet, urine running from his trouser cuff. He stomped his feet up and down, furious at the failure of his body and the lack of remedy for a situation he never thought he would be in, his teeth grinding. He looked like a man who was boiling alive.

All the while Andy Durbin ate his ice cream, sucking the spoon clean with each bite. Lightning blew a tree apart by the levee, again illuminating the inside of the building and a figure at the end of one of the lanes. It also kicked to life a yellow-and-red jukebox, which played an ear-splitting rendition of Chuck Berry's *Promised Land*, sung by Elvis Presley.

It might have ended there. But there are people who are criminals for reasons other than gain, and for reasons they never share. Try the Hillside Strangler or Ted Bundy.

Maybe it was because Andy Durbin let his brother, Eddy, take his fall and do ten hard years at Angola. Maybe he carried guilt over it, or maybe he didn't have guilt about anything and let Baylor Hemmings and his fellow punks stick poor Eddy in the brushes and hot wax. I think Andy had been a puke all his life and had no feelings about anyone, certainly not about selling fentanyl to young girls who have tats on their thighs and dreams in their eyes and cell phones stitched to the sides of their heads. Hey, I got to get out of this. People who sell dope to our kids deserve life in the can or on the hard road and not in our heads.

When you come to think about it, Andy was the perfect guy to drop the trapdoor on a gallows or light the fire under a witch's chained feet or spread plague by filling wells with contaminated rats. When Joan died, I bet his kind were everywhere. And I'll bet they're still here. They just wear better clothes.

Andy set aside his empty ice cream bowl, lifted a small pistol from his belt, probably a .25 semiauto, and began popping at one of the lanes.

I never saw Dave act so fast. He started yelling, "Down! Down! Down!" But he didn't obey his own command. He was standing up in the semidarkness, the only light coming from the jukebox, trying to get his .45 out of his raincoat pocket, pounding his other fist in the air, worrying about everybody except himself. Man, I was proud of him. That was stomp-ass Dave Robicheaux in overdrive.

Hey, I'll tell you a story in the middle of a story. When we were with NOPD, I carried him down a fire escape with two bullets in my back, and it made him madder than hell. He said I should have gotten some kids out first, and when I told him I had, he said I should have gotten myself out. Dave will stand in front of a train if he thinks it will help sick or poor people or people with no power. I think it's because he thinks everybody who's had a break should help somebody else. Maybe that's all right. Or maybe not. I guess it's a good way to be. Hey, who cares? It beats living in Dullsville. As that great American philosopher Bob Seger said, "Give me that old time rock and roll!"

Anyway, Andy started shooting, his tiny shells tinkling on the maple floor, a twisted smile on his face, his eyes merry, his body jerking in four-four time, like he and Elvis were brothers.

The figure with the laser mounted on an assault rifle cut loose. You could hear the .223 casings dancing all over the maple wood. Except the rounds were high. For a little while. Let me explain.

Everyone except me and Dave and Andy was on the floor. I had gotten the .410 cutdown from my belt, but I dropped it. Lauren Bow was making squealing sounds. His wife was kneeling in a pious way, a tragedian to the end. And Baylor Hemmings and a few of his kind were hauling butt for the back door and the levee and maybe a boat, even though the storm was raging and the skylights on the roof were cracking from the hailstones.

I didn't have any doubt who was firing the AR-15. Her superior at the Birmingham Police Department said she'd dropped maybe three Klansmen, but in firefights. She was obviously still under a few restraints. She had not tried to fire into the larger group. Andy was a different matter. I don't know how I feel about this; I'll let you judge. I do not believe he was of low intelligence, nor do I believe he was born different, like the Bible says. I believe he was evil by choice. I think he was an actor, a good one, and greedy. And mean to the core to both animals and children. Why am I so sure? It was his eyes. The intensity never waned. They looked like they were taken from another person and sewn onto his face, and the secrets inside them would go to the grave with him.

You want to know what kind of guys are like that? Don't be surprised. They wear three-piece suits and start wars, but they don't go to them.

Regardless, Andy Durbin's plug got pulled. The shooter of the AR-15 clicked off the red dot, don't ask me why, then took aim and drilled Andy through the forehead. The muscles in his face turned to mashed potatoes, and his body went straight down to the floor, like an inflated rubber tube with a painted face whipping in the air in front of an automobile dealership, suddenly cut off from its oxygen.

The shooting was over, and Elvis got to the Promised Land. Wow, what a song and what a guy. The people lying flat on the floor began to push themselves up and look around, horrified to see Andy and the hole leaking from his head, his eyes still open.

"Where you going, Clete?" Dave asked.

"To get some fresh air and have a chat with Baylor Hemmings and his buds," I said. "They just went out the door."

"Did you see Gracie Lamar?"

"Who?" I said.

# # #

I can't tell you for sure what happened out there in the storm, as would be expected when a lot of things hit your senses at once and your heart is racing and your brain is telling you that if you mess up, your grits will be flying in the wind. Also, my hat had blown away and the rain was pelting me in the head and face until I was almost blind. I had only my .38 snub, and I was about to go up against Hemmings and maybe a dozen of his white-trash followers, although I didn't know how many were packing.

But that's not the point. The world I had entered that morning was not the world I had just run out of. This was not the first time this has happened to me. And I'm not alone in this. I've had friends at my side experience the same thing. Everything about your location changes, disappears, and reinvents itself. The sky, the earth, the woods, the desert, or whatever it is, manifests itself. Just before I got nailed in Vietnam and the navy corpsman dragged me down the hillside on a poncho liner, the jungle looked like it was spiked with candy canes and the stars had turned to Hershey's Kisses wrapped in tinfoil and raining on my head.

Tell *that* to a shrink.

Maybe sometimes your brain overloads and sees what it wants to see. I can't argue with that, but at the same time I don't buy it. For me, the things I saw in the field between the bowling alley and the levee will always be real. I don't care what people say. Why would I make up those things? The details I'm going to give you don't make me a hero. In fact, maybe they'll confirm me as a permanent clod. Who needs that?

The field had turned to marsh, knee-high with mud and saw grass, the sun buried forever, the air filled with flying debris. I could see Hemmings and his men running ahead of me. I had my .38 Special in my right hand, and I could have fired and brought someone down, but I can say I never dropped anyone I wasn't forced to, except for the accident with the federal witness years ago. Also I think the shooter with the AR-15, who was probably Gracie Lamar, had become the model for our situation. She didn't try to pop Andy Durbin until he began firing at her, and even then she gave away her advantage by shutting down the laser and using iron sights or simply pointing the barrel, which has come to be a venerable technique.

I felt like I was running in wet concrete. My lungs were burning, my gallstones squeezing through my bladder, my face stinging, the sky black and filled with sounds like 105s coming out of their trajectory, which is like truck tires roaring down a wet highway. I wanted to sink to my knee and get at least one shot at Hemmings. I owed it to the Jewish mother and her children. I owed it to all the other Jews who died that same day. I would never find peace if I gave up the debt I owed to those people.

How did I acquire that debt? I acquired it the day I learned the lie about the death of Jesus.

The rain looked like spun glass now. I could see Hemmings and his followers running up the slope to the Mississippi levee. They topped the levee and went down the other side, and I tripped and fell in what could have been an alligator's hole. When I stood up, I was soaked in mud, all the way up to my face. I went over the top and had to keep my arm across my eyes because of the rain; I had never felt rain this hard, even in hurricanes. The drops were like ball bearings; I felt like someone had gouged out my eyes.

Then I came down the opposite side of the levee; the entire world had changed. The rain had stopped, and the Mississippi River was no longer the Mississippi River. As far as the eye could see, the earth was a long, widespread collection of forked rivers and elevated claylike plains shining with water. The darkness was gone from the skies, and a lazy yellow sun lay on the horizon. I could see castles and towers and winding roads and villages and peasants in sackcloth and carrion birds circling above open mass graves. There were also corpses suspended from gibbets along the dirt roads, the bones and rags and flesh sunken into weightless balls, like people sleeping.

But I was not going to be stopped by an illusion. I piled into Baylor Hemmings and knocked him down and began beating him with my fists. I wanted to kill him. My knees had him pinned, and the imprints of my blows on his pitted cardboard-like skin reminded me of the roots in the bamboo that grow on the bayou's banks.

But I was careless. He got his hand on a gun and pulled the trigger. The round went straight into my armpit. It was like someone driving a cold chisel into the bone.

Where was Gracie Lamar when I needed her? For a second I thought I would pass out. I leaned forward, trying to keep my weight on Hemmings before he could aim another round. But I didn't know where the gun was.

Under his thigh, a voice said.

"Joan?" I said.

Yes, take his weapon. He's about to kill you.

Then I saw Hemmings lifting it off his shirt. It was a derringer. He almost had the two barrels pressed into my groin. I twisted it out of his hand and almost broke his fingers. I threw the derringer into a mud hole.

All of his men had run away. Their footprints went in every direction. I wondered if his people would spread his seed all over Europe, or wherever we were.

You're bleeding, Sir Clete. I'll try to get you to a physician. Ours are a bit primitive, however.

"I'm all right, Miss Joan."

You're such a funny man. You always make me laugh, no matter what the situation. Can you tell me your plans now?

"I don't think I get you."

Oh, I'm afraid you do. This man is your captive now.

"Yeah, I need to know if this guy has other stashes of poison he'll spread across the country."

I was criticized for letting the looting and killing extend longer than they should have. I don't know if I'm guilty or not. I hope that is not among my sins.

"You were less than nineteen. You're supposed to stop ten thousand drunks from getting out of hand?"

I wish I had done more. I wish I had been kinder.

"Don't bad-mouth yourself, Miss Joan. You're the best there is. Like Dave Robicheaux."

She knew I was kidding, and she knew I knew, and she laughed out loud. *You're a good soul.*

"Look the other way, Miss Joan."

What are you doing?

I flipped the cylinder out of the .38's frame and dumped all six cartridges, then picked one up and held it in Hemmings's face. The wound in my armpit was a pocket of pain, throbbing deep into the bone. I snapped the cylinder back into the frame. "You've got five-to-one odds you don't eat a bullet, Baylor. Ready?"

"No! Please!"

I stuck the barrel in his mouth and pulled the trigger. His face looked like a balloon about to explode.

"Hurray for you," I said.

"What do you want from me?"

"Where are the rest of the goods?"

"There's not any."

I pulled back the hammer. "Are you sure?"

"Yes!"

"I don't believe you." I squeezed the trigger. The hammer snapped on another empty chamber.

This time he screamed and tried to get up, weeping in his impotence.

"Shut up," I said. I opened the cylinder and let it hang in front of his face. All of the chambers were empty. "You get a free pass, asshole. And it's because of someone you probably never heard of. You see all that countryside full of grief and disease? That's the fifteenth century. That's your new home. Beat feet, Baylor. You're on your own."

He stood up, off-balance, staring at the miles of chimney smoke and open latrines and contaminated sewers and drain fields and mortuaries that were little more than bonfires heaped with offal. Then he began running, looking over his shoulder, his shoes slick with mud, falling down again, peasants on the road flinging horse turds at him.

I wondered if he regretted the fate of the six million. I doubted it. But it was time to put away the likes of Baylor Hemmings. Joan of Arc, the Maid of Orleans, was standing less than ten feet from me. Others can say what they wish. She was there. I walked toward her and held her hand. It was small and warm and full of light. I did not know what to say or what to do. The pain she must have endured at the stake was beyond my ability to contemplate. I cannot imagine the level of courage she must have had.

I have to go now, Sir Clete. You know that, don't you?

"But you'll come back, won't you?"

Your wound has to be bound. Go back over the dike. Find your friend Mr. Robicheaux.

"It's a levee."

She shrugged her shoulders and smiled.

"Please don't go," I said.

She raised her hand, then turned into a bouquet of multicolored flowers that blew apart in the wind. In its place was a burned wood post.

EPILOGUE

One day later I woke up in a VA hospital in Biloxi. I could hardly tell people my name. In fact, I didn't even try. Dave showed up, then we went home. On the way back, he asked about Baylor Hemmings. I just shook my head and didn't reply. Sometimes that's the best way to go.

After my armpit healed, I whacked softballs in New Iberia's City Park with a bunch of Black kids whose mothers worked as maids in the antebellum and Victorian homes on East Main. That year we had an Indian summer. The days were warm, and the oak leaves were gold and spinning out of the trees and sometimes blowing high in the sky and drifting down on the Teche, like nature trying to undo its own history. The Black kids thought I was funny and called me big guy. I paid for the snowballs they ate. They still called me big guy, not mister. I liked that.

I didn't tell the Feds anything. I knew better than to lie, because when you lie to a Fed, you're headed for the Gray Bar Hotel Chain. Instead, I told them I had connections in the fifteenth century and I could get them good jobs working in the Paris sewer system. One guy said, "Just keep talking, wisenheimer." Another guy said, "Hey, that's cute, Purcel. Is it true you wear pink slippers with rabbit ears?"

Hey, I didn't have it in for them. I gave up those kinds of resentments. We put the bad guys out of business, Dave and me and Agent Hawthorne and Helen, and let's not forget Gracie Lamar, although she had a habit of leaving dead bodies around. But who's perfect? I know that might sound vain. It isn't. Think of it this way. Do you remember those cutouts of Uncle Sam in front of post offices all over the country? Or if you're not old enough, do you remember seeing a photograph of Uncle Sam like that? He's pointing a finger at you and saying, "I want you!"

He meant those three words. It's the few who put the bad guys out of business. They work for grunt wages and drive Frito trucks and weld bridges and mop hospital floors. They look like Elmer Fudd and Olive Oyl. Don't believe me? In 1942 one navy aviator found the Japanese fleet, got on his radio, and changed the war. John Kennedy himself admitted that we barely escaped incinerating the Earth in 1962. Two men, and only two men, Robert Kennedy and Adlai Stevenson, used a ruse and stopped a nuclear war from happening.

But no more of this. Chen and my temp, Miss Sally, were all right. Agent Hawthorne threw in his badge and ran off with Clara Bow. As far as I know, they're making films in California. I've got another theory about that, too. Gracie Lamar went off the grid. That doesn't slide down the pipe. I think she's in Hollywood; I even saw her in the background when Dave and I were on a set to help these guys make a TV series created by a New Iberia writer.

I bought a small plot in a roadside cemetery south of Jeanerette, just a few yards from Bayou Teche. The trees are all evergreens, the tombstones lopsided and stained with lichen, the crypts sunken into the earth, as though the dead need burying twice. I put the clipping with the photo of the Jewish lady and her three children in a tin box and dug a hole and placed the box in it and shoveled the dirt in the hole. I bought a heavy stone and had it engraved and placed it horizontally on the ground. Its weight was enough that no one would steal it easily. The stone was marble, both rough and polished, and decorated with carved flowers on the edges. The inscription is simple, in case you wish to find it and spend a few minutes in the shade with people I hope I have given a home. The inscription reads: AN ANGEL AND HER CHILDREN REST UNDER YOUR FEET. PLEASE GIVE THEM THE KINDNESS AND PROTECTION THAT WAS DENIED THEM IN LIFE.

# # #

Hey, you guys have gotten your tickets punched a few times, or you wouldn't be reading this. You're either in the club or you're not. The great enemy is time. It wears away stone and collapses arctic ice; it sinks ancient cities beneath the ocean and isolates giant arks on mountaintops and, if we let it, robs the light from our eyes. But the heart is its own measure; if it wishes, it can live forever when you accept the heart as a music box, a magical gift, one that's aways there, like a rustling of the spheres or the leaves bouncing along the pavement deep down in the fall. A rainbow is up there. Don't let anybody tell you there's not.

I said it's only rock and roll? Wrong. It's a poem, brother. Or sister.

If you don't believe me, talk to Dave Robicheaux.

ACKNOWLEDGMENTS

Once again, I wish to thank my editor and publisher at Grove Atlantic, Morgan Entrekin, and Zoe Harris and their colleagues Deb Seager, Natalie Church, JT Green, and Judy Hottensen; the people at the Spitzer Agency, Anne-Lise Spitzer, Mary Spitzer, Lukas Ortiz, and Kim Lombardini; Erin Mitchell, my publicist and copyeditor and advisor who worked with Pamala hand in hand, and Pamala whom we feel is still with us; my entertainment and film advisor Penelope Glass; and my children Jim and Andree and Alafair; and Pearl, my wife, who has been with me for sixty-four years.

I have been fortunate in the kind of people who have helped me during my career. A career is easy to lose. Without dramatics, you can quietly put away your pen or typewriter or keyboard and listen to the naysayers and watch your talent float out the window like a balloon. But I've always been around good people, the kind of protagonists I think you'll find in my books. Every character is a mix of someone I've known, for good or bad but mostly for good. To be an artist is the greatest gift in the world; but the friends of an artist are also a great gift, and I have had hundreds and hundreds of friends whose names should also be on my books. That of course will not happen, but at least I can say to the living and passed-on, thank you, thank you, thank you.

As Woody might say, One Big Union,
James Lee Burke